D0446778

BALLANTINE BOOKS BY KRISTIN MILLER

In Her Shadow

THE
SINFUL
LIVES
OF
TROPHY
WIVES

THE SINFUL LIVES OF TROPHY WIVES

A NOVEL

KRISTIN MILLER

BALLANTINE BOOKS

NEW YORK

A Ballantine Books Trade Paperback Original

Copyright © 2021 by Kristin Miller

Published in the United States by Ballantine Books,
an imprint of Random House, a division of
Penguin Random House LLC, New York.

BALLANTINE and the HOUSE colophon are registered
trademarks of Penguin Random House LLC.

LIBRARY OF CONGRESS CATALOGING-IN-PUBLICATION DATA
Names: Miller, Kristin, 1980- author.
Title: The sinful lives of trophy wives: a novel / Kristin Miller.
Description: New York: Ballantine Books, [2021]
Identifiers: LCCN 2020048734 (print) | LCCN 2020048735 (ebook) |
ISBN 9781524799526 (trade paperback; acid-free paper) |
ISBN 9781524799519 (ebook)
Subjects: LCSH: Psychological fiction.
Classification: LCC PS3613.I53985 S56 2021 (print) |
LCC PS3613.I53985 (ebook) | DDC 813/.6—dc23
LC record available at https://lccn.loc.gov/2020048734
LC ebook record available at https://lccn.loc.gov/2020048735

Printed in the United States of America on acid-free paper

randomhousebooks.com

2 4 6 8 9 7 5 3 1

Book design by Jo Anne Metsch

33614082336560

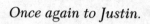

Once again to Justin.

"I'm not afraid to love a man . . .

I'm not afraid to kill one, either."

—GRACE DENT, *The Nightmare Next Door*

THE
SINFUL
LIVES
OF
TROPHY
WIVES

CHAPTER ONE

GEORGIA

PRESENT DAY

The day after the accident
St. Mary's Medical Center

Pain is the first thing I remember. One moment I'm sleeping the soundest sleep anyone has ever slept. In the next, pain bites at the tips of my toes. Sharp, piercing sensations crawl up my body, slinking over my skin, torturing every nerve ending until I'm paralyzed. I try to suck in a jagged breath, but lead sheets crush my chest. I'm flattened against a firm mattress. I'm cold. So unbelievably cold.

Panic lashes through my veins.

I can't open my eyes or my lips. I can't speak or move. My strength is gone, completely sapped from my muscles.

Beep.

Knives pierce my eardrums as the sound goes off again. Swallowing is an effort. A jagged-edged rock has taken up residence in the back of my throat. I'm so thirsty. My lips are unbelievably chapped.

Beep.

Without warning, the nightmare floods back in violent, vivid color. Flashing lights and blood and screams create a chaotic painting against the backs of my eyelids. Agony follows, and grief too.

The accident.

Something terrible happened. I—I didn't stop it. I could have—God, I should have—but I didn't. What have I done?

It strikes again—that cold, wretched feeling that sours my gut. Guilt. I could've done something, opened my mouth and changed the sequence of events that catapulted me into this dark place. I could've changed everything. I held the future in the palm of my hand. But I didn't act, didn't try hard enough.

This is my fault.

Beep.

The annoying bleat morphs from something intrusive and foreign into something familiar. A machine I've heard before, when my first husband, Eli, slipped and tumbled down our spiral staircase. He landed on the bottom, arms and legs broken in awkward angles like a demented starfish. His head had hit the tile hard and oozed blood from the crack in his skull all over our Grecian tile. An ambulance rushed him to St. Mary's Medical Center. The doctors tried all they could to save him, but their efforts were in vain. The following year, Andrew, my second husband, had been dead on arrival. Not much the doctors could do after he swallowed that bullet. I found *him* in our office, his brains staining the back of an Italian leather chair I'd given him for Christmas.

Beep.

I know that noise. I'm in the hospital. The knowledge only increases the adrenaline surging hot through me.

"Open those curtains, would you, Sheree?" someone says from beside me.

I'm here! I can hear you! I want to scream. But I can't. My lips might as well be stapled shut.

"There, that's better," the same nurse says after another shrill chirp from the machine. "She's still really pale, though."

"Do you think her color is off because of blood loss?" someone asks from the other side of me. This voice is softer. Sweeter. "Or lack of sunlight from being stuck indoors? Look at her nails, Karen. She's definitely not the outdoorsy type. Maybe she's always this pasty white."

Pasty? Have I truly lost that much blood? My pulse races at the thought.

Beep . . . beep . . . beep.

Something tugs on my arm. It's an IV. They're upping my medication.

How long have I been here? It could be hours after my wedding reception, or a month later. There's no way for me to know. It feels as if I've been sleeping my entire life. Consciousness slips away as blobs of inky darkness threaten to pull me under. My thoughts knock together clumsily like shapes in a kaleidoscope, changing and smearing until time and dream and reality are inconsequential. Is *he* here too? Tucked away in the room next door in the same situation? Too many questions swirl through my brain at once and I can't make sense of any of them.

"You know," Karen says, "she kind of looks like that woman."

"Which one?"

"The woman all over the news," Karen says, the IV jerking in my vein. "The one who killed her husband, married another guy right after, and then killed him too. I think it's her."

Beep.

"Oh, I'd almost forgotten about her," Sheree says. "They

say she pushed one down the stairs and shot the other one while he was working in his office." She's beside me now. The side of my bed slumps as if she's leaning over to get a closer look at me. "Yeah, she kind of does look like her, doesn't she? What were they calling her?"

"The Black Widow."

"That's right. Hard to tell what she looks like with those bandages on her face."

Oh, for the love of all that is holy, please don't let my face be covered with scars. I wouldn't want to live if I've become disfigured.

"Did you hear if the other woman made it?" Karen asks. "The one who was hit by their car?"

"There was no way that poor woman could've survived. They had to have been going fast." Sheree's voice lowers. "When they brought her in, she was really messed up. Did you see her? The officer said she flew thirty feet. Cracked her head open on the asphalt."

"What was she doing in the middle of the road?"

"No one knows." Sheree sighs heavily, as if whatever she's thinking has taken a physical toll on her. "But that's not the worst of it. I've heard that the woman's husband—the one driving—was killed on impact when they veered into a tree."

"Oh my God," Karen says as she pats my hand. "She's going to be devastated when she finds out."

Denial flares in my gut. That's not right. They're mistaken. I'm not—we hadn't—Robert couldn't have died. That's not possible . . .

Beepbeep . . . beepbeep.

"It gets worse," Sheree retorts. "I overheard the officer outside her door talking to a detective last night. They're going to have a lot of questions for her when she wakes up, and who knows? They might try to arrest her for murder."

Murder? No—this can't be happening. As a heavy dose of medication deluges my blood, I fall into a deep, coma-like sleep—one plagued with nightmares of shattered glass and blood-soaked skin and screams bubbling from the pit of hell.

CHAPTER TWO

BROOKE

SIX DAYS BEFORE THE ACCIDENT
Sunday

"The area is an architectural dream, with Italian Renaissance, Elizabethan, and Mediterranean influences," the real estate agent says. "There are only forty homes in Presidio Terrace, all located around one street that makes the shape of a lasso."

Or a noose, I think, though I don't dare speak.

"There is a twenty-four-hour guard at the front gate, and anyone using the pedestrian entrance must show proper identification." The agent leads us through the formal dining room, featuring a table that could easily seat thirty. "Not even Google Earth can get in here. The community association negotiated for this area to remain unseen from all maps. There is a security system on the home as well, of course. It features cameras for every door, sensors on every window, and a panic button in each bedroom. It was created by the Secret Service."

"Really?" Jack says, finally acknowledging the agent's presence. It's as if she'd been beneath him all this time and not worth speaking to. "Interesting."

She nods excitedly. "The level of security here is quite extraordinary."

Jack lets his arm fall heavily around my shoulder, and I'm not sure why but it feels fatherly. As if I'm a child he's trying to shield from something heinous. At fifty, Jack is twenty-two years older than I am, though he's aged incredibly well. I gaze up at him, admiring how smooth and tight his skin is, even though he doesn't do anything special to maintain it. He's clean-shaven, with one of those hardened jawlines that must've manifested after years of clenching his back teeth. He takes care of his body too. I've dated twenty-year-olds who didn't have the muscles he's got. But his hair and eyes give his true age away. We've been together only a year—and married for ten of those months—so of course I didn't know him when he had a full head of dark hair, but to me, his silver hair only enhances his sex appeal. And his eyes—they're crisp blue and full of light and vitality, but when he smiles, which he doesn't do often, tiny lines splinter from the corners. I won't mention the size of his—*ahem*—wallet, but that's impressive too.

"Top level security is what we're looking for. Isn't it?" He squeezes me against him, indicating that I'm not supposed to answer that. *Stand silent and smile.* I do as I've been previously instructed. "I anticipate I'll be spending most of my time at work—that's why we moved here. To be closer to the hub of innovation. I need to make sure my wife is protected when I'm spending long hours away from home. This place is hers."

"Lucky lady." The agent smiles at me. I return the gesture without showing my teeth. "This way," she sings, "to the kitchen."

My stilettos click-clack over the tile and echo through the

cavernous kitchen. I won't be cooking, so I'm not interested in this room. The counters are quartz and the appliances are all stainless steel. It's pretty, in a simple way. The sink's faucet is hooked like a swan's neck, and the cabinetry above the stove is beautifully detailed. Actually, the entire thing resembles the kitchen in Jack's Virginia Beach home.

His previous home is gorgeous and while his business is based in tech—he's the CEO and principal engineer of a major search engine company—and he could technically run it from anywhere in the world, Jack says it's time to move to the city where his headquarters are. I thought it wouldn't hurt to own two homes, one on the East Coast, one on the West, but he insists on selling it. Reminds him too much of his ex-wife, I think. They divorced a year and a half ago after twenty years of marriage. He's looking to put their loveless marriage and nasty divorce behind him. I'm completely onboard with that idea. Last week I mentioned something about taking a trip to California, to blow off steam. Being an army brat means I lived in half a dozen states growing up, and California has always been my favorite. I've visited two times in the last five years, though both trips had been more for business than for pleasure.

A single mention of how much I missed the Northern California ocean air, and here we are, one private jet ride later, seriously looking at homes. He says the timing lines up perfectly with his desire to expand the company. I can't argue. I wouldn't dare.

"All of this will have to be redone. Obviously," Jack adds, skimming his hand along the counters. "The colors aren't to our taste."

Aren't they?

"That's the great thing about this place," the agent says.

"There's enough room in your budget for you to make all the changes you want. This way. Follow me."

Jack said he would hire a full-time staff for whichever California home we choose, if that's what I want. But everywhere we go people recognize Jack. He's been featured on the covers of *Wired, Popular Mechanics, PC Magazine,* and *Computerworld.* He's also been featured on a few select *Forbes* lists, but since those were based on net worth, rather than the empire he's built himself, he didn't pay much attention. Jack doesn't like to acknowledge the fortune he received from his parents—they invested early and smartly in Apple, Amazon, and Time Warner—but it must be on everyone's mind when they meet him. People don't forget your name when the word "billion" is attached.

Because of his wealth and prestige in the tech world, we always have to smile and wave and speak enthusiastically, as if we've been waiting all day to have a ten-minute-long conversation about who-cares-what with someone wanting their big break in the industry. I don't want to feel like I'm being watched in my own home. I'm hoping he'll let me take care of the place—the inside, at least. The home is expansive, but as long as we have regular housekeeping services, I should be able to manage the rest.

It's not like we have children running around, muddying everything up.

It's just going to be me most days. The thought is enticing, to say the least. I love spending time with Jack, but there's something about having the day to myself that tickles me down to my toes. I'll have all day to research, to get some serious work done on my book, or do absolutely fuck-all, if the mood strikes me.

Although Jack hasn't spoken the words, I know this is the

home we'll buy, and I'm happy with that plan. It's the only home I've seen that's ticked all the right boxes. Jack is after the security and privacy, and for those things, nothing rivals this place.

Peeking out the kitchen window over the sink, I steal my first glimpse of the backyard. It's landscaped beautifully, with a pool, a spa, a cabana on either end, and trees lining the edges for privacy. I can definitely imagine summers spent back there. Alone. Curled up on the lounge, computer on my lap, margarita on the table at my side.

"The community board is active, as you would imagine in a place like this," the agent says, letting her hand drift over the banister as she leads us upstairs. "So there are rules that must be followed if you intend to purchase the home."

"What rules?" Jack stops dead. "You didn't mention that before."

There's the husband I know, resistant to any kind of order.

"Nothing too onerous. This way to the master. You must see the view."

I stop a few stairs above him and extend my hand. He clenches his jaw and follows reluctantly, taking my hand as he passes.

"These rules are going to be a deal breaker," he says with a groan, and leads me down a hallway wide enough to fit a car through.

As the agent pushes open two oversized doors simultaneously and stands back with a smile, the room washes in light. The bedroom is enormous, with a cathedral-like ceiling, a chandelier in the center, thick crown molding, and a window with a sprawling view of the Pacific Ocean and Golden Gate Bridge.

"Before we go any further, I need to hear about these

rules," Jack presses. He's standing in the center of the room with his arms folded over his chest. "What are they and who makes them?"

The agent turns, her blond hair falling over her shoulder. "It's about the front of the home, mainly. Grass can't be longer than two inches. Garage doors cannot be left open for longer than five minutes at a time. Cars must be parked in the garage overnight—not in the street or the driveway. No music over seventy decibels. Things like that."

Nodding, Jack seems to chew over her words. "Those aren't too cumbersome. Who makes them?"

"The Presidio Terrace Homeowners Association. It's run by a few of the wives in the community." She checks her phone. "Erin King, who lives across the street, is the president. Georgia St. Claire—I'm sure you've heard of her from the news—lives next door, to your right, though you can't see her home from here. She's the secretary."

"Why would we have heard of Georgia St. Claire?" he asks. Then he repeats the name, thoughtfully. "St. Claire. Is she married to the governor?"

"No, no, nothing like that." The agent lowers her voice as if telling a delicious secret. "She's the Black Widow." When Jack stares blankly, she prattles on. "Oh, it's just a nickname the press has given her. She's had two husbands pass away in the last ten years, and some say she's killed them. She's already lined up her next future dead husband too. Got engaged this summer. Robert Donnelly is still alive for the time being, but there are bets as to how long that'll last."

Talk about morbid gossip. I'm all ears.

"I don't know that I want my wife associating with a husband-killer." The corners of Jack's mouth kink up in an attempt at a smile. "What if that kind of behavior rubs off?"

"Mr. Davies, I'm sure that's not the way it works and—"

"That was a joke," he says flatly. "Brooke wouldn't dare associate with someone nicknamed the Black Widow."

But I don't even know her. How could I say who I would or wouldn't hang out with? Surely I'll make up my own mind. And it's not like Jack will be around to police me.

"There's more of the house to show you: the gym, the upstairs office, a handful of other bedrooms. If you'll follow me?" The agent glances at me out of the corner of her eye, and then continues the tour. "I wouldn't let Ms. St. Claire's presence sway your decision to purchase the home, Mr. Davies. I can assure you there are plenty of reputable women on the street for your wife to associate with."

I was wondering how long it would take for them to leave me out of the conversation completely. It's as if I've become invisible, a ghost walking the halls. I must have a talent for disappearing in plain sight. I'm impressed with the agent, actually. Within my husband's inner circle it usually takes only a few minutes to start ignoring me, and she's nearly finished giving the tour. Points for making an attempt.

After she's shown us everything the magnificent home has to offer, Jack moves the conversation to other couples on the street. He covers the husbands' occupations and the length of time each couple has lived in the community. Listening intently, though pretending not to care, I stand in the backyard near the pool, relishing the warm California sunshine on my cheeks.

"All right, Brooke," Jack says with a tone of finality. "Sounds like you could make some friends in the neighborhood." He's at my side again, though this time he doesn't touch me. Clearly he's interested in the home and ready to negotiate. His demeanor has completely changed. It's all business now. "You'll be happy here. You can get involved in the board too, if you'd like."

Realistically, we'll be here only a year tops before we move on to the next best house in another enticing neighborhood. Moving is in my nature, and the thought of putting permanent roots down in a place like this has the blood freezing in my veins.

I smile brightly, playing the part of a billionaire's wife, and nod enthusiastically. He nods decisively in return.

"It's done," he tells the agent. "I just have a few other questions for you, about the security system. Brooke, I'll meet you at the car."

As he takes her by the elbow and leads her back into the house to talk business, I take in my new backyard. Flowering bushes and walkways leading to hidden places and fountains and birdbaths. It's going to be peaceful here. I can feel it. Following a tiny shaded path on the left side of the house, I tiptoe from one stone to another, beside towering ferns that take my breath away. The path leads me out front, near Jack's and the agent's cars. A few houses down, a blond woman scoots along her driveway on her hands and knees. She's holding something and from here, it appears as if she's edging her lawn with scissors. *Odd,* I think. What's she going to do next? Measure the blades with a ruler?

I'm waiting for her to do just that when a woman directly across the street yells, "Good morning!"

She takes a break from unloading groceries from the trunk of her Tesla to enthusiastically whip her arm back and forth over her head. I can't remember what the real estate agent had said her name was, but I like her immediately. "Are you looking or buying?"

"Buying," I holler back, and then check over my shoulder

for signs of Jack. He's nowhere to be seen. "My husband's inside finishing up the details."

"Oh, how exciting!" The woman strides confidently across the street without a single teeter on her heels. Her platinum-blond hair, a stark contrast against her black pencil skirt and matching jacket, blows in the breeze behind her as she approaches and extends her hand. "Allow me to introduce myself properly, then. I'm Erin King, president of the Presidio Terrace Homeowners Association."

"My name is Brooke," I say, shaking her hand. "Brooke Davies."

"Let me just say, right off the bat . . . your husband is a genius."

I squint, perplexed. "You know Jack?"

"Not personally, but I doubt there's a single person in Silicon Valley who doesn't know *of* him. Besides, not many can afford this neighborhood, and people of his magnitude love the privacy it offers. I recognize you from the news," Erin says. "They like to bring up your husband's nasty divorce and his hasty marriage to—well, to you. Kids?"

"No, not even on the radar." I try not to sound upset by her probing into our personal life. "You?"

"God, no." She makes a scrunched face as if she's tasted something gross. "Mason hates kids. Loathes them. That's why we moved here. No children on the street."

"Is that because people aren't allowed, or—"

She laughs sweetly. "Oh, that's not part of the community's bylaws or anything. Can you imagine? Limits to procreation." She laughs harder now, and I wonder if she's on a mood-lifter. "Most people who can afford these homes are older, so their kids are already grown and out of the house. Except for me, of course. I'm thirty-five. I would assume you're in your early twenties, but I won't dare ask. Have you met her yet?"

"Who?"

"Georgia."

"No, you're the first one I've met on the street."

"Oh, you *have* to meet her." She clasps her hands over her chest. "You're going to *die* when you realize how sweet she is. Not like the media makes her out to be. Everyone thinks she killed her husbands, and I mean *everyone*. Have you heard anything about her?"

I shake my head. "Not much."

"I'm sure the agent told you some things." She moves closer, invading my personal space. I resist the urge to back up. "Georgia's been married twice. Her first husband died shortly after they were married. She pretended to be devastated, but we all know the truth about how she really felt. Took her only a year to find husband number two. Seems like it's easier to find a second spouse than the first. Well of course your husband would know all about that. You don't mind my talking candidly, do you?"

"No, not at all." I fold my arms over my chest guardedly, though I can't help but smile. I love her fast chatter and the ease of our discussion. I don't feel like I could say anything wrong to Erin. She'd simply eat up any mistakes in the conversation and bury them with beautiful new words. "It's no secret that my husband had a bit of . . . overlap in his relationships."

"Overlap." She nods, grinning ear to diamond-dangling ear. "I like that. Anyway, the second time, Georgia married for money, just like the first. She was miserable from the start. I didn't think she'd marry again. I mean, she certainly doesn't

need the money at this point. But then she found Robert—
the guy she lives with now—and she simply *adores* him.
They're getting married next week."

"Really?" I look up into Georgia's windows for signs of life.
Not a curtain breathes against the glass. "That's great. Once
I'm settled, I should send her a congratulatory bottle of cham-
pagne."

"Oh, she's going to love having you live next door. Just a
heads-up: they're getting married on Saturday, so things are
going to be crazy around here the next few days. I've never
seen Georgia this happy. Even through all the wedding-
planning madness she's got a smile cemented on her face.
Robert's really into his yacht, but he treats her like a queen, as
I'm sure your husband treats you."

Sure. Like a queen. Locked in a palace.

"What about your husband?" I need to turn the tables before tears gather in my eyes. "What does he do?"

"Mason's a plastic surgeon. He's responsible for these,"
she says, pointing to her full lips, "and these," she adds, tap-
ping her cheeks, "and getting rid of all of these lines." She
traces an imaginary line from one side of her forehead to the
other. "I don't like to boast, but my husband is brilliant."

Judging from the perfect roundness of her breasts, I'd
wager he took care of those as well, though I don't ask. I
had mine done last year, and the doctor went a little fuller
than I'd originally wanted, but Jack is happy, which means I
am too.

"Well you look amazing," I offer. "Good enough for the
movies."

"That's what I do. Not movies, but television." She drags
her hair over her shoulders and squares up to me. "Erin King,
KFLAG evening news. That's how I recognized your face. I

did a special on you during last year's Tech World Conference. Your husband gave the keynote."

"You're a news broadcaster? That's amazing. I could never talk in front of bright lights and a camera. I prefer the shadows."

She tilts her chin to catch the sunlight. "It's taxing at first, having to be perfect all the time, hitting all the right angles and saying all the right things, but I find, with practice, it simply becomes a part of who you are."

"I understand completely." Behind me, the front door closes. "It was great meeting you, Erin. Since we're going to be neighbors soon, I look forward to continuing our conversation another time."

She's across the street before Jack rounds the corner, and for that I let out a huge sigh of relief.

"What do you think?" he says once we're inside the safety of his car. "Do you love it? Is there anything about that homeowners association that strikes you as strange?"

I think about the rumored husband-killer, the bubbly gossip Erin, and the woman cutting her lawn with scissors.

Tilting my chin to catch the light, the way Erin had moments before, I say in my sweetest voice: "I love it, darling. I wouldn't change a thing."

As he backs out of the driveway and we pass the home next door, where the rumored husband-killer lives, I wonder if she's about to marry a man who pretends to be strong in public, but desperately requires his wife's opinion in private. Or maybe he's a man who demands perfection at all times, or at least the impression of it.

Above all else, I wonder if she's already plotting her future husband's death.

I'll have to bring over a tray of cookies and find out.

CHAPTER THREE

ERIN

MONDAY EVENING

I love my job, I love my job, I love my job.

Staring into the mirror backstage at the newsroom, I smooth the fine lines around my eyes and wonder if it's time for another laser treatment.

"Look at these things. They're huge, and they weren't here yesterday," I tell Monique, my stylist. She's working a straightening rod like it's a magic wand. "Do you see these lines? They showed up out of nowhere. Should I be worried?"

Monique doesn't even entertain my concerns. The station must pay her well. "You're beautiful, Erin. I don't know what's gotten into you today. You've been talking about your ass since you walked in. Now your face?"

I meet her gaze in the mirror. "The house across the street from mine is being purchased by a tech industry mogul and his new toy."

"Ah," she says, whipping that wand through my hair. "That explains it."

"That explains *what*?"

"The sudden concern that you're past your prime."

"You know," I say defiantly, "that's not even it. I don't care about my age—it's merely a number like everyone says. But this woman—she can't be more than twenty-eight or so—looks, I don't know, I guess she looks fresh, and I look tired."

"It's because she's a mistress," Monique says flatly. "That's her job. She's supposed to look fresh, otherwise she won't catch fish. No one wants sour bait."

"Is that what I am?" I squeal. "Sour bait?"

"Not you, calm down." She taps me on the head with the brush, and then checks the clock. Another few minutes before I'll have to head out. "What I mean is, her only worry in the world is staying hydrated, working out, eating right, and looking good so she can catch a man."

Dropping my hands in my lap, I look up at Monique. "But I want to do all those things too. Can't I do all that and have a career?"

"Maybe some people can." She shakes her head definitively. "But you? Absolutely not. You give everything to your job. It's who you are. And that's not a terrible thing, Erin. You dive wholeheartedly into whatever venture is in front of you. That doesn't make you sour bait. It makes you decisive, a go-getter. You're vicious, Erin. You're a freaking piranha!"

"I—I'm a what?" I whirl around in my chair. "Out of all the fish in the sea, that's what I am? A piranha? Those things are hideous. I don't want to be that ugly thing."

I want to be like Brooke, young and naïve and fresh-faced. I want to turn heads with my tight body. People say the good years fly by, and man, they aren't kidding. I used to be that way . . . and I'm not sure what happened.

Monique pinches her eyes closed. "You know what I meant."

"Ted and Erin, you're due on set," someone calls over the speaker.

"Why does his name always come before mine?" I wonder aloud as Monique finishes up. "Have you ever wondered that? Ted and Erin, Ted and Erin, never Erin and Ted."

"What'd you eat for lunch today? Something spicy?" Monique stands back to admire her work. "You need to focus, Erin. Seriously. Forget the mistress. Forget Ted. Focus on what you need to do."

That's just it. I don't know if I can. As my chest grows tight, I wonder about the last time I had a facial. Maybe that's why Brooke's face is so flawlessly smooth. I bet she clears her schedule for her skin care routine while I'm stuck here in the studio. I should get a massage. Not one of Monique's pitiful shoulder rubs either. But I'm constantly thinking about the next show, the network's schedule, the ratings, my followers on social media. If only I had all the time in the world to focus on what really matters: me.

"I could be a trophy wife if I had the time," I say decidedly. *I could be like her.*

"Of course you could, Erin," Monique says, leaning against the hair station. "But would you really want to?"

"What do you mean?"

"Does a shark want to be an eel?" Lifting her brush as if it's a beacon of truth, she says, "Hell no, because he's too busy chomping things, causing massive bloodshed, and swimming around to intimidate all the smaller fish. He doesn't have time to be thinking about what an eel's up to. He's a shark. That's all he knows."

I hear what she's saying. We each have our role to play, and it's easier to look at another woman and think about how easy she seems to have it. Working mothers can fight guilt over not staying home to raise their children, and stay-at-home mothers often wish they had ten minutes of adult interaction so their only conversation of the day didn't revolve around Timmy's potty schedule. But it's only fantasy. We're only seeing the downfall in our own lives and comparing it to the glossy veneer of someone else's. Is that why I can't stop thinking about Brooke? Because I want to rewind the tape and go back to when Mason and I were first moving into the neighborhood, the future sprawled out in front of us?

Is it so terrible that I want to have it all? A fulfilling job where I'm respected, and also plenty of time to be at home working on my house, my health, and my marriage?

I don't know that I'd want to be a trophy wife *permanently*. It's only that suddenly things seem unbalanced, as if I've been neglecting the aspects of my life that Brooke seems to have perfected.

By the time I'm on set, the heat of the lights making me sweat, cameras cued up, Ted beside me doing his disgusting throat exercises, a realization settles over my shoulders like a heavy cloak. I want to spend more time with Mason, working on us, to go back to the way things were before. I want to have the time and energy to wake up in the morning and have coffee with him before he heads to the office. Maybe we wouldn't fight so much if I didn't spend every waking second worrying about my upcoming segment. This job definitely ages people. I think it has something to do with the glare of the lighting.

Maybe I could take some time off. Even a week would be good for my soul.

"Did you eat something bad?" Ted asks after a rather loud and disgusting gurgle.

"Excuse me?" I skim through the notes for the show.

"You look like you're scowling. That weird vein is protruding from your forehead again." He points, leaning forward. "Right there. You don't feel it?"

After the injections, I don't feel much of anything up there. But it's certainly dickish of him to point it out.

"And, uh, did Monique see you today?" Shielding his eyes from the lights, Ted searches the people milling about behind the camera. "She couldn't cover those lines by your eyes? I'm sure the camera will pick those up. You might want to do something about that. Can we call her back in here?"

I love my job, I love my job, I love my job.

The lines by my eyes couldn't be as pronounced as he's making them out to be. He's a jerk, that's all. An egotistical blowhard who, for God knows what reason, has hated me from the moment I transferred from a rival news station.

Monique rushes over—Ted wasn't exactly speaking quietly—and dabs powder on my face. "You all right, girl?"

"Don't I look all right?" I give her my biggest, brightest smile.

"You look great. Remember: focus on what you need to do in this moment." She lowers her voice to a whisper. "You can address the trophy wife thing with Mason later." She retreats behind the cameras and gives me a thumbs-up.

"Trophy wife, huh?" Ted clears his throat awkwardly. "I think at this age you're more of a participation trophy." He snickers at his own joke.

I whirl on him in my fabulous spinning chair. "How are

you doing today, Ted? Boyfriend break up with you? Oh, that's awful. Wardrobe couldn't get your size right? Pants two sizes too small? Riding up in the crotch and making your peanut-sized balls shrivel away to nothing? Terrible. Hate to hear it. Do your fucking job, Ted, and leave me the hell alone."

"Whoa." His eyes widen in horror. "PMS with a side of possession? Haven't seen that look on you before."

I've had it with Ted's attitude and the hot glare of the lights, and the way I'm always under pressure. It's exhausting, and—you know what? I'm over it. I need a break.

I meet Monique's eyes and hear her say, "Oh no," but I can't stop now. Something's gotten into me today and there's no damming the flood of water now.

"Ted, you're a tool." I stand so fast, my chair tips over behind me. "Fuck all y'all. Except you, Monique—you're my girl. I'm out!"

No one tries to stop me as I clear out my room, pack up the car, and drive out of the lot. I don't know whether to be offended by that, or satisfied. I must've been so resolute in my decision—determination was certainly written all over my face—that everyone knew there would be no changing my mind. I'll call tomorrow, of course, demanding a week—maybe a month—off.

For now, I'm free. No job. No restrictions.

On the drive home down the Embarcadero, I check my reflection in the mirrors and notice that my face looks ten years younger when I smile, so I do it all the way home. I roll the windows down, slide the moonroof back, and blast hip-hop until my speakers rattle. I've never felt more alive, more refreshed, than I do in this moment. Salt-N-Pepa and TLC holler through the speakers and I'm singing about pushing things and chasing waterfalls and feel like a teenager again. I haven't talked to Mason yet. I'm going to surprise him—tell him I walked out, and it felt fantastic. He had a meeting tonight—won't be home for another two hours.

He'll be so surprised.

I stop by the store on my way home, something I haven't been able to do in years. I pick up spinach, cucumbers, tomatoes, an avocado, cheese, olives, and crackers. I stroll through the aisles with new eyes, taking everything in. The people seem kinder in the evening, opening my doors for me, offering a cart. My steps feel lighter over the glossy floor. The checker even hit on me—and he was solidly in his twenties. I saw the flirty gleam in his eye when he asked if he could help me out with my groceries. I'm already feeling younger and more vibrant, the way I'm sure Brooke does. I feel instantly changed.

I just walked out on my job.

Can they tell?

Before heading home, I make a quick trip into the wine boutique and purchase a bottle of their most expensive red. I don't even check the price. Then I pop into Chocolatier Azul and pick up their largest box of gourmet chocolates. Mason likes the orange peel chocolate laced with spiced rum, so I make sure our box has at least four of those. I prefer the mousse-filled chocolates decorated with patterns that look like lace. The prettier the chocolate, the better.

And tonight is for celebrating.

Thrusting my arm out the driver's window, I wave to Malik at the gate, and fly down the street to our home. Looks like Brooke and Jack have already settled in. The moving truck that was here this morning has already gone. I'll have to invite her over tomorrow. We can pop a bottle of champagne and have mimosas at Grounds & Greens to celebrate her new home and my sabbatical, when I'll proudly become Mason's trophy wife. I can introduce her to Georgia. I've never known Georgia to turn down mimosas.

Our home is cavernous and quiet, but as I make my way through the rooms, lights turn on when they sense my presence. An orange and red glow emanating from the setting sun bleeds through the living room windows and streams over the foyer tiles, making them appear as if they're on fire. In the kitchen, classical music cues on. The station is set to Mozart, Mason's favorite. Within seconds, the home is full of warmth and sounds and I can't wait for Mason to come home.

I get to work quickly, pouring a hefty glass of wine before chopping the veggies and dumping them into an oversized bowl. I display the chocolates on the rock-cut crystal Tiffany plate Mason got me for Christmas last year and set it in the middle of our dining room table. As I'm pouring my second glass of wine and feeling completely satisfied with myself, lights sweep through the kitchen windows. The garage door opens.

Mason's home.

I snap a quick selfie with wine in my hand, a smile on my face, and the delicious spread behind me. I select a dark, smooth filter. Perfection. #Datenight. #Mainsqueeze. My followers will love it. I'll have a thousand likes within the hour.

I fill a glass with Mason's favorite rum and wait at the garage door for him to enter. The door opens. He's frowning.

"This is a surprise," he says, pushing past me into the foyer. "What are you doing home?"

My smile doesn't falter. There's nothing that can get me down tonight.

"Well that's a story to tell," I say, watching him disappear into his office. "Let's talk over dinner and drinks."

"Give me five minutes," he calls out.

I take the time to arrange the table, tame my hair—the windows-down thing isn't the best idea after I've had my hair styled—and wait for him at the dining room table. Exactly five minutes later, he enters looking rested and refreshed, in a white polo, black slacks, and house slippers.

He kisses me on the forehead. "Sorry I didn't do that earlier. You took me by surprise."

"It's all right." I watch him sit across from me and eye the salad. "I'm glad you're home."

"Me too. It was a long day. Four meetings, two liposuctions, and a reconstructed nose job. Mariah made this?" He sifts through the chunks of avocado. "I didn't see it in the fridge earlier."

"No, I prepared it myself," I say proudly, diving in. "I went to the grocery store and everything."

He knows this is a big deal. I don't think I've stepped foot in a grocery store since before we were married five years ago. Our personal chef, Mariah, does all the shopping, prepping, and cooking. It definitely takes the load off my shoulders. But tonight, ambition got the better of me. And who knows? Maybe I'll take on more of that role during my time off.

"Look at you, being productive." He smiles in that way that makes me tingly inside. "It's good. I'm proud of you."

He's so handsome when he's playful, his dark eyes twinkling with mischief.

"So tell me about your day," he goes on, between sips of rum and bites of dinner. "How'd you manage to get off so early?"

Setting down my fork, I temple my hands over the table in front of me and take a deep breath. "I walked out."

He stops chewing for a moment, and then struggles to

swallow the food he's shoved in his cheek. "What do you mean, you walked out?"

"I sort of quit, I guess. On the spot."

He squints at me, as if that'll help him understand. And then he sets down his fork. "You quit working today, or . . . permanently?"

"Well I don't know yet. I didn't really say. I just left. But from the way I'm feeling right now, I'd like to take at least a week off. Maybe a month. I'm going to play it by ear."

"Did you find a better job?"

"No, that's not necessary. They're not going to fire me. They *need* me, Mason. I'm simply going to demand a short sabbatical to recenter my priorities."

He chews slowly. "What do you plan to do during this . . . sabbatical?"

I take a gulp of wine to soothe the sudden tick in my nerves. "I'm going to be a stay-at-home wife."

"But we don't have children, Erin."

"Obviously, Mason."

"If you aren't staying home to take care of children, what would you be doing with your time?"

I smile sweetly. "We have a house to take care of."

"Erin, give me a break. You're going to start vacuuming and dusting and mopping and cleaning bathrooms? You've got to be joking. It's not that I don't think you can do it, because when you set your mind to something, I know you can. It's just—Erin, I don't want my wife doing those things. You don't need to." His voice softens. "That's why we work so hard, so we can enjoy our lives, rather than spend all our time dealing with stuff like that."

"I could take care of you," I offer, thinking of Brooke and her smooth skin and flouncy dress and stiletto heels on a

Monday morning. Slowly, swaying my hips a little more seductively than normal, I move around the table and plop myself on Mason's lap. He squirms for a second, and then
readjusts as I run my fingers through the fine, black hair on
the back of his head. "If I didn't have to think about work," I
whisper into his ear, "I could think about working other
things."

He makes a low, throaty sound as he buries his head in my
neck. "Well I certainly like the sound of that."

I nip at his earlobe. "We would actually have time together
in the evenings."

"And if it didn't work out," he says softly, caressing my
back, "you could always go back earlier than planned."

I peck his cheek. "I suppose I could, sweetheart, but why
wouldn't it work out?"

"It might throw off my routine." He goes in for a kiss.

I pull away. "What routine?"

He stares at my mouth. "All these years you've been working nights, I've come to like how my evenings play out. I come
home to a quiet house. Dip in the pool and do some laps. Eat
dinner. Have a beer. Watch sports. It's nice."

"And me doing those things next to you *wouldn't* be nice?"

"Don't put words in my mouth, Erin." He gently nudges
me off his lap and takes his plate to the kitchen. I follow him,
desperate to see this through. "That's not what I said." He
faces the sink as if he can't even look at me. "All I'm saying is
it'll be an adjustment. I wish you would've said something to
me about it first."

"I need your *permission* to take a break from working
now?"

"No, but we make decisions together. You should've con-
sulted me."

When he finally turns to face me again and his jaw is set in frustration, I'm not sure I made the right choice in walking out. If I hadn't been hasty, I might've been able to formally request time off. I've asked a few times before, and have been granted only a day off here and there. Nothing like what I'm thinking now. Perhaps we could've negotiated fewer hours working each day. I could review notes for the upcoming day at home, rather than at work. I could become a part-time broadcaster and a part-time stay-at-home wife. Maybe that would've worked out better?

I can run through the options with the station in the morning.

Folding my arms over my chest, I lean against the island. "The only thing is . . . the way I left, they might not want me to come back so soon."

"It was your damn mouth, wasn't it?" He charges at me a step, and then stops. "What'd you say to screw things up this time?"

"I told Ted he was a tool."

"Jesus," he says, and smothers his face with his hand. "He is a tool, but I bet he didn't take that well."

"That's not all."

He peeks at me through his fingers.

"In the heat of the moment, I might've said, 'Fuck all y'all.'"

Without a sound, Mason lowers his hand and stares at me with his mouth open. And then he bursts into a roar of laughter, bowled over, hands on his knees. He shuffles across the kitchen, barely able to breathe in his fit of hysteria, and lifts me off my feet.

"Y'all?" he blurts, laughing into a snort. "You're not southern!"

I smack him on the shoulder. "I know that, *Mason*, it just came out!"

I squeal as I kick to be released, but he doesn't let me down. He carries me upstairs hollering "fuck all y'all" in between hoots of laughter. And when he drops me onto our bed and we strip out of our clothes, we have the best sex we've ever had. Somewhere between orgasms two and three, I swear I acquired a southern accent.

CHAPTER FOUR

ERIN

TUESDAY

This is not my usual morning routine.

I would usually make a cup of coffee and scurry off to my office, where I would run through emails while watching the morning segment. Mason would read his paper in the kitchen and then head up to shower. Before leaving for work, he'd pop his head into my office and blow me a kiss goodbye.

Today, though, I'm perched on one of the stools at the kitchen island, reading an amazing self-help book downloaded onto my e-reader, and tipping back my first cup of coffee, when Mason enters. I'd been anticipating this moment—when Mason would stride into the kitchen and say "good morning" and kiss me on the cheek and we'd gush about how wonderful it is that we can be together this way. He'd ask what I'm reading, I would ask him the same, and we'd hold hands across the table until he had to leave for work.

I've dreamed about how these days would go, when I could give him my full attention in the mornings . . .

Only he doesn't say a word as he marches through the kitchen and pours a cup of coffee without acknowledging the fact that I've brewed enough for both of us, *thank me very much*. Rustling the newspaper to the sports section, he splays it open on the table. Then he plops in the nearest chair—the one where he'll sit with his back to me—and flips furiously through the pages, pausing only to drink from his steaming cup.

"Happy Tuesday," I say, moving to join him. My cup makes a loud clanking sound when its bottom rim hits the table. "How'd you sleep?"

"Good."

I wait for him to say more. When he doesn't, I grab my phone and my book and sit at the table across from him. "What are you reading?"

"The newspaper."

Arranging the mug and book just so, I snap a picture of my morning view, with Mason's head buried in the paper, and vibrant streams of light cascading through the windows. I choose a filter that whitewashes everything in a pure glow. #Morningvibes. #Lovemylife.

After checking my text messages and missed calls— nothing from the station, but it's still early—I glance over at Mason, who's remained unmoving, and silent. My phone pings with new likes.

"I'm reading *Get Out of Your Mind and into Your Life*," I say, feeling a flush of warmth on the back of my neck. "It's really great. Talks about how, as humans, it's in our nature to overthink things, but that causes our lives to be full of stress, and our relationships to be strained." I tuck hair behind my ear in a way that's not at all fidgety. "It gives tips and tricks on learning how to slow down and just be. Really experience each moment as it's presented to us."

"Mmm."

"I can't remember the last time we had the morning all to ourselves this way," I say, beginning to sweat. "It's nice that I get to be out here with you, isn't it? No more hiding away in my office. No stress."

"Mmm."

"Don't you think?"

On a burdened exhale, he flattens his hands over his newspaper, causing the shirt to strain across his chest. "Erin, what are your plans for today?"

"I wanted to read a bit longer," I say excitedly. "Maybe have another cup of coffee with you. Then Georgia and I are going for a walk. Thought I'd introduce her to Brooke, the woman who moved in across the street. Have you had the chance to meet her?"

"Not yet."

"She's married to that famous tech guy who, about this time last year, was caught up in that scandal about his wife and his mistress. *She's* the mistress-turned-new-wife, if you can believe it. Anyway, after that—who knows? Maybe breakfast at Grounds & Greens, or a pedicure. And you know Georgia's going to need help with *something* having to do with the wedding. She's down to the wire and can't possibly do everything herself. She'll probably need my help with a few last-minute things. Don't forget, tonight's the party."

He sips his coffee. "Umm-hmm."

Something about his tone tells me that he's not really listening. "You remembered the party . . ."

He looks up, lost. "What?"

"Georgia and Robert's prewedding party. On his yacht. To-night at six," I say and watch confusion, and then panic, shift over his face. "Don't tell me you scheduled—"

"I remembered." He flips angrily to the next page—the comics section, which he never reads. "Still don't understand why they can't have a bachelor and bachelorette party like normal people."

"Because she's been married before."

"Back to back," he says, giving me side-eye.

"You can't blame Georgia for that."

"That's debatable." He folds his paper noisily. "Just don't understand why it's on a workday. They could've at least picked a weekend, so those of us who still have jobs could properly enjoy ourselves."

"It's only a sunset cruise under the Golden Gate." I brush my hands over the bulge of his shoulder and down his back. "You'll work a full day, come home and change, and then we'll head out. You'll be in bed by midnight."

"And up again at four."

"It means a lot to Georgia that I'm there. She needs me." I shrug, only one shoulder in a way that should be cute as hell, and tuck another strand of hair behind my ear. "She's my best friend."

"You need to stop that."

I frown. "What?"

"Fussing with your hair. It's annoying."

"Oh." I move the hair from behind my ear and let it fall limply to my shoulder. "I didn't even realize I'd done it," I lie.

His jaw clenches. "It's become one of your nervous tics."

"*One* of my tics? I have others?"

He fusses with the paper as if it's wet and he's shaking the droplets off. "Why don't you get things going for your day so you can leave me to my morning paper."

I stare in disbelief as he flips a page so hard he tears the paper. Tension balloons through the space between us as he continues reading. It's as if I'm not sitting right next to him, waiting expectantly for him to apologize for being so callous. This is not the way I'd wanted my first morning as a trophy wife to go, and I wonder if Brooke has these kinds of days, when her reality doesn't live up to her fantasy. I'm sure she doesn't. I'm sure her mornings are smooth and perfect, just like her hair. My phone pings with another like, confirming that my life is the one everyone wants to be living.

"I'll leave you to it then." I don't know what else to say, and I don't want him to be mad. "Have a good day."

"You too," he says, though he pushes out the words as if they're a burden. As if he's frustrated with something I've said or done.

Darting up the stairs and blinking back ridiculous tears, I run into the closet and, on instinct, reach for a long-sleeve, straight-leg jumpsuit with a plunging neckline. I take a step back with a jolt. Nearly my entire side is filled with business attire. Pants and pencil skirts. Blazers and tailored suit jackets. Tie-neck and button keyhole pleated blouses. I love every single outfit. They're power colors on the spectrum from black to gray and back again. No weird patterns or polka dots or splashes of color. Against the back wall, meticulously organized racks of stilettos stare at me. If I quit my job permanently, I wouldn't have to wear any of these ever again. I always put my professional foot forward, unless Georgia and I are on one of our walks. Even then, I stick to my power colors, just in case. I never know when I'm going to run into someone who recognizes me from the show. Keeping viewers interested in *me* is crucial, which means I always have to be on point. I'm the reason they tune in, after all.

Why haven't they called?

I check my phone again for messages. Still nothing.

I'll probably be getting calls from the station manager by noon, begging me to return. I can almost hear Monique now.

They can't do this without you, she'll say, and I'll be able to hear her smile over the phone. *They're paralyzed with fear. They know ratings will plummet without you. You have to come back.*

Who knows what might happen? I could ask for more money for my return, for putting up with Ted all these years. My impulsive decision might just be the best thing that ever happened to me.

Feeling a surge of pride, I slip into black leggings, a matching sports bra, and a billowy red tank. Snapping a quick picture of my reflection, I post it to all of my social media accounts and then shove the phone into the side pocket of my leggings. I'm in my shoes and out the door before Mason finishes reading whatever article has captured his attention.

The morning air is crisp and cool as the foggy marine layer rolls in from the bay, and I'm grateful for the reprieve. I'd started to become stifled in the house, as if the air was too sticky to breathe. As fresh air fills my lungs, I push down Mason's sour morning attitude. It's a blip on the radar. Nothing to dwell on. Georgia has lost two of her husbands, yet she manages to remain cheery, even though her insides must be rotting with grief.

As I'm striding across the street, Brooke pulls into her driveway. I wave enthusiastically when I reach the sidewalk, but she must not have seen because she doesn't return the gesture. I stare at the majestic, White House–like pillars on Robert and Georgia's entry as I knock on the door. One of the things I love about this neighborhood is the ideal spacing between the homes. Far enough apart for beautifully landscaped yards to create a peaceful and somewhat isolated atmosphere, yet close enough that if I'm standing in my driveway, I can *almost* hear conversations drifting over from the yard next door. The street is smooth, newly paved, and much wider than in a usual neighborhood. Six cars could probably line up across without brushing against one another. Feeling like I have eyes on my back, I turn around in time to see Brooke pop the trunk of her car. She is sunshine incarnate, with a canary-yellow dress cinched at the waist with a blue ribbon and polka-dot heels.

She must wake up gaggingly perfect.

Has she had a chance to read the homeowners association handbook yet? I wonder. Surely the real estate agent gave it to her. Brooke must know about the five-minute rule for the garage door. How unseemly would it be if everyone kept their garages open whenever they wanted? I glance at my watch and note the time.

Georgia swings the door open wide and slams her heel into her left tennis shoe. "I'm nearly ready. Two minutes?"

"Sure," I say, following as she hops inside. "No problem."

Shoving on her right shoe, Georgia dashes up the winding staircase and disappears into the last door I can see from the entry. Somewhere upstairs, Robert whistles. It's a tune I don't recognize. High-pitched and erratic. He emerges from the door nearest the staircase wearing nothing but a towel. From my angle far below him, I can see *everything*.

"Oh my God." I shield my eyes with my hand, but it's too late. I've already glimpsed all that tan, wet skin. Bare chest. Thick legs. A generous shape outlined in the darkness beneath his towel. "I'm so sorry, I didn't—I didn't know— I didn't mean . . ."

"Erin, what a surprise." He stomps down the stairs. "Didn't hear you come in."

My nerves bundle into chills at the base of my spine as the image of his muscular chest spins on a hyperloop through my brain. He's lean around the middle, even for his age. Glistening gray hair slicked back on his head. If I caught a glimpse of him in the window at Saks, I'd easily mistake him for a younger version of Robert Redford. They even share the same name.

"I swear I didn't see it—*anything*," I stammer.

He stands close, evaporating all personal space. He's not trying to be creepy or sleazy, I've learned. He's simply one of those people who likes to taste the breakfast on a person's breath.

"You here to see Georgia?" he asks.

Versus the alternative that I'd be here to see . . . *him*?

"Yeah, uh-huh, yup." I tuck my hair behind both ears nervously. And then drop my arms when I remember Mason's comment about it becoming a tic. "She said she'll be right back."

"Shouldn't you be locked away in your office?" he asks. "Isn't that where you usually are at this hour?"

"How would you know my schedule?" I mock defiance. "Have you been keeping tabs on me?"

Light flickers in his light eyes. "No, why? Do you want me to?"

There's no denying his eyes are beautiful, piercing in their intensity. He must be Italian or Greek, though I've never asked. Even without his multimillion-dollar bankroll, I'd say he has undeniable sex appeal. Why he's never been married is anyone's guess.

And believe me, we've been guessing.

When Georgia started dating Robert last year, she thought he might've been a little small beneath the belt. But after she sealed the deal, she was quick to announce that that wasn't the reason he'd remained single after all. Crazy mother? Nope. She visited from Oregon last Christmas and is kind as can be. Mental issues? He either doesn't have them or hasn't let his crazy flag fly yet.

For now, at least, it appears Georgia has finally found herself the perfect guy.

All I know is he better mind himself. Men who cross Georgia get the ax.

Literally.

"Did Georgia tell you the scoop?" I fish my phone out of the leggings' pocket and begin skimming Instagram simply so I don't have to look him in the eye. "I walked out on my job yesterday. So until they call, begging me to come back, my insanely busy mornings are a thing of the past."

I lower my gaze to the floor so I don't get sucked into his eyes again.

"Interesting. That *is* news." Thick droplets of water run down his legs and pool at his feet. "Bet Mason will love having you home all the time."

The way he said the word "love" has the hair on the back of my neck standing on end. There was a hint of sarcasm to it. As if Mason wouldn't like me to quit my job.

"He does, actually," I say smugly, and scroll through my

messages. Surely Monique's called by now. "We had coffee together this morning. We read the paper. Talked about a book I'm reading. It was good."

"You and Mason talked about your book." He nods slowly, disbelieving. "Sounds lovely. So what are you and my wife plotting, other than my imminent demise?"

I laugh nervously because most people in Presidio Terrace already think Georgia is plotting how to kill Robert and inherit every penny in his Swiss bank account. She and Robert hadn't dated long before he proposed. She'd moved him into her Presidio Terrace home—the one she's owned since marrying her first husband, Eli—faster than Robert could say "prenup." Weeks later, wedding invitations went out to everyone in the homeowners association. Two hundred of the most notorious, wealthiest people in California will be gathered in the Julia Morgan Ballroom, watching Georgia marry her next victim. Gossip circles her all the time, as one could imagine. It's not every day that a woman has two husbands die strangely, back to back.

"You've got such a dark sense of humor, Robert." I resist the urge to smack him on the shoulder playfully. "Your wife and I will be hanging out today. Probably grab a bite to eat. Thought I could help her with some last-minute wedding planning. Can you believe you'll be off the market in less than a week?"

"Guess I should make sure I've taken care of everything I need to." He leans in as he whispers, "And everyone."

Did he mean—could he have meant . . . no he couldn't have. "Wha—what about you? Plans today?"

"I'll be at the dock." He plants his hands on his hips as if he wants my attention to drift to the bulge in his towel. "Need to make sure she's ready for her showing tonight."

"Her," I parrot, holding back a laugh. "You're still calling it 'her.'"

He doesn't flinch. "Boats are women."

"Does *she* have a name?"

"*Maxine.*"

"Oh, *Maxine.* Classy." I can't help but grin at the ridiculousness of it all. "So *Maxine* is getting a wax. Don't you have someone you can pay to do that for you?"

He laughs, and his abs twitch. "How would you feel if your husband hired someone to sleep with you?"

"Excuse me?"

"Mason," he repeats, water dripping from his chin. "How would you feel if he neglected your needs so bad that he had to hire someone—me, let's say—to sleep with you?"

"I—I don't know. Angry? Betrayed?"

But it was a knee-jerk answer. As his question roots in my mind, something about the implication has set my insides tingling. Mason and I have been together fifteen years, since Stanford. Sex has always been good between us, but lately when we're in bed at night, he doesn't reach for me the way he used to. If I really think about it, our encounters in the bedroom are occurring less and less. Before last night, the previous time we slept together has to have been three weeks ago. I don't want to sleep with Robert—and not just because I wouldn't do that to Georgia—but I'm a sexual creature. Are *my* needs really being met if I'm sleeping with Mason only once every three weeks? Are his?

"That's exactly how my boat would feel," Robert says darkly. "Betrayed."

"Your boat has feelings now?" Georgia jogs down the stairs with confidence, her raven-black hair fanning behind her. Only she's not wearing black—she's wearing nearly every color of the rainbow: pink-and-purple striped tank, blue swirly leggings, and highlighter-green shoes. Nothing matches, but somehow, as always, Georgia pulls it off with finesse. "Great. The hunk of metal has evolved into a sentient being."

"She'll never replace you, my love." He lifts her hand and plants a gentlemanly kiss on her knuckles. Her ring catches the rays of morning sun and sends a glint of blinding light shooting into my eyes. "You're my number one."

"I better be." Tilting her head lovingly, she flicks his bare stomach. "Did you have a good swim this morning?"

He drops her hand. "Would've been better if you'd joined me."

"I told you I had plans." She gestures at me. "Robert, meet Plans."

I nod as Robert winks at me, a flash that's so quick, if I hadn't been staring directly into his eyes, I might've missed it. "You're still coming tonight, aren't you?" he asks. "Bringing Mason?"

I smile tightly, remembering the terseness of our earlier conversation. "Of course. We wouldn't miss it."

And then he's gone, tightening the towel around his waist as he struts upstairs. I'm sure Georgia hadn't heard what he said. She couldn't have. She wouldn't be smiling as brightly if she'd heard the way Robert came on to me.

"I love that man to death," Georgia says, jerking open the front door, "but I'll never understand his obsession with that boat."

As I step onto the front porch, I see Brooke has left her car in the driveway. And her garage door is still open, gaping like a gutted fish.

"Have a few minutes to run next door so I can introduce you to our new neighbor?" I ask, fighting the urge to fiddle with the hair draped over my shoulder. Inside, my veins rattle with irritation. "I saw her unloading groceries earlier. Seems she forgot a few in the trunk. Come on. You'll love her."

"Will I?"

"She said something about buying you champagne as an early wedding present. Let's see if it made her grocery list." I loop my arm in Georgia's as if we're Thelma and Louise, off to do something naughty. "While we're there, you can judge the hell out of her décor. I know how much you enjoy that."

"And you can nag her about leaving the garage door open." As Georgia spots the malevolent twinkle in my eye, she pats my arm. "I'm glad you're on my side, Erin. Shall we?"

Just like that, all thoughts of Robert and his innuendos evaporate from my mind.

CHAPTER FIVE

BROOKE

Please leave me alone.

One quick glance at Erin's face when I pulled into the driveway earlier, and I know she's itching to barge in on what would've been a peaceful morning. But Jack's limo left for his company's headquarters only an hour ago, and I simply want time to write, and work on my book. It's due in a week, and while I'm nearly finished, something isn't right. It's like a puzzle with all the edges complete, but a few pieces in the middle don't seem to fit into the overall picture. I haven't fleshed out my lead character's motivation either. That might be the problem. Usually, I wouldn't be worried about the deadline— a week is more than enough time for me to get the words down—but with the chaos of the move, I feel as if I haven't had a moment to spend in my characters' heads. My fingers are itching to get back to the keyboard.

After the success of my first mystery, my editor, Lisa Maestretti, has been nudging me to finish this book, and finish it fast. The tone in her monthly check-ins has shifted from enthusiastic to worried. I can hear the doubt in her words. She doesn't think I can do this. I don't think I can do this.

The words aren't flowing like the first time.

It's as if someone's robbed me of them completely.

No matter what it takes, I need to devote a couple hours each day to new pages. Routines get the work done, and that's how I'm going to make this deadline. Later, after I've slopped words onto the page, I'll have time to schmooze with the neighbors.

First things first, though.

I get to work putting things away. Vodka, champagne, and orange juice. Coconut water, honey, and tea. Enough vegetables to fill the drawer in my new high-tech refrigerator. Fruit for the counter. Oranges piled into a gorgeous citrus pyramid. Premade salads.

The house echoes with my every step over the tile, every click of the pantry door. The house is furnished, but empty— the way Jack likes it. Couches, but no decorative pillows or blankets to encourage comfort. End tables, but no lamps or candles or magazines. Pictures on the walls, but nothing too personal. I would've preferred to set out pictures of us on Cape Cod, or preparing to board the private jet, but Jack wouldn't care for it. Instead, the pictures are abstract. Colors splashed here and there, dotting the canvas. Nothing to attract the eye.

"Minimal clutter keeps the energy clean," Jack had said, draping his arm around my shoulder before he left. "There's nothing worse than walking into a house and feeling choked by the crap people call 'decorations.' *People* should make the home, not the things they put in it."

I completely agree. When Jack thinks about our home, he should think of me in this peaceful space, waiting for him with open arms. He shouldn't be worried about the lawn that needs to be mowed or the things that still need to be put away on his side of the bed.

This is the first place we've had together, and I need to make sure that when he walks through the front door, he feels as if he can breathe here. I want him to feel relaxed, to *want* to come home to me. I don't want to be like Patricia, his first wife, who put her needs above his. She was so busy trying to build a career in politics, she left their house a disaster. Rather than support Jack's ambition to make his search engine a household name, she would delete important events from his calendar and erase missed calls from his phone. Even after all the lies and sabotage, despite what the media would have people believe, Jack had wanted to work on their marriage. But Patricia had been unresponsive. Cold as ice. It's no wonder Jack had been starved for affection when we met.

Sunlight washes through the dining room, over the white-marble table that can seat ten. I doubt there'll ever be more than two people eating at any one time, but Jack insisted we be prepared to serve ten at all times.

It must appear that we entertain often, he said. Even though we won't.

I'm still getting used to what it takes to be a billionaire's wife, and I'm not sure I'll ever fully understand. I'm well accustomed to the lengths people go to in order to reach perfection. My mother, determined to get me out of the house, had signed me up for beauty pageants starting at the age of twelve. One pageant turned to a half dozen, and soon we were driving all over the country. It wasn't until my dad started hitting the bottom of the bottle seven nights a week that I realized the pageant trail was not only for my benefit. It got my mother out of the house as well.

I couldn't have known it at the time, but my pageant training prepared me to be married to Jack. It's as if I never left the spotlight. It's all about the image of perfection, keeping up the charade, even if things are melting down behind the scenes. A comment or move that may seem insignificant at the time could blow up years down the road and ruin a future business partnership that could be worth millions.

I can't imagine the weight Jack must bear.

I'm about to steal upstairs and start writing when someone knocks on the back door—the one leading to the garage. Who would come through that way? It could only be one person.

"Jack," I push out nervously.

God, he's going to be so upset if he forgot something and had to turn back.

I turn the handle cautiously, and peer into the space between the door and the jamb. Erin, the woman from across the street, and a dark-haired woman stare back at me.

"Brooke?" Erin says, her wide smile showing a set of straight teeth too large for her mouth. "Can we come in? I wanted to introduce you to Georgia. It'll only take a second."

"Sure, I—I'm sorry, you startled me."

"I told you we should've gone around front, but you had to make a statement," Georgia whispers to Erin. Her shirt is so fluorescent pink, it's nearly blinding. "If this is a bad time, we can come back later."

"No, no, it's fine, but . . ." *Had I put the grocery bag away or was it still resting on the counter? Is everything in order?* "Come on in," I say, but they've already wormed their way inside. Erin and Georgia spill into the kitchen, smiling and full of noisy energy. Georgia is stunning in bright shades of pink and purple, blue, and green—seems magazine-worthy, with ocean-blue eyes that pop against the fairness of her complexion. She's carrying a paper bag and sets it on the counter.

"You left it in the trunk," Georgia says, pushing it toward me. "Thought you might've forgotten it."

She must have balls of steel to grab my groceries and bring them in for me. Or maybe that's just what California neighbors do. It was probably a kind, welcome-to-the-neighborhood gesture that I quickly mistook as being pushy. Erin's probably the envy of everyone at her news station. I bet she often acts first and thinks second, and easily commands the attention of her peers at KFOG—or was it KHOP?

"Thank you. I appreciate that." A giant bottle of Baileys, enough to put me into a deep coma, stares up at me from the brown bottom of the bag. "I'll put this away later. I'm Brooke," I say to Georgia, extending my hand. "You are?"

But I already know. How could I not?

"Oh, I'm such an ass." Erin smacks her forehead. "I suck at introductions."

"Georgia. Nice to meet you." Smiling sweetly, Georgia scans the dining table set for people who'll never come, and the ninety-inch television we'll never watch mounted above the fireplace we'll never light. "Love what you've done with the place. It's minimalistic. Peaceful. Energy's clean."

So this is Georgia. Rumored black widow and husband-killer. Next-door neighbor. A woman who's somehow managed to harness the colors of the rainbow and pull them off without looking tacky. She's petite, maybe a size four. Narrow waist. If she doesn't have breast and butt implants, she's certainly blessed with natural voluptuousness. She doesn't appear to be wearing much makeup, but her eyes are bright, her skin smooth, and her mouth tilts up at the edges with the hint of a smile.

She reminds me of one of the girls I would've seen at pageants when I was young, someone who truly loved the spotlight, who sought it out. Someone very much the opposite of myself. I never wanted the attention. I was only using it to cast a light where I wanted people to look at the time. If people ogled my silky hair extensions, my nails, my tan, or the lightness of my eyes, they weren't looking at the rest of my ugly life that was ripping apart at the seams.

"It's a work in progress," I offer.

"Aren't we all?" It's clear from the hitch of her eyebrows that her question is rhetorical. She strolls through the living room and stops in front of a red and white abstract painting with blue threads attached to the surface. "What do you have here?"

"Forgive the intrusion, but I must ask," Erin says, setting her cell on the table before sliding onto the nearest stool. "Did the real estate agent give you the Presidio Terrace homeowners association handbook? I was curious if you'd had a chance to read it yet?"

"I'm sure she gave us the book, yes." Though I have no idea where I might've put it. "But I haven't had a chance to look through it yet."

"Here she goes," Georgia says from the living room. "This painting is good, Brooke. It makes me think I'm locked in some kind of dream state."

Erin glances into the living room. "Looks like a painting of sticky fog, to me."

Georgia won't let it go. "Did you purchase it new from the artist or from an auction?"

"It was a wedding present from Jack," I say. "I'm not sure where he picked it up. It's called *Reflection*. There's supposed to be a bunch of faces in there or something, but I can never find them."

"There's something about it." Georgia kinks her neck in the opposite direction like a confused canine. "I think I've seen it before, but you know how these abstract paintings are—study too many, and they all start to blend together. Maybe—I'm not sure, but Andrew might've had a print just like it in our office at some point. He changed things around so much, it's hard to be sure, but it's familiar . . ."

"Her ex-husband was shot in their home, in his office," Erin declares without lowering her voice. "Georgia was home in bed. Didn't even know there was an intruder until the gunshot. You must sleep like the dead!"

Georgia waves her off as if she's annoyed.

"Oh, that's . . ." I don't know what to say. "Terrible. I'm so sorry."

"Don't be." Georgia glances at me over her shoulder. "You didn't kill him."

Does Georgia talk about her exes often? I wonder. Do their names spill off her tongue effortlessly or does she keep their secrets tucked close to her heart?

"Brooke, what I was going to say before Georgia derailed the conversation with talk of her dead ex is that we have a strict rule about not leaving garage doors open for more than five minutes at a time." Erin checks something on her phone, her lips downturned in a puzzled sort of frown. "Wouldn't want the other neighbors to get the wrong impression of you from the start. We want everyone to know that you care about our neighborhood, as I'm sure you do."

"Yes, of course." The transition from Georgia's ex-husband's murder to my garage door startles me. "I—I didn't mean to—"

"It's fine. I wouldn't imagine that you did it on purpose." Erin reaches across the island as if to soothe my anxiety. "You'll need to pull your car in and close the door as soon as we leave. It's not like we're going to penalize you or anything if you don't. I simply thought you could use the reminder."

"She will fine you though," Georgia says darkly, returning to the kitchen. "Don't respond quickly enough and you'll find a fee envelope in your mailbox. She takes her job very seriously. This job, that is. As for the one she just walked out on, that's another story."

"You quit your job?" I startle. "At KHOP?"

"It was KFLAG, thanks for listening, but yeah, I did. Well sort of." Erin snaps and the crisp sound echoes through the kitchen like the crack of a whip. "I wanted a sabbatical, so I took it. I had an epiphany yesterday: I couldn't put up with Ted's condescending attitude for another minute—he's my coanchor, damn him, and he could've at least treated me as his equal. Anyway, I walked out and am taking today off. Maybe the week. Perfect timing for Georgia's wedding and all. I absolutely expect them to call any minute and grovel to get me back."

"Oh, I'm sure they will."

"Erin and I were headed out for a walk," Georgia says, beside me. "And then we planned on hitting up Grounds & Greens. Want to come?"

I'm still trying to process why a woman like Erin—so professional and composed—would walk out on her job. "Grounds & Greens? Wha—what is that?"

"If the neighborhood's built like a nest, with the houses swirling round and round, it's smack in the center—the egg, as it were," Erin says. "Each morning they serve mimosas so strong you'll be able to put up with *anything* the rest of the day . . . even your husband. Not that you have to do that, of course. You're one of the lucky ones—your husband is a workaholic."

"Oh, he used to be, but now that we're closer to his offices, I imagine he'll spend more time at home." They're staring at me strangely, as if expecting me to go on. "He'll travel to the satellite branches in Seattle, Sacramento, or Los Angeles now and again, but for the most part he'll be here."

"You sound happy. How lucky for you." Georgia groans softly. "I need a drink. Thank God Grounds & Greens serves the best mimosas."

Erin and Georgia exchange a quick glance as Erin's phone pings. Erin slides her cell out of the side pocket of her leggings and swipes her finger over the screen. Her eyes track quickly as if she's reading a text message.

"They want to see me first thing tomorrow morning." She smiles smugly. "They can't run the show without me, and now they know it. I bet they're going to beg me to come back immediately, and be so disappointed when I request the week off."

Georgia gives her a high five that echoes through the house. "They can't live without you."

"I'm happy for you," I say. I know how thrilled I'd be if I had a job that valued my expertise. Instead, I'm suffering from a serious case of impostor syndrome. "Now we have cause to celebrate. First round of mimosas on me!"

"I'll hold you to that." Georgia grins. "But don't mention it to Erin's husband. He doesn't like it when she drinks this early in the morning. He'd kill her if he found out."

"Not like you killed *your* husbands," Erin retorts, and for the first time I sense a bit of animosity between them. The tension in the air thickens.

Georgia rolls her eyes. "Of course not. No one can kill with the finesse that *I* do."

I stare at the sharp angles of Georgia's nose and chin, at the way her eyes give no hint of the truth away. Why would she joke about her ex-husbands' deaths so callously? Surely she doesn't want everyone to think she's guilty. That'd paint a target on her back. She's almost larger than life, a character who's vibrant in the colors she wears and dark in her humor. Deadly beautiful. The hint of an idea niggles at the back of my brain. I could make Georgia a character in my story. A true Black Widow. I'd have to change her name, of course, but it's been so long since I've heard the familiar heartbeat of my muse, I'm eager to keep her alive.

"Let me change into some workout clothes," I say eagerly.

After I've pulled my car into the garage and secured the door, we start off on our walk. We're not three minutes in before Erin starts gushing about her therapist, Dr. Theresa Wilson. I wonder if Georgia's ever been to therapy, and if she opens up about her husbands' deaths. I'm intrigued, my thoughts racing as I breathe life into a character in my head. Does she grieve like a normal widow? Does she take any re-sponsibility for their demises? What type of woman would joke about killing her husbands? I prefer writing about savvy characters, especially women, who think they have the world on a string.

"Where are you from originally?" Erin asks me, her stride eating up the sidewalk. "Virginia, like your husband?"

She's really thorough in her research. "I don't know that I'm really from anywhere in particular. When I was growing up, my family moved every six months for my dad's work—he was in the army. I guess you could say I call Louisiana home, since we were there the longest, but I lived in Virginia most recently. That's where I met Jack."

"I love the South," Georgia says dreamily.

"No, you love southern men." Erin rolls her eyes. "It's the accents. You already have one on the line, G. Focus." She laughs, and then turns her sights back on me. "Were you seeing anyone back home?"

"Other than my husband?"

"No, not a man—a therapist," she clarifies. "Do you have a shrink?"

"No." I keep my pace in time with theirs. "Do you?" I ask Georgia.

"I don't trust therapists," she says sharply, then points out a dark blue home on the corner. "Senator Baldwin lives there and his wife holds *all* the power in their relationship. She sleeps with the pool boy every Wednesday afternoon while her husband is at the office. They see Erin's therapist."

She nods. "They referred me."

"We all have issues," Georgia says. "Some of us need to talk through them, others are more adept at managing them on their own."

"And others simply pretend they don't exist," Erin chimes in. "Not that I would know about that. The couple in that house with the red door didn't get approval to have it painted. I don't care that it's the same color it was before, they still had to get approval. They thought they could just ignore the issue and it'd go away . . . so I called them out at the last homeowners association meeting in front of everyone. You should have seen their faces."

"Three-hundred-dollar fine," Georgia says, laughing. "Pennies to them, but still. It was the principle."

"Those people with the gray garage door fight, but only after two A.M. so their neighbors won't hear," Erin says. "Apparently if the wind is just right, and Georgia opens her windows on that side of the house, she can hear every word."

"It's juicy," Georgia agrees, nodding. "You should be able to hear it too. Might make you feel a whole lot better about your own marital issues."

"I don't have marital issues," I say, pulse quickening.

"Of course not," Erin and Georgia say together, and then they giggle.

It's true. Jack and I are happy. We love each other. I can't imagine my life without him. What I do have are book issues. Characters who won't behave. Plot holes that won't fill themselves. And it occurs to me that not once has Erin or Georgia asked what I do for a living. Our conversations have revolved around Jack and therapy and Erin's work and Georgia's dead husbands. Par for the course of my life. I find a strange sort of comfort in being overlooked as just another pretty face.

As we follow the sidewalk toward the guard shack, the attendant runs out the back door waving a small white envelope over his head. "Ms. St. Claire! A delivery for you."

"Early wedding present?" Erin asks.

Georgia shakes her head as we cross the street. "We said no presents, remember?"

The attendant meets us at the curb. "Someone dropped this off about an hour ago. I was waiting until the mail came to walk it over."

"He delivers our mail by hand?" I ask Erin.

"Only Georgia's." Erin leans in to whisper in my ear. "She must offer him some incentive. It's not hard to guess."

"She's sleeping with the—"

"Shhh," Erin says.

"It's no problem," Georgia says kindly, taking the envelope. "Thanks, Malik."

Malik. That's right. For the life of me, I couldn't remember his name. He looks like a sweet man who tries to please,
with a soft smile, and squinty eyes hidden behind his unfash-
ionably square glasses. His uniform—a collared polo shirt and
khaki pants—is faded a bit on the edges. I can't imagine Georgia sleeping with the guy. What could he possibly offer her
that her fiancé—or her previous two husbands, for that
matter—couldn't?

As we continue our trek down the sidewalk, Georgia tears
into the envelope and pulls out a piece of cardboard, smooth
and white, the size of a wedding RSVP card.

"What the ever-loving-fuck?" She stops and covers her
mouth with her hand. The color drains from her face as she
turns the card around. "Another one?"

TIME IS RUNNING OUT. PAY WHAT YOU OWE is
scrawled in thick, black ink.

CHAPTER SIX

BROOKE

As Georgia takes a call just outside the front doors, a waiter escorts Erin and me to seats near the window overlooking a wide lawn and gravel flower beds filled with potted hydrangeas. Beyond the grass, sidewalk, and narrow lane, gigantic houses bathe in the orange-red glow of morning sunlight, their pillars long and smooth, their hues vibrant.

"Is it hot in here?" Erin asks, fanning herself with the menu. "No? Just me. My temperature is off lately. Not sure what's happening—and don't you dare say menopause." She laughs nervously and glances up at the waiter, who's staring at her quizzically. "Mimosa with light strawberries for me. Nothing to eat. For Georgia, a mimosa with raspberry, sugar rim, and a warm bagel—lightly toasted—with pepper and cream cheese. Brooke?"

"Sure." When the waiter disappears, I say, "I don't think

anyone has ever ordered for me before, the way you just did for Georgia."

"That's what friends do. Your husband doesn't order for you?"

"No," I say, nor would I want him to. "Never."

Her eyebrows hitch as if she can't believe it. "Mason doesn't either. I just didn't think Georgia would want us to wait. Here she comes."

"Sorry," Georgia says, relaxing into her chair and flicking the card into the center of the table. "I needed to report the threat to the police. Can you believe it? I mean, I have no idea what the person is referring to. I don't owe anyone *anything.*"

"And I'm sure if you did, you would pay it," I say, trying to comfort her. "When you first saw it, you said 'another.' How many threats have you gotten like this?"

"What would you say, Erin? Five? Six?"

Erin thanks the waiter as he drops off our drinks and Georgia's food. "Has to be over ten by now. Started shortly after her second husband died."

"Ten?" I squeal.

"Erin, I didn't know you ordered for me," Georgia says, dismissing my shock. She takes a quick, sloppy bite of her bagel, smearing cream cheese onto the corners of her mouth. "You're the best. Pure gold."

"No, if I were the best," Erin says after a long sip, "I would've been camped out at the police department, demanding they find whoever is responsible for sending all those things."

"That wouldn't help," Georgia says, dejected. "The threats would keep coming."

"The police have to be able to do something." Tipping back the mimosa, I think about what I would do if I were in

Georgia's shoes. "You should take this in and have them check for prints."

"I did that for the first few, of course," she says. "Nothing ever came of it. They're clean. Every one. At this point it's a waste of my time to keep going down to the station. Now they say, as long as the threats aren't escalating, I shouldn't be concerned."

"You're being harrassed," I say, incredulous. "If they don't act, when will it end?"

"The problem is, they don't have a thread to start pulling." Erin leans over the table, anxious, fingers twirling around one another. It's as if she's getting ready to play Clue. "If only they had an idea of who it could be. You have tons of enemies. Your ex-husbands' families, for starters. They hate you."

Georgia drinks heartily. "Let's not dig up the past."

"What about the hermit on the corner who glares from her living room window every time we walk by?" Erin asks. "It was probably her."

"It wasn't anyone who lives in the neighborhood," I say quickly.

Georgia looks to me. "How do you know?"

"Because they didn't leave the note on your doorstep. They left it with that Malik guy. That means they couldn't get in to deliver the note themselves."

"She's clever," Erin says to Georgia. "All of them have come through the mail, haven't they? Well except for the one that was left on your car when you were out shopping."

I can't help but smile. "The message is disturbing, but at least you can sleep easy knowing whoever it was can't get in."

"Deep down, I've always had suspicions about Penny— you know, the woman two houses down who cuts her grass with scissors?" Erin fans herself with her napkin. "She's always wound so tight. Wouldn't take much for her to snap. I appreciate her adherence to the rules on keeping up the lawns, of course, but damn, no one has to go to those lengths."

"She's not the first person on the terrace you've driven crazy," Georgia says, laughing loudly. "Remember Veronica?"

"Ohhhh, I loathed her," Erin says, crinkling the napkin in her fist.

"Who's Veronica?" I ask.

"A woman who lived right over there." Georgia points to a gray house that looks exactly like the others on the street. "She had a mad crush on Mason, Erin's husband, and when she discovered he was a plastic surgeon, she went to see him as much as possible. She must've had twenty surgeries last year alone."

"What happened?"

"Nothing," Erin says quickly, but the bite in her tone gives away her jealousy. She takes a long, hard drink, draining her second mimosa. "Her marriage was on the rocks, but mine was solid. Always has been. She tried to get my man. She failed. And then she and her husband moved away because there were better insane asylums in Texas, apparently. End of story."

"What else should I know about the neighborhood?" I ask, feeling nervous for the first time since I sat down. I'm not even sure why my insides have gone all jittery. "Anyone I should stay away from?"

"Honestly?" Erin raises her empty glass. "Us."

And we all laugh.

"Truer words were never spoken," Georgia says. "We're not the best influences. Everyone in the neighborhood would agree."

"I think you're both great," I say. "I wasn't in Virginia long enough to make friends. I was only there a month when I ran into Jack at some random bar outside of D.C. Once we met, we were pretty much inseparable."

Erin's smile falters. "What about family?"

"Not in Virginia," I say. "My dad died right after I graduated high school, so it's really just my mom, and she still lives in Louisiana, in the house I grew up in. I talk to her on the phone as much as I can, but with Jack's career, we don't really have time to see her very often (I have a brother who lives in Florida, but we have very different views on life."

This is not entirely true. We have time to fly down to visit my mother, but I don't really have any interest in going back. I think that's partially thanks to the way my parents raised me. Growing up, moving so often, I never really felt like I could get my footing in any one place. I left behind friends, boyfriends, schools. After a while, I started to enjoy the endless possibilities of a new place. I could put a period at the end of one sentence and move on to another, brighter, better one. I could become anyone I wanted—a character from a story even. I think that's what made me want to become a writer. Watching ordinary characters living out their extraordinary lives became a weird little pastime that I absolutely loved. The other reason I don't want to go back home is the way my father died, and the way my mom looks at me. But I doubt Georgia and Erin are ready to hear that story yet.

I glance around the quaint shop, which smells of coffee and baked goods. The tables are empty, save for a woman sitting in the corner feeding pieces of her biscotti to the teacup Yorkie tucked under her arm. Now there's a character I could develop into someone amazing . . .

"Oh my God," Erin says under her breath. "I can't believe she brought that thing in here. Do you recognize who that is?"

I turn around completely, and Erin smacks my arm. "Don't look at the same time as Georgia. Too obvious."

"It's Pam—the labor and delivery nurse who moved into the neighborhood last month," Erin explains, and snaps a picture of her mimosa before diving in. "She lives around the corner. Married to a lawyer who defended that guy who killed someone last year—I don't remember the name. Anyway, she's certifiably insane. Maybe she's the one who wrote that card."

"You don't know that she's insane," Georgia snaps. "I think she's sweet."

Making a dismissive sound, Erin leans closer and motions for us to do the same. "I hear she thinks that dog is a human. Takes it everywhere—even to bed with her, if you know what I mean."

I stifle a laugh by smothering it down with my drink.

"This gossip is as cold as my first husband's grave," Georgia says. "Can we talk about something else?"

"Fine," Erin asks. "Have you talked to Robert about Maxine yet?"

"Before you assume my husband's having an affair," Georgia says, leaning toward me, "you should know that's his yacht. They have a special relationship. And no, Erin, I haven't brought it up."

"You need to fight for a place in his life," Erin says fondly. "He should be waxing your ass as much as he waxes that boat."

I've spent only one morning with these women and I love them already.

"Does your husband have a yacht?" Georgia asks me.

"Or a hobby you absolutely despise?" Erin adds quickly.

I shake my head. "No to both."

"Lucky you," Georgia says, breaking off a chunk of her bagel. "I hear your husband is quite the computer geek."

"Thank you?" I say with a chuckle as I fiddle with my hands in my lap. I'm always so nervous when the conversation starts to veer toward Jack's business. I don't know much about technology and find myself tuning out when Jack rambles on about this person needing that information for this meeting, and that guy needing money for this investment. It's not so much that I'm not interested as that I'm afraid of sounding stupid. "News really travels fast around here."

"It's the neighborhood," Erin offers. "You can hardly sneeze without hearing 'bless you' come from half a dozen surrounding houses."

"It's no secret how we found out," Georgia says. "I used the same real estate agent when I bought my place ten years ago. She called to fill me in on the details after your walkthrough. She said your husband bought the house *for* you . . . not *with* you. Interesting choice of words, I thought."

My insides squirm like I've swallowed worms. She smiles but takes a swift drink before she laughs. Erin giggles, the high-pitched sound like daggers to my ears. When Jack said we'd be house hunting, I started researching neighborhoods from Sacramento to San Francisco, all within driving distance to Silicon Valley. From the moment I spotted Presidio Terrace, I knew it would be a perfect fit. Yes, he bought it for me. It was his final decision, as the moneymaker in our household. But our home was my absolutely first choice. Its location is prime. I wouldn't have moved into any other home in any other neighborhood.

"Not like you can judge," Erin fires at Georgia. "You bought your house for no one but yourself. Andrew didn't mind moving into the house you lived in with Eli."

"That's true," Georgia corrects. "And Robert doesn't mind either."

Suddenly, the stories I've heard about Georgia begin to take shape. Eli, her first husband, had fallen down the stairs. Cracked his head open. Andrew, her second, had shot himself in their office. How could Robert be comfortable living in the same home where her previous two husbands had not only lived but died? How could she?

"It all boils down to loyalty," Georgia says quietly, and Erin stills beside her. "It's important to make sure the ones you keep closest to you are the people you can trust wholeheart-edly, and that includes those who live within earshot. I trust Erin with my life. I enjoy having her close to me. Each of my husbands knew they'd have to wheel my lifeless corpse out of this neighborhood—I'd never leave willingly."

I look to Erin and expect her to smile cheekily or gush about how much she trusts Georgia as well. Only, she doesn't. She's watching me carefully, and I'm suddenly keenly aware that Georgia's conveying a message, and I'm supposed to be paying attention.

"I think it's nice that you allowed your husband to pur-chase your home for you," Georgia goes on. "It shows the level of trust in your relationship."

"Or the level of control," Erin says under her breath.

"Excuse me, I don't mean to bother you," someone says from across the restaurant. It's Nurse Pam. She's left her table and is walking closer, her slip-ons silent over the tile floor. She stops only when she bumps against the table with her thighs. "You're Georgia St. Claire, aren't you?"

With a little flip of her hair, Georgia looks up and beams. "I am. We met last month when you moved in, remember? I brought you over a welcome basket. Erin, my friend here, had her personal chef bake the cookies."

Pam frowns. "I know about you—after we got settled, I Googled your name and read all about how your husbands were killed. I've been sitting over there minding my own business, but I wouldn't forgive myself if I didn't say something— the way you sit here talking about your ex-husbands is revolting. You should be ashamed of yourself."

"Yet you RSVP'd to my prewedding party tonight," Georgia says sweetly, her smile not faltering. "You said you were coming."

Pam's chin lifts confidently. "Harold and I are attending to show support for your husband-to-be, the poor man. It's not assigned seating, is it?"

At that, the light in Georgia's eyes dims. For the first time since I've met Georgia, I feel bad for her.

"Pam," I say, interjecting before this conversation completely derails. "If you're going to be two-faced, at least make sure one of them is pretty."

Cursing, Pam spins around, collects her things from her table, and pushes out the café doors. Erin smothers her laugh with her hand while Georgia simply stares at me with a smile on her face.

Once she's gone, Erin lets loose. "Brooke, you're gold. Solid gold. I can't believe you just said that. Georgia, can you believe she just said that? Oh, that was too good. I wish I'd snapped a shot of the expression on her face so I could look at it again and again. I always had a strange feeling about Pam, from the moment she took those cookies and didn't even say thank you. Georgia . . . there's no way she's coming now, which means you have two open seats for your party."

"I do, don't I?" Georgia says after a pause. She hasn't taken her eyes off me the whole time. "It's a sunset cruise around the bay tonight at six. A little dinner and dancing. Your husband is invited too, of course. It'll be perfect. The men can run off and talk about golf or boats or whatever, and we can stay behind to drink and gossip. You in?"

Jack's going to be exhausted, if he can come at all. The entire time we've been together, I don't think we've ever been invited to something because of me. IT and tech conferences? Sure. He's been the keynote speaker plenty of times. But we're being invited to this because of me. I'm not sure how he'll respond.

"Sure," I say coyly. "Sounds like fun."

"I wish we didn't have to be stuck on Robert's yacht," Georgia says, "but we'll deal with it the best we can."

"Enough about Robert's yacht . . ." Erin groans. "Something has to be done, Georgia. Frankly, I'm just tired of hearing you complain about it."

"I should just light the bitch on fire," Georgia says darkly. "After the wedding, of course."

"You're not serious." I let my gaze flip between them. They're unreadable. I can't tell if they're malicious or simply have dark senses of humor. "You must be joking."

"Oh, I want to help." Erin bounces up and down in her seat and claps her hands. "You know how I like reconnaissance missions. I could sneak out there at night to make sure the job is finished. Just say the word."

"Done deal," Georgia says, raising her glass. "Bonus points if the captain goes down with the ship."

I'm taken aback, gaping at the casualness in her tone. She'd just put a very informal hit out on her soon-to-be husband in a very public place. Does she realize that? Anyone could have heard her just then. She could be in some serious trouble. Or is her sense of humor so dark that she simply doesn't care who overhears?

Georgia and Erin clink their glasses together and wait for mine to join theirs. For the first time in as long as I can remember, I'm thinking about characters and plots and I'm excited about going out and meeting new people. And it's all because of these two sinful women. I clink my glass against theirs as Erin pulls out her phone and takes a photo of our hands lifted high, morning light reflecting off the rims of our empty glasses. She hashtags it #3Musketeers and #Sinking-LikeTitanic.

I don't know why it occurs to me now, but suddenly I know what's missing from my manuscript in progress—a character readers will either love, or love to hate. I know exactly how I'm going to fix things now. And someone who looks a lot like Georgia, and talks like her too, is going to land on the page.

CHAPTER SEVEN

ERIN

Can't wait to see you in the morning, I text Monique. *Do you know if they'll want me on air for tomorrow's segment?*

Tossing my phone onto the edge of the bed, I check my reflection in the full-length mirror next to our dresser and smooth down the lines in my dress. I've chosen my favorite for tonight: a little black dress, three-quarter-length sleeves, form-fitting, with a slight flare at the knee. It's always made me feel like Audrey Hepburn. I tie a simple string of pearls around my neck and feel like I can take on the world.

My phone buzzes.

I didn't know you were coming in, Monique texts back. *It'll be good to see you. Not the same without you here.*

Not the same without me.

Precisely as I thought. No one has my energy, my pizzazz. But why wouldn't she have known that I was coming? Surely they would've told her I was returning . . .

When the door to the bathroom opens and Mason emerges in a black suit and tie, I have to catch my breath. Sometimes that man still takes my breath away.

"You look great. Very sophisticated," I say, straightening his tie. I'm nearly bursting to tell him the news—I'll be going back to the station, but not until after this week, and Georgia's wedding, is over. And if I'm feeling feisty, I'm going to demand more pay. Maybe more comprehensive benefits. Who knows. "I always love you in black."

He looks me up and down. "Is that what you're wearing?"

"Yup." I give a twirl, my arms raised over my head like a slightly uncoordinated ballerina. "What do you think?"

"I've seen you in it before." He shrugs as if he's unimpressed. Doesn't he see I'm wearing pearls? "Didn't you wear that thing to Georgia's first wedding?"

That . . . *thing*?

He disappears into the closet to slip on his shoes, and I check my reflection again. Boobs sitting at attention. Spanx tightening the soft curves of my stomach. Smoothing my fingers over the wrinkles at the edges of my eyes, I think about the last time I wore this dress. It wasn't to a wedding.

"Oh God," I say, suddenly recalling. "I wore it to one of their funerals."

"Thought so," he calls from the closet. "I've never liked that dress anyway."

I flinch as if he's struck me. "You've never said anything about it."

"I'm saying something now." He emerges from the closet, ready to go, and checks his phone. "Five minutes. I'll be waiting downstairs."

As I'm sifting through clothes that are too bright or too plain, too dark or—God, not that one—too gaudy, I find the perfect dress buried in the corner. It's from Saks, a robe dress, navy blue, long sleeves, deep-cut V-neck, and a ruffle on the side. I'm sliding into my shoes and prancing downstairs when I hear Mason's voice drifting from the kitchen.

"I can't talk long. Only another second. I told you why." His voice deepens. "I'm sorry. I completely forgot about tonight." He pauses, two pregnant beats. "I'll make it up to you, I promise."

My heart clenches into a fist as I tiptoe closer. The palms of my hands slicken with sweat. He can't be talking to another woman—he'd never cheat on me—and yet, something about the tenderness in his voice, and the sincerity in his apology, has me second-guessing my gut instinct. I hate to jump to conclusions. Like Georgia said earlier, loyalty is the most important part of a relationship, whether that's a friendship or a marriage.

I slink onto the last stair and then descend to the floor. My heel clicks against the tile.

"She's ready." He's all business now, his tone sharp. "I'll be in touch."

When he turns the corner, sliding the cell into his breast pocket, he sees me and smiles sincerely. "Hey, gorgeous." He kisses my cheek. "That's much better."

I gaze up at the handsome angles of his face, searching for signs of infidelity. Isn't that where I'm supposed to see it? The shiftiness of his eyes and the smile that's a little too forced? But it's not there. He's simply my Mason.

I take his hand in mine and let him lead me to the car. We're at South Cove Yacht Harbor by quarter to six, and when his headlights sweep over the dock, I spot Georgia immediately. It's as if the light fixates on her magnetically, illuminating every perfect curve, every windswept highlight of her hair. A group of people huddles around her. As Mason parks, I see Brooke on the arm of a man whose hair is slicked to the side, his back ramrod straight. He gives a handshake here, a fake smile there, like a politician. A thumbtack would probably have more personality.

As Mason escorts me toward the main group, and a wave of laughter carries on the cool sea breeze, he smiles through his teeth. "We're not staying the whole time. I don't know any of these people and I have work I could be doing."

"You know Georgia and Robert. That's all that matters. Besides, we're going to be on the bay, sweetheart. It's not like you can just walk off into the water." I feel him tense beside me. "Can you work from your phone?"

"It's not ideal."

"Does it have to be 'ideal'?" I make air quotes. "Or can you make it work for one night?"

His steps pound on the concrete as we approach the dock. I pray he gets over his attitude before we reach the rest of the group.

"I'll figure it out," he mumbles.

But I can tell from his tone that he's not happy about being here. Maybe if he weren't so busy, he would've remembered about tonight. I love that his business is booming, but how much longer are we going to have to sacrifice our time together for his career? I'm about tired of it. If Mason weren't slaving away at his desk, he would've been ready to go tonight, and eager to have a date night together. He's always busy lately, always cramming in appointments first thing in the morning and after hours.

I completely forgot about tonight, he'd said over the phone.

It hits me then. He had other plans. That's why he'd apologized. I don't even know how to ask without sounding paranoid and ticking him off.

As something in my heart bangs like a boat against the dock, I go for broke. "Who were you talking to earlier?"

"When?"

"When I came downstairs."

He waves to Robert, who's leading everyone down the wood planks to where his yacht is berthed. "The office. They wanted me to reschedule a meeting. Not all of us have the liberty of walking out on our job. Some of us have to pay the bills."

Out of the corner of my eye, I watch Brooke and her husband blend with the rest of the group. Coiling his arm around her waist, her husband whispers in her ear. She laughs, throwing her head back like a woman in one of those vacation commercials where the couple is having the time of their lives. She's smiling, glowing actually, and I can't help but glance at Mason. He's scowling. Checking his watch. Sighing heavily and rolling his eyes. He clearly wants to be anywhere else in the world, rather than boarding Robert's yacht . . . with me.

When Georgia sees me, I squeal to match the volume and pitch of her squeal, and Mason plugs his ears. She jogs over precariously on her stilettos so that her heels don't fall between the planks of the dock and wraps me up in a bear hug. God, she smells good. She's always smelled like roses and sunshine, even after each of her husbands died. I don't know how she does it.

"I'm so glad to see you." She links her arm in mine as if I'm her date, then glances over her shoulder at Mason. "You don't mind if I steal your wife away for a while, do you?"

He gives a dismissive kind of wave. "It'll break my heart, but I'm sure I'll manage."

Georgia whisks me into a group filled with people I don't recognize and quickly begins introducing me as her best friend. I meet Robert's yacht buddies, coworkers, and a few married couples from our neighborhood. It doesn't take long to forget Mason's attitude. Once he's on the yacht and having a good time, he won't even think about leaving.

"You look fabulous," I gush, whispering in her ear. "I've never seen this dress on your before."

Georgia does a twirl, gently pulling the ocean-tinted dress away from her sides. "It's an Elie Saab. Remember that day you came over to sunbathe and we sat beside my pool reading *Vogue*? It's the one that made me moan and stroke the page just as—"

"Robert came out to see what we were up to," I finish for her, remembering the image from the magazine perfectly. "He bought it for you?"

"He remembered, all on his own," she says, her tone deliciously dark. "Isn't he to die for?"

He is, it would seem.

I glance behind me at Mason, who's slipped away from the main group to hover over something on his phone. Mason would never buy me a twelve-thousand-dollar dress, which is exactly what that A-line, square-necked, beaded gown with satin stripes was on sale for. And he'd certainly never remember which dress had me moaning with delight, only to buy it as a surprise.

Maybe it's because Robert and Georgia are still in the courting stage. That has to be it. I remember when Mason and I were getting ready for our wedding, we couldn't keep our hands off each other. We had actual bachelor and bachelorette parties—not a prewedding celebration like this—and we both found a way to disappear from our respective parties to have sex. When we reappeared an hour later, cheeks pink, lips flush, no one even knew we'd been gone.

It's times like those that I miss—when we could keep our little secrets from the rest of the world, and it was just him and me.

Now that Mason and I have been married five years, some of the shine has worn off. Our marriage is the piece of jewelry that's been sitting in my box, unworn and forgotten for too long. It's collecting dust, and a little dull, and if I were to decide to wear it one day, I'd put the time and effort into cleaning it up. I'm sure if I brought up my feelings in therapy, Theresa would say it's about time that the newness wears off. There's got to be something like a five-year itch I haven't heard about. I'm sure I'd have to do something outlandish to bring back the spark, and then everything would be fine again.

But I'm tired of being the one to put in all the effort.

I want him to woo me, to buy me a twelve-thousand-dollar dress that makes me feel like a million bucks, to whisper in my ear and make me giggle.

I want him off his damn cell phone.

"Brooke!" Georgia exclaims and embraces her the same way she did me a few minutes earlier. I'd thought her excitement was genuine . . . appears I was mistaken. It rubs me the wrong way, though I swallow my feelings with a smile. "Glad you could make it. Mr. Davies, it's nice to meet you."

He's taller than I'd realized from the broadcast we'd covered about him. Or perhaps he's simply standing straighter. His eyes are piercing blue, almost white, and he examines

Georgia critically before finally extending his hand. His skin is smooth.

"Pleasure's mine," he says, shaking as she puts her tiny hand in his. "I've heard so much about you."

Georgia kinks an eyebrow seductively. "Oh, I'm sure only the good things."

After oohing and aahing over Brooke's strapless cocktail dress and another round of squeals and hugs, Robert calls everyone to the second berth, where he's docked his life's joy: *Maxine*. The yacht looms over us, luxurious and sleek, with a sharp, pointed bow. Long, narrow, blacked-out windows on the sides look like glossy insect eyes watching us. Before we board, he raises his arms triumphantly and gives a speech, gushing over its glory. Hundred feet long. Cruising speed of sixteen knots. Five generous staterooms that can sleep twelve, along with a master suite on the main deck. Jack lifts his hand as if he's commanding a meeting—bless his soul—and barks out a statement about a monitoring system that can enhance the yacht's security. Robert assures him that it already has its own state-of-the-art security system. Best money can buy. Jack nods, giving his approval. Full dining room that seats twenty comfortably. Sundecks in front and back.

"All aboard," he says cheerily. "Any questions?"

"Where's the bar?" Mason asks to riotous applause.

Please don't let him get drunk tonight and make a fool of himself. Please . . .

As we step onto the back sundeck, between multiple rows of lounge seating, Georgia tugs me close. "Before we all meet in the dining room, can you follow me to the master suite on the main deck? I need a witness."

"That sounds backwards," someone says from behind me. "Murderers usually want to minimize witnesses."

It's Jack. He looks proud of his little joke, with a smug smile splashed on his handsome face. Beside him, Brooke looks mortified, the color draining from her cheeks. She hangs her head and sighs.

"What good would it do to kill him now, sweetheart?" Georgia bats her eyelash extensions at him. "We're not even married yet."

CHAPTER EIGHT

ERIN

Laughing tightly, Georgia squeezes me against her, almost as if she wants protection as our group fills the dining room. Mason heads straight to the indoor bar with Jack and Brooke, and I watch him say something—I'm sure it's a joke he thinks is witty—and they laugh, clinking their glasses together. The rest of the group fills both the indoor and outdoor dining tables, lounging back onto the sea-blue cushions, diving into conversation about their jobs, the yacht, how smooth and calm the water appears. A fire has been lit in the center of each of the tables, casting warm glows over their faces.

As the yacht pulls away from the dock, silently slicing through the water, Georgia leads me to the master bedroom. It's modern and airy, and doesn't feel like we're on the water at all. A king-sized bed is in the center, while a dresser rests against the far wall, and two chairs and a table sit beneath a wide span of tinted windows. Outside, the docks disappear and are replaced with San Francisco's colorful cityscape. Somewhere in the dining room, piano music begins to play.

I wonder why Georgia has such an aversion to Robert's yacht. If Mason were to have something like this—an obsession that stole his time away from me, but one we could enjoy *together*, I wouldn't have a problem at all.

I'm about to ask Georgia why she's whisked me away from the party when Robert enters, securing the door quietly behind him. It hadn't occurred to me earlier, but he must've hired someone to captain the yacht so he could be present for tonight's event.

"This is it," he says and meets Georgia at the chairs. She sits in one of them delicately and begins flipping through the papers he's placed on the table in front of her. "Let us slay this big fat elephant in the room once and for all, shall we?"

Hesitant, not exactly sure what I've walked into, I perch on the edge of the bed and watch Georgia's face drop.

"I thought we'd talked about this," she says sweetly. "When did you have the lawyers draw it up?"

"This week." He begins signing sloppily, the pen whirling over the paper. "In the event of a divorce, you receive one million dollars for every year we're married."

"I see that." She flips the pages slowly, her gaze skimming over the legalese. "And five million for every child we have."

He looks up at her. "I know we've had this discussion, and you don't want children, which is fine by me, but if something happened, you and the child would be covered. The lawyer thought it was a brilliant contingency plan."

"Right," she whispers, and keeps reading. "Better safe than sorry."

Does Robert hear the sarcastic inflection of her voice? Does he know that at this very moment she's like a serpent, rearing back, waiting for the perfect moment to strike? Because I know Georgia well enough to realize when she's about to swallow a man whole.

"You get to keep the engagement ring, and any other jewelry I purchase for you over the course of our marriage." He's talking quickly now, ready to get this over with. "The same goes for gifts. Those are all yours, no matter what."

"Very kind of you." Georgia glances at me, but it's only for a second, and I know she's about to go in for the kill. "Other than that, it says here that any assets accrued before we were married are to remain ours. You want yours donated to . . ." She flicks a page over. ". . . a whole list of charities: EduReform, UNICEF, PETA, Better Healthcare, and . . . what's this one?"

"Water for India. They need it." He folds his hands in his lap. "My lawyer recommended splitting up my fortune rather than dumping it into one place."

"Very generous of you."

As if he's suddenly picked up on Georgia's irritation, he pats his lap. "Come here, baby."

Keeping the agreement in her grasp, she moves to his lap. He swivels the chair so they're facing the cityscape rather than looking at me. I get the urge to leave, but Georgia asked me here for a reason, and my instinct says that reason hasn't come to fruition just yet. Robert cradles Georgia lovingly, and she rests her head on his shoulder. If I were reporting this encounter, and my photographer was with me now, he'd record the way Robert brushes his hand gently up and down Georgia's back. I'd talk about love and sacrifice and all that comes with it.

To keep from staring at them, I scroll through my social media accounts, yet I'm not really looking at anything in particular. Instead, I'm hanging on every word that comes out of their mouths.

"What's the matter?" Robert says into her ear. "You're not angry with me, are you?"

She nuzzles against his chest, her gown fanning over his legs and onto the floor in a sea of beads and shimmering sequins. "I'm not angry, but . . ."

Using two fingers, he tilts her chin up so she's looking him square in the eye. "But what, my love?"

If I weren't married to Mason, I'd fall in love with Robert this instant. I'd thought before when watching Jack with Brooke that perhaps the shine in my marriage had simply worn off. But this—Mason has never made this type of romantic gesture. Disappointment and jealousy twist my stomach into a knot.

"I want to spend the rest of my life with you, G. More than anything in this world. Signing this means that I love you for you, and you love me for me. To hell with the money."

She stiffens in his arms. "Robert, I don't see it that way at all. I know you love me, and you know I love you. But signing this means you don't trust me. It means you're just like every other person in this damn city—you think I killed them."

"You know I don't think that."

But I just might . . .

"Don't you see? That's exactly what signing this document proves." She strokes the back of her hand down his cheek, and as her ring catches the final rays of the setting sun, the diamond sends flecks of color starbursting over the ceiling and walls. "If you ask me to sign this, it proves that you have doubts about my integrity. I would never"—she chokes back a sob—"I would never hurt you, Robert."

Oh, she's good.

His gaze turns tender, as if she's hurt him immensely. "I don't think you're capable of hurting anyone, baby. You're the kindest, most generous woman I've ever met. I'm not scared for my life, or my future—that's not what this contract is about. It's about eliminating the pressure of thinking about your money, our money, or what would happen in the case of divorce."

She pulls away from him slightly. "So that's what this is about? You think I'm going to divorce you and take you for everything?"

His grip tightens on her upper thigh, his fingers digging into the beading, as she tries to stand up. "I'm not going to lose you, Georgia. You're the best thing that's ever happened to me. If this thing makes you feel like I don't trust you, then fine. Tear it up."

"Don't play with me," she says weakly.

"Here. I'll do it." He snatches the papers from her hands, tears the contract to pieces, and then tosses them over his shoulder. "It is my pleasure to erase all the doubt from your mind."

Cupping his cheeks in her hands, she plants a long kiss on his lips. "I love you, Robert. I've never been this happy before. I can't wait to make you mine."

And I know from her tone that she's telling the truth. Some of what she said earlier was blowing smoke. And she wasn't about to cry, the way she wanted him to believe. But when it comes to her level of happiness, she's being forthright. Robert makes her happy. I've never seen her skin glow this way, and it's not from the colors of the setting sun.

Robert leaves the master suite, grinning broadly, his shoulders pulled back as if he's just completed a great feat.

"Thanks for being a witness to that. I needed someone to

see that it was his idea to do away with this stupid thing, and not mine." She kicks the shreds of prenup with the toe of a diamond-dusted Jimmy Choo. "Ready to party?"

"Absolutely."

It really is too bad that no one can see how Georgia works a man. How she can make him believe anything she wants, and truly make him think an idea was his, when it was in her master plan all along. If I want to fix the issues in my life, I'm going to have to take a page out of Georgia's sinister playbook.

CHAPTER NINE

BROOKE

It really is a magical night.

I've met so many people I couldn't have had I stayed home, cooped up in the house. Convincing Jack to come with me, after he'd been in terrible meetings all day and hit traffic coming home, had taken some work. But I'm glad he's here, on my arm tonight. Usually I'm the one on *his* arm, being introduced to *his* friends. I was looking forward to the shoe being on the other foot. He'd declined Mason gracefully when he suggested they go "shot for shot" at the bar. He'd expertly ditched out of a hushed conversation when it began to veer toward Georgia's past husbands.

I've never loved him more.

Robert had had dinner catered, and we ate eggplant rotolo, chicken cacciatore, and tiramisu as we sailed beneath the Golden Gate Bridge. I had three—or maybe it was four— glasses of some kind of strawberry mango cocktail. Don't know the name, but they were delish. We danced on the outdoor deck, beneath the twinkling twilight, and toasted Georgia and Robert and their union just a few short days away.

The weather had been refreshingly cool all evening. Jack had offered his coat when a chill came over me, while I was talking to Erin on the back deck. Even though I would've been fine without his warmth, since he offered in front of Erin and another Presidio Terrace wife, I'd happily accepted.

It's all about creating that fairy tale. I may not write romance, but that doesn't mean I don't read it, and everything in those books is about making people think that the happily ever after of their dreams is within arm's reach.

I like doing that with Jack.

Pretending we have it all.

From the lounge chairs on the bow, Georgia, Erin, and I point at clusters of stars and try to guess their names. A few times, they crack up and smack each other around playfully, apparently sharing some kind of private joke, and it makes me wish I had that type of friendship in my life. I tip back another drink to keep the delightful fizziness bubbling through me.

"Can you believe what he wanted me to sign?" Georgia says, still laughing. "There was no way that was happening. Only thing I'm donating is this boat."

Although I don't know what she's referring to, her words get me thinking.

"I must confess," I say, slurring a little, curling my legs beneath me, "I was expecting your husband's yacht to be a busted heap."

"Because I hate it," Georgia says sweetly, sipping her ice-blue cocktail. "Understandable, but I don't despise this thing because it's run-down. It's a terrible sap on his energy that he could be spending on me."

As a strong gust of wind whips around the yacht, Erin nods as if she understands completely and tucks loose strands of hair behind her ear. "Quality time is important. That's one of the reasons I was so excited about having a break from work. If only Mason would do the same—even for a week. I understand why he can't, of course, he's got a business to build, but still." She tells us about the text message from the station, and how she's planning to go back after Georgia's wedding. Then, when she's done gushing about how much she loves her job, she looks to me. "What did you do before you met Jack?"

"Same thing I do now. I write books."

"What kind of books?" Georgia asks, turning toward me completely.

Now I have her attention. Funny how it happens that way. Jack says I'm his eye candy, the trophy on his arm, until people ask what I do for a living, and suddenly my interesting factor blasts up ten degrees.

"Murder mystery, mainly."

A hot rush of blood heats my cheeks. I usually blush when people ask about my writing, but this is partially fueled by the liquor surging through me. I'm so thankful that my publisher handles promotion. My weakness, even in my pageant days, was the way I wilted in the spotlight. Writing, I can handle. Promotion, I simply can't.

"*Murder* mystery?" Erin sits up straighter, plants her feet on the ground, and leans closer. "Oh, Brooke, you just became my favorite person on the planet. Have you thought about being published?"

Despite the cool drink, a fire breaks out in my stomach. "I am published, actually. My first book came out last year. I'm already working on my second."

"What's this one called?" Georgia asks quickly.

"*The Nightmare Next Door*." My lips are so numb I almost bumble the title.

"Sounds wonderfully sinful," Erin says with a dark laugh. "How's it going?"

I chew on the side of my lip. "I must admit I'm a bit stuck."

"We can help! Put us in the book!" Erin exclaims, as if the idea just jolted through her like lightning. She pulls a strand of hair over her shoulder and begins twisting. "I can be the lead. Gorgeous, of course. Make sure you only mention my best qualities."

"Then you should leave out her anxious tics," Georgia quips.

"I do *not* have tics." Erin drops her hair and folds her hands in her lap. "If Brooke wrote *you* into the book, she'd probably want to leave out the strange ways your previous husbands died. That'd make you look simply terrible. Guilty as hell. On the other hand, it'd make really interesting reading material. We could tell Brooke all the gory details and let her decide. What do you think?"

"Erin." Georgia speaks a single quiet word. A warning. "Have you seen Robert anywhere? Would you mind fetching him for me? I sent Mason to search for him earlier, but he didn't have any luck."

Erin rises slowly. "Sure. But you shouldn't be worried. Unless someone pushed him overboard, he's here somewhere."

Georgia looks out over the glossy water, and a few boats puttering around in the distance, her dark hair whipping about her face as the yacht picks up speed. I want nothing more than to ask about the gory details Erin had mentioned. They would make interesting writing material. I could use the book to expose her dirty laundry. I'd substitute other names, of course, but she would know. And I would know. The rest of the world would simply fall in love with an enchanting character hiding behind a murderous veil.

Jack and I would have to move to a different neighborhood after the book releases, but that won't be for another year, about the time I'll want to be moving on anyway. We have plenty of time. Anything can happen by then. My fingers itch to get back to the keyboard, but first, I need background. I have to dig around and figure out what really happened to her husbands. Excitement buzzes through me.

After Erin traipses down the spiral staircase leading below decks, Georgia says, "Do you put people you meet into your books?"

I smack my lips together, enjoying the way they tingle. "Not usually."

"That's good," Georgia says, "because people would be cautious around you if they thought there was a possibility that they could land in one of your novels. They'd watch their words more carefully. They wouldn't want you to get too close . . . they might even view you as a *threat*, rather than a friend. Oh, there's my fiancé. Would you excuse me?"

As she excuses herself and practically skips into Robert's open arms, I lean back and stare up at the night sky. *I hear the threat,* I say to myself. *But I don't care. Not at all. Nopenoppity.*

Because I know for a fact Georgia is hiding something. And she doesn't want anyone to learn her dirty little secret.

Alone on deck, I realize I have yet to see the water. When I reach the edge of the bow, cocktail in hand, I feel a little like Leonardo DiCaprio declaring himself the King of the World. Only I'm a Stranger on *Maxine*. Doesn't have the same ring. I laugh at the stupidity of my silent joke. Georgia would be Mistress of *Maxine*, wouldn't she? That sounds much better.

Perhaps I should be setting my next book on a yacht, much like this one. There could be a party, a struggle. My lead character could disappear, which would lend to the suspense. Where could someone hide a body on a yacht? I bet there's a captain's cabin, or lower quarters where someone could fold a body into a closet until everyone disembarked.

That's probably how I would do it.

From out of nowhere, strong hands clutch my waist and jolt me forward, as if to push me overboard. Screaming, I drop my cocktail into the dark water roiling below and rear back, attempting to elbow the person behind me.

Jack barely ducks out of the way. "Whoa, you're dangerous with those elbows!" He wraps his arms around me protectively and pulls me back from the edge. "I just saved your life, you know."

Fighting off the surge of adrenaline, I rest my head back on his chest. "No, you almost pushed me over."

"We're the only ones out here," he says darkly. "Who would know the difference?" And then he barks out a laugh and squeezes me tight. "Don't be mad. You know I was just teasing. I would never let anything happen to you."

Something inside me twinges, but it must be a dump of adrenaline in my gut. Jack would never hurt me. I'm safe.

"Then it's a good thing you were here to save me." I spin around in his arms so that I'm looking up into his dark eyes and realize my entire body has gone tingly. "I was plotting. You know all those puzzle pieces I told you about earlier? I'll have to rewrite some things, but I know how I'm going to make them fit now."

"It's about time," he says.

Jack brings his stare to mine, and his face blurs in the moonlight. Sometimes it seems as if he has two faces—a dark, shadowed one and a really freaking handsome one that catches the light perfectly. The dark face looks mean, with a twisted half-nose and demon eye. The other half, I want to kiss until I pass out.

"I told you a change of scenery would do you good," he says from the handsome side of his mouth. "I'm glad you're back on course. Now you won't be so stressed all the time."

Nope, I'd been wrong. That came out of the demon side. They're blending into one now, and I can't see a clear division. That happens sometimes though, doesn't it? Sometimes he can be so sweet, and other times I think not. But he's my Jack, and I love him no matter what. Thick and thin and all that other stuff I vowed.

"I have some research to do first," I say, my words melting together, "so that'll take a few days before I dive in. Hanging out with Georgia and Erin has been amazing for my muse."

"I'm proud of you, Brooke." He tucks a strand of hair behind my ear, the way I love. "Perhaps you'll get even more inspiration this weekend. We're invited to their wedding."

"What?"

"You know how much I hate repeating myself. You shouldn't have had that last cocktail. You've had more than enough." He drops his hands from my waist and shoves them in his pockets. "I was about to say that I was having a drink with Robert, we got to talking, and it turns out we have a few associates in common. He wants us to come to the wedding on Saturday. I'll make sure I'm not working."

"Associates?"

"No one you would know." His jaw tightens. "People from work."

And I know that's the end of that conversation. Whoever those associates are, he doesn't want me to know anything about them. He'd say it was to protect me, but I'm not so sure. Sometimes I think he simply likes to keep secrets, to hold things over my head because doing so keeps me in the dark and makes him seem powerful.

"Anyway, I told them we'd be happy to accept the invitation. We're getting close to docking," he says, as the boat's motor quiets to a hum beneath us. "Let's go inside with the others and thank our gracious hosts for this evening. We don't want to seem antisocial."

As we enter through the sliding doors, I realize everyone is ready to leave. In my state, I hadn't realized how close we'd gotten to the dock. Where we'd embarked is right there—we'll be anchored up in a few short minutes. The entire group is huddled near the doors on the opposite side, talking and laughing and saying goodbyes. Erin and Mason are in the corner near the bar, having a quiet conversation. It could be my vision blurring again, but Mason doesn't seem happy. His lips are pressed so firmly together, they've gone white. He nods finally, throwing his hands in the air as if he can't be bothered, then points to his phone and disappears into the crowd. When Erin turns to me, she grins broadly and makes her way over.

"Mason's heading into work to get a few things done. Always busy, that guy. You're staying, aren't you?" she gushes, crossing her hands over her chest. "Tell me you're staying. We'll have so much fun."

"Staying?" I ask.

"Overnight. Onboard. Georgia invited us exclusively. Everyone is leaving but us." She nudges her chin at the guests ready to disembark. "What about you?"

"Oh no, I'm afraid . . ." Jack begins, but Erin touches his shoulder to cut him short.

"You have to stay. It'll be Georgia and Robert, of course, and unfortunately Mason has to take a work call, so he'll be gone, but if you both stay, it'll be a real party. We're going to dance all night, maybe play a few rounds of Truth or Dare. It'll be a blast."

Truth or Dare? Oh, I'd love to pick Georgia's brain . . .

Jack gently takes my elbow, a sign I'm supposed to leave with him. But I don't want to leave. I want to get as close to Georgia as possible, and I want this happy-fuzzy feeling inside me to keep going strong.

"I don't think so, Erin. Maybe another time," Jack says, moving toward the main group as the yacht docks. "But thanks for the offer."

Without thinking about the consequences, I blurt, "He's right, he can't stay tonight, but I can! Count me in."

Erin squeals happily, bouncing up and down on her designer heels. Jack glares at me from the demon side of his face.

"I know you have to leave for work early, sweetheart," I say, brushing my hand down his shoulder, "so I'll hitch a ride home with them in the morning. That way you won't have to worry about how you're going to pick me up."

He frowns. "You aren't prepared to stay. You didn't bring a bag or anything—all you have is your dress."

"This place is a floating hotel, Jack," Erin says matter-of-factly. "Georgia has everything stocked for guests. Complimentary pajamas, robes, toiletries. You don't have to worry. She's safe with us."

"I'm sure she is," he says, his tone laced with sarcasm.

Erin tugs me away from Jack's side and says, "It's settled then! She's ours now. We'll take good care of her. Georgia!

Look! Brooke is staying! And don't worry, Jack: I'll have her home early, because I have to run to the station in the morning, if you remember."

Georgia seems to glide over the floor as she separates from her husband's arm and joins us. "Looks like it'll be just the three of us tonight."

"And Robert," Jack says. "Don't forget about your doting fiancé."

Georgia lifts her hand in a dismissive wave. "He drank so much, he'll be passed out in bed, dead to the world, in an hour flat."

CHAPTER TEN

BROOKE

I should be exhausted, but I'm wide awake.

Warm in bed in my stateroom, I feel the yacht slowly rolling side to side as it slices through the bay. I've been searching Google for anything I can find on Georgia and her dead exes since Truth or Dare ended and we called it a night.

I check the time. Two A.M.

My head hurts from the hours of staring at the screen. Or maybe it's the cocktails . . . or a sloppy combination of both. Either way, I'm fighting the migraine from hell as I try to piece Georgia's story together, and I still wouldn't be able to force myself to sleep a wink if my life depended on it.

The deeper down the rabbit hole I go, the darker Georgia's past seems.

She was born into a middle-class family in Livermore. Lived in the California Bay Area her entire life. No siblings. Mother was a financial adviser for a local bank. Father worked as a software developer for an IT company. On the surface, it appears she had a stable home life.

But when I search for her mother's name, an obituary pops up. Her mother and father were killed while on vacation in Australia. Freak boating accident. Georgia was sixteen at the time, and on the boat with them. Most likely watched her parents die. Only she and the captain of the boat survived.

That's another thing Georgia and I have in common: I watched my father die as well. It does something to a person. It changes them, and not for the better. In the middle of the night, I see my father's face, screaming in terror, though no sound comes from his gaping mouth. I wonder if she has visions of her parents' deaths too.

The tragedy would explain why she doesn't like *Maxine*. Suddenly Georgia's seemingly-illogical hatred of Robert's yacht isn't so illogical after all.

Lawyers must've gotten in touch with Georgia after her parents' death because she sued the boat company and won an undisclosed settlement. I can't find anything on Georgia after that—no college records or any old social media accounts that would show what she was doing from the age of sixteen to twenty-three.

Until Eli Dalton came into her life.

At a young and vibrant twenty-five years old, Eli sold his software development company to Compaq for $150 million. *Forbes* called him an "up and comer" in the tech scene. Just days after the news broke about the multimillion-dollar deal, Eli met Georgia at a charity event in the city. Their wedding eighteen months later made national news. Cost him a fortune. She strutted through the church in a one-of-a-kind, form-fitting Oscar de la Renta, dragging the diamond-studded cathedral veil behind her. The pictures are breathtaking. She looked like an angel. Celebrities copied the style of the dress for their own weddings for years afterward. Five hundred people attended.

And then there was the prenuptial agreement. According to its provisions, the only way Georgia was getting out of that marriage with Eli's money was if he died before her.

A year later, Eli slipped and cartwheeled down the staircase—Georgia's staircase, as she bought the house alone. Public records show that her name is on the deed, and her name alone. Eli had landed at the bottom of the stairs, arms and legs broken in awkward angles like a demented starfish. At least that's what the city paper had reported. Georgia had called 9-1-1 immediately—she claimed—and they'd rushed Eli by ambulance to St. Mary's Medical Center.

Five years later, at thirty years old, Georgia met Andrew St. Claire in Hawaii. He was attending a charity event benefiting sea life, and she was donating millions of Eli's hard-earned dollars to adopt a pod of whales.

He must've thought Georgia was adorable, the way she fawned over the sea life that she'd seemingly had no interest in seven years earlier. Andrew had inherited his fortune, and had been a different kind of rich his whole life. He didn't have anything to prove, as Eli had. He'd outbid her on the pod, and then adopted them in her name.

I couldn't even write something in a book that cute. Readers would claim men like him don't exist in the real world.

Not even a year later, Georgia and Andrew were engaged. They were married on Waikiki Beach at sunset, just before her thirty-second birthday, with only his closest friends and family in attendance. She walked over the sand in a silky and elegant Vera Wang dress that, again, caused a stir in the fashion community. The images are magazine-worthy. Andrew placed a flawless ten-carat diamond on her finger. It was twice as large as the one Eli had given her.

Again, a prenup signed.

But sadly, according to one article, Andrew had "swallowed a bullet eight months after he married Georgia. She found him in the office of her home, his brains staining the back of an Italian leather chair she'd given him for Christmas that year."

How she convinced these handsome, single, wealthy men to marry her and agree to hand over their millions should they die is beyond me. But neither of them had any family that they'd been especially close to. No children. No nieces or nephews that I can find in my hours of research.

I don't have to guess where Georgia met Robert Donnelly.

A charity event at the yacht club, approximately four years after her second husband's death. Georgia's now in her mid-thirties, two husbands down with the next one on the line.

I'm deep into a fashion article speculating about the style of Georgia's new wedding dress when something bumps against the side of the boat. It's jarring. The sound of metal on metal.

We've hit something.

I sit up, scared, listening.

Another thump. This time, it's softer. Not metal, but the yacht's definitely hit something. Another bump knocks against the hull.

It's as if the boat is rubbing against the dock, but that's not right because we're still moving. I feel the hum of the engines all around me. I open the closet, where I'd found the silk chemise earlier, slip into the matching robe, and sink my feet into the plush slippers. Peeking into the hall, I listen for more thumping, and look to see if anyone else has heard it as well.

Nothing out here. All quiet.

I close my stateroom door and hear it again. Right outside my room, but on the *outside*. This time, I lift the blinds and peer out the window. It's black out there. Blinding black. I can't even discern water from sky, and yet there's something bobbing beside the yacht. Isn't there? It can't be my imagination. Another thump, just beyond my field of vision.

Clutching my phone, I text Georgia and Erin.

Either of you up?

I wait a few minutes, staring out the window into the blackness, when something *definitely* moves outside. It's a shadow—no, it has a smooth form. It's something bobbing in the water. A silhouette of something large marring the smooth, inky dark.

My heart begins to pound as I head into the hall. I think I remember Georgia saying her stateroom was the one at the end, but now, with the migraine piercing my skull, I'm not sure. The room across from me was Erin's . . . right? Or had she been in the one beside me?

"Erin?" I whisper into the dimly lit hall. "Georgia? Anyone awake?"

The smooth purr of the engines answers me. As I tiptoe through the dining room and living area, where the party had been earlier, it's cold and dark as a tomb. The curtains are all closed, table reset for breakfast.

A chill creeps up my spine. I should go back to my room, lock the door, and try to sleep.

There it is again. A bump of something against the side of the boat.

Unlocking the sliding glass doors that go onto the front deck, I shove back the glass. Wind blasts over the bay, sending goosebumps scattering across my skin and my hair flying around my face. I tighten my robe and tuck my hair into the collar as I step outside. With only the light of the moon illuminating the deck, I tiptoe around the lounge chairs and peer down the length of the right side of the boat—had Robert called it the port side? Or had this been starboard? I'm not really sure.

There's nothing there. Bench seating. Small table for drinks. A ladder going down to the black water below.

A series of waves rock the yacht unsteadily, sending gusts of sea spray into the air, wetting my face and robe. It seems as if the boat's motor grows louder, echoing through the night. I grip the railing, and then, when the yacht seems to steady, I swipe my eyes and peer into the darkness. The outline of a boat bobs over the waves, a stone's throw away from the yacht.

Doubting my vision, I rub my eyes again, clearing the sea spray, and peer harder. It's definitely a boat. Smaller than this one by a long shot. Maybe only twenty feet. It looks like one of those black rubber boats I've seen in movies—the ones the military trains on. It's moving away from the yacht, and if I'd seen it earlier, it wouldn't have caused concern.

But it's sailing in complete darkness. No one seems to be in it. At least not that I can make out from this distance. Not even the moonlight reflects the metal of its hull. It's the epitome of a ghost ship, and by the time I'm wondering if that's the thing that had bumped against our boat, it's gone.

To be sure, I glance over the side of the yacht toward my stateroom window. There's nothing there that would bump against the window, but it's water level. Maybe it was a log floating in the water. Or debris of some kind. The boat might've just been some fishermen out for a late-night catch. If there was one in the vicinity at all.

With one last search for the ghost ship on the horizon, I

head back inside, closing the sliding doors behind me. When I turn around, someone's standing in the center of the dining room, cloaked in shadow.

I gasp, but can't breathe—the air has frozen in my lungs.

"What are you doing up?"

It's Georgia. Her tone sounds strange. As if she's suspicious rather than simply curious. And she doesn't have that familiar sleepy rasp to her voice. It puts my walls up.

I point toward the starboard side. "I heard something out there, banging against the side of the ship."

"Really?" She folds her arms over her chest. "I didn't hear anything." She pauses, and then, "Did you find out what it was?"

Pulse spiking, I swallow hard. I don't even know why I should be nervous, but something about this whole situation has me wanting to go back to bed, and fast. "No, but I saw—at least I thought I saw, a boat close to ours, but moving away. That direction."

She takes a slow step closer. "You *thought* you saw a boat?"

"Yeah, I couldn't be sure." I look to where it'd disappeared into the dark. "It didn't have any lights."

"Are you feeling all right? I know you said you weren't feeling well earlier. Was it your head?" She's still moving closer, and for a split second, when she reaches her hand out, I'm not sure what she's going to do. But she rests the back of her hand on my forehead to test my temperature. "You're cool. No fever."

My heartbeat thumps in my ears. "I think I'm going to head back to bed."

As I pass her, she mumbles, "Sleep like the dead, Brooke."

I stop, turning around to stare at her silhouette in the dark. "What did you say?"

"Sleep your pretty head," she says, unmoving, hands hanging oddly still at her sides. "Good night, Brooke."

But I know what I heard—at least I'm almost sure what I heard—so I lock my stateroom door and climb into bed, certain I'm not going to sleep a wink the rest of the night.

CHAPTER ELEVEN

ERIN

WEDNESDAY

I have a little over an hour to get to my appointment at the station.

Plenty of time considering Georgia is the best hostess in the world. I don't have to run home for a thing. It's as if she knew Brooke and I would be staying overnight on the yacht. The closets are stocked with a variety of clothes and sandals in a range of sizes. I choose black Bermuda shorts, a floral blouse with a flouncy tie near the neck, and black wedges. I'm not going to tell her just yet, but I'm totally keeping this outfit. I spend the next twenty minutes in the bathroom that's rather large for a yacht. Flipping my head over, I tousle my hair and run my fingers through in an attempt to give it that beach-wave look. I use generous amounts of skin cleaner, eye cream, toner, and moisturizer, yet still don't feel awake enough to speak to my boss.

I shouldn't have drunk so much last night. I still have bags under my eyes, and no amount of cream is going to fix that.

Georgia had told Brooke and me to leave our dresses hanging in the closets—that she'd have them delivered home later. What a treat. She really knows how to make a guest feel special.

As I step into the hall, I hear her voice carrying from the dining room. "What do you mean, he's not here? He has to be here. This is a ship. There are only so many places he could be hiding. I'm not messing with you, Raul. Look *everywhere*."

Raul—the one who must've been driving the ship during our foray last night—nods obediently and disappears belowdecks. Georgia turns to me, eyes wide, hands in her hair.

"What's the matter?" I ask.

She nearly collapses into my arms. "Robert's not here."

"What do you mean?" I pull back to read the desperation in her eyes.

"He's gone." Her eyes shift from the left to the right side of the ship. "When I went to sleep last night, he was beside me, and when I woke up in the middle of the night, he wasn't in bed. I thought he might've been sleeping in one of the guest quarters, but just now Raul said those rooms were unused. Robert's not answering text messages or any of my calls either. It's like he's vanished off the face of the earth."

Despite Georgia's anxiety, I'm not panicked. At all. What a change of pace, isn't it? Is this how I look when my anxiety gets the better of me? A little ragged, nerves frayed, like I'm about to rattle apart? Anyway, I'm not freaked out because Robert takes off all the time. He's kind of a nomad, that guy. There have been a few dinner parties at Georgia's that I can recall specifically where we thought he'd gone to bed, but in reality, he'd taken an Uber into the city to frequent his favorite pub. It wasn't a big deal. She'd get a little peeved, but that's how he is. A free spirit or bird that didn't want to be caged kind of thing.

"Okay, let's calm down," I say, smoothing my hands along Georgia's arms. Her skin is cold to the touch. "We're going to find him. It's possible he drank too much last night and passed out somewhere."

She nods, borderline hysterical. "That's true."

I've never seen her this panicked, not even when Eli and Andrew died.

"Or maybe he was ready to disembark right when we docked," I offer. "It's possible he took off without telling anyone. You know how he can be."

"You don't think that—"

"No." I put up my hand, stopping her. It's best not to breathe life into terrible thoughts. "That's not possible."

Her eyes are wide, concerned. "Are you sure?"

"Positive."

She distances herself from my embrace and paces in front of the windows. "Then why isn't he answering his phone? He always answers when I call. I tracked him using the locator thing on our phones, and it shows that his phone's battery is dead. Last registered location was under the Golden Gate."

I don't know how to respond. She's right—it's not like Robert to decline her calls, or to neglect to charge his phone. All the times he's disappeared on us during parties, when Georgia's called, he's picked up his cell right away to ease her fears.

Brooke enters the room in khaki shorts and a white top, looking fresh-faced and clear-eyed, even after the night of drinking we had. I hate her now more than ever. Why can't I ever look like that so effortlessly? Simply being near Brooke makes me feel old.

Georgia seems to come alive and rushes to her. "Did you see Robert last night?"

"What? Yeah. Of course." She stops when Georgia charges closer. "We all did."

"No," Georgia spits, pointing toward the outdoor deck. "I mean when you got up last night. Did you see him?"

Brooke frowns quizzically. "No, I didn't see anyone but you."

Now I'm confused. "What are you talking about? When last night?"

"Brooke thinks she saw something in the water at, like, two in the morning. I heard someone moving around out here, and came out to see what was going on. She'd just come in from outside. And you didn't see him? A weird splash in the water—anything?"

She shakes her head. "I'm sorry, Georgia, I wish I could say that I had. I just thought I saw a boat, that's all. And I can't even be sure about that."

Making a whimpering sound, Georgia begins punching numbers on her cell.

"What are you going to do?" I ask.

"I'm calling the police. He might've gone overboard. I have to do something. We're getting married in three days, and I need—hello, this is Georgia St. Claire and I'm calling to report a missing person. My fiancé . . ."

As she paces, I stand beside Brooke, who smells like lavender, vanilla, and sunshine. She must've gotten the expensive goodies. I wonder why Georgia didn't put that deliciousness in *my* stateroom? "Will you stay, Brooke? Take care of her? I have to run. My meeting, remember?"

"You're not . . ." She glances back at Georgia, who's rambling on to dispatch about our location, and what transpired last night. ". . . worried about Robert?"

"No way." I hitch my purse over my shoulder. "He probably skipped out as soon as we docked to go have breakfast. You'll see—he'll show up. Will you tell Georgia I'll call her later?"

"Yeah, of course."

Heading out, I turn back to Georgia and wave. She tries to ask me something—probably where I'm headed in the middle of her crisis—but I can't stay. I have a meeting to talk about how amazing I am, and how much they want me back.

When I reach the end of the dock, I spot the Uber waiting for me and slip inside. I text Georgia on the way to the station, letting her know I'll call her when I'm finished. She'll understand. Besides, Brooke is there, so she won't be alone.

The station comes into view on the right a short drive later. I probably could've walked here, had I not been wearing wedges, had I gotten up an hour earlier, and you know, actually enjoyed exercising. Nonetheless, the building itself is five stories tall, stuck between two brick industrial studios, and painted dull gray with red awnings. I pay the fare on the app and exit the car, taking a moment to stand on the sidewalk and gaze up at the building as if I'm seeing it for the first time.

"I've missed you," I say, as a car honks down the street. "Home sweet home."

Inside, the lobby's quiet, as usual. I throw a wave and a smile to the receptionist—never actually gotten her name—and head into the elevator, doing a little jig to "What's Love Got to Do with It" as it plays through the speakers. When the doors whisk open, I weave through the cubicles toward Bill Hardwick's office. I look for Monique, or the camera guys, but don't see them just yet. They're probably waiting for me in my dressing room. They're going to be so surprised to see me.

Striding into Bill's office as if I own the place, I close the glass door behind me and spread my arms out wide. "Tell me how much you miss me."

Bill looks at me over the top of his black-rimmed glasses. He's got to be in his sixties, the skin on his face sagging, jowls hanging loosely on either side of his mouth. He's been at this company so long, he's starting to look like the building. Gray hair. Gray suit. Red tie. "Thank you for coming in. Take a seat."

He motions to a square leather chair in front of his oblong desk, and I sit delicately on the edge, clasping my hands in my lap so they don't fidget. This was not the welcome I'd been expecting. While Bill and I haven't been what I would consider friends, we're closer than his current demeanor is letting on. We banter back and forth. We give each other hell. He's sarcastic with a dry sense of humor, and I've always enjoyed working for him. The serious line of his mouth is not giving me good vibes.

He takes a long sip of his steaming coffee and then leans far back in his chair, folding his arms behind his head. His dress shirt stretches over his belly, nearly popping the buttons. "Want to explain what the hell happened on Monday?"

"Of course." I'd fully planned on having to explain myself, and I have my story ready to go. "I was having a terrible day, and—"

"Piss on your day, Erin." He jerks forward so hard his chair gives a sharp snap. "We all have bad days. I'm always having a bad day. Yet I get my ass to work, I don't complain, and I get the job done. You don't see me flippin' the bird and walkin' out of here, do you?"

"No, but you don't have to sit and listen to Ted run his god-damn mouth."

"Christ, this is not about Ted!" He smacks his fat hands on his desk. "This is about you, Erin. You're a professional—at least I thought you were. You disappointed me. I expected more from you."

An awful tingling sensation crawls up my spine.

I'm not here because they want me back.

"I'm sorry I let you down," I say, changing my approach.

"You walked out, Erin. On air."

"It won't happen again."

"Goddamn right it won't."

I'm fired. My insides sour. "Bill, I'm so incredibly sorry for letting you, the station, and my coworkers down. My bad day, or Ted's attitude, was no excuse for my terrible behavior."

He shakes his head. "You were my favorite, you know that?"

There's still a crack in his defenses. He likes me, he always has. "Do you want me to beg, Bill? Is that it? You want to see me on my knees?"

A light flares in his dark eyes. But wait—*take it back, take it back, take it back.* That's not what I meant, and now he might want—now he thinks that I'm offering—*oh God.* I spoke too fast, let my mouth steamroll over my thoughts. And now the sexual innuendo's out there and he's staring at me, trying to decipher my intent, and my palms are hot and my head is swimming. What do I say? I'm married, he knows that, he's met Mason at our Christmas parties. Bill's married too, to Shirley. She's sweet, great family, two kids, longtime marriage. He can't think that I'd get down on my knees and . . . *God, please, no.*

"It's an interesting proposition," he says, unmoving, as if

he's suddenly turned to stone. "I've always wondered if you were too good to beg."

I'm sweating. My thighs are sticking to the seat. I don't know how to respond, so I sit silent, staring, waiting for the verdict.

"You know I can't slide you back into your normal time slot, don't you? We've replaced you with Hillary Gleaves. New girl on the scene. Came to us from our sister network. She's real . . . perky."

I nod slowly, willing the moisture to return to my mouth so I can stop swallowing cotton. If they've replaced me already, that means I'm finished.

"So you realize that if I find you a spot elsewhere, that's very generous of me, because I don't have to accept your apology. I don't have to do a goddamn thing for you if I don't want to." He rolls his fingers along the smooth curves of his coffee mug. "I'd be doing you a favor. I could just as easily kick you out of here and tell you never to come back."

"I understand." Isn't there air-conditioning in this place? Has it stopped working since I left? Good God, it's downright sticky in here. "I'd be happy to work in any time slot, with anyone. Even Ted. I'd promise to be on my best behavior."

He stares at something on his computer screen as if it's captured his attention. Or perhaps whatever he's about to say next is making it hard to look me in the eye. "If I do this for you—if I put my neck out this way—I'd expect you to return the favor at some point. You'd have to do something for me."

Yup, it was the second part. He's uncomfortable, and can't look at me. But it's not stopping him from asking for what he wants, the pig. I throw up a little in my mouth, quickly swallow down the bile, and cover my revulsion with a cough.

"Wha—what would I have to do?" I ask.

He smiles tightly. "We can decide that later. No need to rush into an agreement now. But the offer I have right now might not sit well with you."

You mean like this whole conversation?

"Are you still friends with Georgia St. Claire?" he asks.

"Yes," I say. I'm afraid to say more. If I start rambling, I'll sound like a tool. "I am."

"Good." He takes another long drink. "I want you to cover the story. Her past husbands' deaths, her new fiancé, the wedding, all of it. No one's been able to get an interview from her, but something tells me you can."

My heart pounds in my ears. "You want me to betray my friend."

"Not at all. I want you to do your job. You're a journalist. If you uncover a few skeletons in her closet, then all the better. Given your access to her, it should be easy to rattle a few bones around. People have covered her story before, so it's not like you'd be the first one to give her the moniker the Black Widow. But we'll be the first to get an interview, and that'll make up for your bad behavior . . . especially if her fiancé dies. We can only hope."

"That's not very nice. She caught a good one this time."

"And the last ones weren't?"

Eli and Andrew were plucked from the same cloth. They both loved Georgia, but much too intensely. Love quickly flipped to obsession, and neither wanted her to remain the vibrant firecracker she'd been when they were dating. The only difference between them was the amount of time it took to make the first blow. According to Eli, he wasn't an abuser because open-handed slaps didn't count. The bruises on her cheeks spoke otherwise. He hit her the night of their wedding, when she said she was too tired to pleasure him. Andrew didn't start pushing her around until they'd been married a month. He'd claimed it was her fault, that she pushed his buttons until he exploded. He said she was manipulative and should've known better. I think she should've known better than to marry him. She doesn't talk about those marriages much. I wouldn't either. Not many good memories there.

I blow out a shaky breath and swipe my hands on the shorts I took from her an hour ago. "She's not going to like this."

"Maybe not," he says, "but under the circumstances, this is the only position I can offer. I'm sure she'll be busy with wedding planning this week, and I want you by her side as much as possible. Do whatever you have to, but get that interview. When you have the date and time, let me know and we'll send Monique and a camera crew. If we can get cameras to the wedding, that's even better. We'll run the special after this weekend. You always said you wanted to take your career to the next level, Erin. This is your chance. I guess the only question you have to ask yourself now is, how bad do you want it?"

I excuse myself from his office and head back out onto the street. That didn't go at all how I'd expected, but I also might have just received everything I wanted. Without a set schedule to work, I'll have more time to spend with Mason. I don't have to work with Ted anymore. I'll have my own segment, my own special. I won't have to come into work this week. All my focus will be on Georgia and her over-the-top wedding, a mere three days away.

But at some point Bill's going to want his favor repaid. And I have no idea how I'm going to respond when that happens.

CHAPTER TWELVE

BROOKE

I haven't left Georgia's side since Erin walked off the yacht. She hasn't wanted to be alone, and I don't blame her. Raul and Erin are on the same page. They think it's typical of Robert to take off without warning. Only there are a few things awry that can't be explained away.

One is that, wherever Robert went, he left his wallet and keys on the bedside table in the yacht's master suite. If he, in fact, decided to head to a pub, or anywhere really, wouldn't he need money or an ID? Georgia is continuously checking the tracker app on her phone, and claims Robert's phone battery is dead. She insists his last known location was on the ship, as it sailed beneath the Golden Gate Bridge. Or perhaps that's the last time it updated. Either way, he needs his phone, and he left his charger behind as well.

The other strange thing that can't be accounted for is Robert's Porsche 911 Carrera convertible, still in the parking lot.

I suppose it's not strange that it's there, in the literal sense, because he left his keys behind. But if he "left," as Erin suggests, why wouldn't he have taken his car?

Georgia gives me a lift home, using the keys he left behind, and asks me to come inside. When she'd called from the yacht, the police responded that they'd meet her at her residence to take a report. Jack will be working most of the day, and although I really need to squeeze in a few hours of writing time today, I don't want to leave her alone.

Especially since the police are coming.

The writing can wait, at least until they've gone.

As Georgia escorts me into the grand entry, I take everything in. Intricate detail in the oversized tile. Crystal chandelier overhead. Winding staircase. An airy living room that bleeds into the dining room, which flows into the kitchen.

"In here," she says, and leads me through gigantic doors on our immediate left. "Hurry. They'll be here any minute and I want to be ready."

I don't know what she means, but I follow her inside anyway. It's an office, and if rooms had genders, this one would most definitely be male. Black leather furniture. Cherrywood desk and matching bookshelves. Models of yachts and mechanical books everywhere. A lamp on the corner of the desk and a thick book splayed open in the center. Laptop closed on the far corner. Dark, cigar-colored rug in front of an electric fireplace.

"Grab that chest for me, would you?" she says with a snap. "The small wooden one on the lower shelf by the door."

As she strides around the desk and slides into the rolling chair, I notice that she's comfortable in this space. Perhaps I'd been wrong in my earlier assessment—this could be her office. Out of curiosity, I eye the blood-red walls, ornate crown

molding, and wonder if Andrew had shot himself in this office
or whether that had been in another. Had his blood splattered
across the windows looking out over the lawn behind her?

"Brooke?" She looks up at me. "The chest?"

"Sorry, I was just thinking how beautiful this space is."

"In times like these, it's important to remain focused."

Times like these. A husband gone missing? Police on the
way? I'm not sure what she means, but I locate the small
wooden chest latched with a gold lock and set it on the edge
of the desk as she brings the laptop to life.

"Do you need me to do anything else?" I ask.

"Yes," she says sharply. "Watch the door. Tell me when you
see their car pull up. I don't want to be caught unaware."

Standing in the doorway, feeling more like a criminal's
lookout than a friend, I watch her sift through the top drawer
of the desk and come out with a tiny gold key. She unlocks the
chest, pops it open, and begins digging. Then, laser-focused
on the screen, she taps the keyboard furiously, referring back
to a single sheet of paper pulled from the chest. It's so small,
hardly larger than a receipt. There's calmness in her move-
ments, smoothness in her urgency that's absolutely captivat-
ing. Whatever she's doing, it's important, and I want nothing
more than to ask her about it. But I know I can't.

I'll have to come back in here later and search through the
chest myself . . .

A single unmarked Charger pulls up to the curb.

"Georgia," I warn softly. "They're here."

"One minute." She pounds the keyboard, a determined
gleam in her eyes. "Okay. Sent."

She pushes a few more buttons, slams the laptop lid closed,
replaces the key and the chest, and is at the door before the
officers have made it up the driveway. She brushes her hands

down her vibrantly floral dress. "Thanks for being with me today. I appreciate your help."

"No problem," I say.

And then she transforms before my eyes. A moment before opening the door, she was composed—definitely concerned, but not frazzled in the slightest. It appeared as if something had gone terribly wrong, but she had a firm handle on how to fix it. But the moment before Georgia opens the door, she changes. Her shoulders roll forward, ever so slightly, causing her to appear frail, like a victim who can't take another beating. Her eyebrows pinch together with worry, and her voice—even that changes by rising an octave.

"I'm so glad you're here. Thank you, Officers, come in," she says, her tone laced with fear. "The living room is this way."

She leads us toward a couch that's been perfectly staged with pillows and throw blankets, its cushions firm and clearly not for comfort. The detectives sit beside each other as Georgia and I take the chairs opposite them. Georgia introduces me as her "good friend" who was on the yacht when Robert went missing.

"I'm Detective Basil Linard," the handsome one says. His features are sharp, his nose pointed, skin deeply tanned. He's in a deep blue suit and tie, while the other, a younger officer with blondish hair and boyish features, is in slacks and a thin-striped polo shirt. "This is Officer Pangburn. What can we do for you, Ms. St. Claire?"

She wrings her hands together in her lap. "I told your dispatcher that I need to file a missing person report. My fiancé, Robert Donnelly, disappeared sometime last night, and we need to find him. Our wedding is Saturday."

Linard pulls an iPad from the crook of his arm and taps the screen. "We were informed of that. I'm sure the dispatcher told you that we generally encourage waiting twenty-four hours before filing that kind of report."

"Even when I *know* something's gone wrong?"

He looks up at her, his gaze icy. "Dispatch didn't inform us that there was any foul play involved, but if you have any information of the sort, we'd love to hear it."

Georgia looks to me. "Brooke saw something. Tell them."

"I—I don't know what I saw."

The detectives turn their gazes to me.

"I . . ." My throat suddenly dries. "I woke up when something started banging on the edge of the yacht near my head. I went out on deck and thought I saw a blacked-out boat in the distance."

"You *thought* you saw?" Linard parrots.

"Yes, I mean, I can't be exactly sure. It was dark, and my head hurt pretty bad. I was fighting a migraine." Georgia rolls her eyes, so I go on. "But something had been making a noise—it's possible the boat somehow connected to ours, and Robert was taken."

Detective Linard taps his iPad. "What side of the yacht did you witness this?"

"The starboard. Or, the right, whichever that is."

"Time?" He glances up at me, then back down to his notes as I relay the story again. "Your head was hurting. Had you been drinking that night?"

"I had."

"And you?" he asks Georgia.

"We all were," she says quickly.

"I wasn't asking about everyone," Linard says pointedly. "I was asking about you, specifically."

"Yes, I'd been drinking."

"And your fiancé?"

"He'd been drinking as well. It was our prewedding party, but it hadn't been in excess, and I don't know what that has to do with the fact that my fiancé is missing, three days before our wedding. You should be out there searching for him. If he's been taken, you're wasting time here, when the kidnappers could be getting away."

"If he's been kidnapped, the people who took him will be contacting you for a ransom. If that happens, call me immediately. Here's my card." He hands it to Georgia, who eyes it wearily. "But there are many possibilities for what happened to your fiancé."

"Such as?" Georgia asks.

"One is that your husband had too much to drink and fell overboard. That may've been the sound you heard," he says to me. "If you were still inebriated when you went to sleep, it's possible there hadn't been a boat in the distance at all. It may've been an alcohol-induced hallucination."

Crossing her legs, Georgia taps her foot in the air. "If that's the case, you should be searching the bay for him. He could be out there somewhere."

"If he went overboard last night," the younger one pipes up, "he's already deceased. If the cold didn't get him, the sharks did. If that's the case, his body will wash up in the next week. Rushing out there right now would be pointless."

Georgia makes a tiny whimpering sound into her hand and looks as though she's going to cry. I watch her to see if it's genuine, but I can't quite tell. A single tear rolls beautifully down her cheek. Detective Linard's gaze flicks to mine, and I instinctively know he's wondering the same thing.

"Thank you, Officer Pangburn," Linard says, turning to him, "for outlining such a grim prospect, but there's another, less menacing option we should consider first."

"Which is?" I ask, while Georgia's silently sobbing into her hand.

"He might have gotten cold feet."

Georgia glances up through her fingers. "You think he doesn't want to marry me?"

"It might be a simple fight-or-flight reflex," Linard goes on. "Happens in nature all the time."

"And I'm the threat closing in on its prey," Georgia says flatly. "Is that it? I'm the predator?"

"Not the predator, per se," Linard says carefully, "but you've lost two husbands before him. It's quite possible he faced that fear last night . . . and needed some time to himself."

"The Black Widow," Officer Pangburn says quietly.

"I don't like you," Georgia says, pointing straight at his chest. "You can go."

She sits straight-faced, pointing at him until Linard motions for his partner to wait by the door. Then, once he's out of earshot, Georgia seems to soften again.

"I had nothing to do with my previous husbands' deaths, and deep down, Robert knows that," she says, pleading. "He's never once mentioned being concerned. Why now?"

What Erin said about Robert taking off without telling anyone, and showing up sometime later, echoes through my head, but I don't want to intrude on their discussion. I'm here for Georgia. And to watch the show.

"I'm not sure the reason he'd leave, but you told dispatch you didn't notice he was gone until after you'd docked," Linard says. "If that's the case, it's quite possible he walked off without saying goodbye. We don't have reason to believe he's in the water somewhere, or that he's been kidnapped. Not yet."

"Walked off?" Georgia leans out of her chair now, pleading

with her hands open, palms up. "Without his wallet or his keys? Exactly how far do you think he'd get, Detective?"

"Anything is possible at this point, Ms. St. Claire, which is why we're not going to write up a missing person report." Rising, Linard tucks the iPad beneath his arm. "Keep trying your fiancé's cell. If you don't hear from him by tomorrow morning, call me immediately."

"This is ridiculous," Georgia says beneath her breath as she follows him into the foyer. "I can't believe there's nothing you can do."

"One more thing," Linard says before he walks out. "Do you have access to view your fiancé's checking and savings accounts?"

She pauses, hands on her hips, and I'm not sure what she's measuring.

"I do," she says finally. "Why?"

Linard nods. "Watch them closely. You said he doesn't have his wallet, but he may still have ways to move money. If you see anything, let us know. You have my card."

When Georgia closes the door, she sags against it and slides to the floor, hugging her knees against her chest.

"I'm going to make you a drink," I say, striding toward the kitchen. "A strong one."

"You're an angel," she calls out.

As I find my way around her kitchen, I wonder if Georgia's an angel as well, only one of death rather than salvation. Something tells me the detectives were thinking the same thing.

Robert did not have cold feet.

And he's not coming back.

CHAPTER THIRTEEN

ERIN

"Thank you for squeezing me in today. I came straight from the news station." I lounge on Theresa's couch and stretch my arms over my head. "You'll never believe what happened."

"I'm sure you're going to tell me." Thin legs crossed, glasses teetering on the edge of her nose, Theresa flips through her planner. "But before we begin, can we discuss your upcoming appointment? You have an hour block scheduled tomorrow afternoon with Mason. Would you like to keep that or cancel because you called an emergency meeting today?"

"Keep it. You know we can't make our marriage work without you," I say decidedly. "We'll be here."

Mason and I have been seeing Theresa together since last year, when I begged him to work on our marriage. Every now and again, it feels as if Mason pulls away. It's usually when he feels swamped at work and begins to take out his aggravations on me. It's not fair, and he's acknowledged that, but it still happens. It's nice to have a mediator truly hear me when I feel like the rest of the world doesn't. And then she simply interprets my jumbled thoughts and translates them to Mason in a way he understands. Works for me, for us.

"Done." She closes the planner and rests it on her lap. "I sent invites to both you and Mason regarding the appointment, just in case."

"You're amazing. What would we do without you?" I try to relax into the leather cushions, but the back of my neck is sticky with sweat, and it's making me itchy. "Did you crank up the heat today?"

She shakes her head, though not a tendril of dark hair escapes the bun on the top of her head. "Same temperature every week. Are you uncomfortable?"

"There's something"—I rub the slickness on the back of my neck—"wrong with me lately. Since I walked out on my job, I've been sweating more than normal. Is that strange?"

"Everyone sweats at different levels, and yours most likely stems from nervous energy. But we're going to stop in this space for a moment and focus on the real issue: you walked out on your job?" Her tone is high-pitched, disbelieving. "That's a new development. You hadn't mentioned wanting to do that before. What brought it on?"

I talk about Brooke moving in and looking all fresh-faced, and Ted, the jerk-off. Theresa is quiet the entire time, save for the little sound of encouragement she gives when I start to trail off. Leaning back, I gaze up at her blue ceiling and wonder who chose that color. It's the most hideous blue I've ever seen. Not quite blue, not quite purple. It's like a bruise taking shape.

"But Brooke has turned out to be really nice," I say, "and I think we're going to hit it off well."

"I'd like to focus more on the decision to walk out on your job, and less on Brooke," Theresa says. "Do you regret your decision to take a sabbatical or have you embraced it?"

"Well that's why I wanted to see you today," I say, the words tumbling out of me. "In my head, I'd planned it all out. They'd call me in, and say they were sorry for pushing me to my breaking point, and I would demand a week or two off—you know, to help my friend Georgia with all her last minute wedding details—and then I thought I'd maybe ask for a pay raise. Make them really prove to me how much they want me, you know?"

"And that's not how it went today," she says, sensing the disappointment in my tone. "You had a fantasy built up in your head, and then today you faced the reality. Tell me about it."

"Bill called me into his office and told me they'd already hired someone to take my place, someone young and fresh." I can nearly taste the bile as it rises from my gut. I repress the urge to tug on a strand of loose hair lying over my chest. "But he wants me to do a feature segment instead. He said this could be my big break."

"That's wonderful news, Erin," Theresa says, but she doesn't get it.

I jolt up to sitting. "He wants me to do a special on Georgia."

Her lips twist. "I see. Did you agree?"

"I did," I bite out between clenched teeth. "But there's a catch."

"Which is?"

"I think my boss wants a sexual favor in return for giving me a second chance." There comes the bile again, rising hot and fast. I think I'm going to be sick. "And the worst part—the part that makes me hate myself—is that if he'd made me choose right then and there: the job for the job, you know . . . I would've done it. My tit for his tat."

I hide my face in my hands as Theresa says, "Oh, Erin."

"I'm a terrible, wretched person," I mumble, sick inside.

"You're not terrible for wanting your job back so desperately. You would do anything to regain your position at the station, that's clear. It's the cost that should worry you," she says, her voice soothing to my ears, "because it means your boss crossed a serious line. You should report him immediately."

I look up at her. "He was careful. He didn't actually say the words. It was implied. He would deny it, and say he meant something else entirely."

Folding her arms over her chest, she leans back in her chair. "Yet the implication was clear enough that you were ready to drop to your knees."

My chest is tight. "Yes. What does that say about me?"

"You didn't do it, Erin. You didn't do anything wrong."

Yeah, but I'm almost positive I would have. I don't speak the words because she'll simply repeat what she just said, and we'll go round and round. I don't have the energy for games.

"What do I do when he comes calling for that favor?" I ask.

"Reject him, and then report him," Theresa says flatly. "If he's doing this to you, he's probably done it to countless women before you. And if you don't say anything, he could do this again to another woman after you."

She's right, I know she is.

But being the first one to stand up is harder than it seems. "Have you told Mason?" she asks.

"No, and I don't know if I will." Because thinking about how he would react scares me. He's likely to charge into the station and beat Bill's ass, and I'm sure Bill would press charges. That's the last thing Mason needs right now. "How can I do a special on my friend? I can't subject her to the scrutiny, not right before her wedding."

"It won't hurt to ask her," Theresa says. "You could even tell her what happened with Bill. Maybe she'll understand and agree to do the interview to save your job. She knows how much your work means to you."

My heart returns to its natural rhythm. "I hope so."

Theresa leans forward. "Erin, you're a professional. You're worthy of having your own special air on television. You have an amazing husband who loves you, and the respect of your peers. You can do anything you set your mind to. Say it."

"I can do anything I set my mind to," I parrot, without feeling the words.

"Good. I want you to say that to yourself every morning and every night. Words are powerful things, Erin, and eventually those words will become ingrained in you, and you'll believe them with your whole heart. Are you feeling better?"

"A little." Not so much. I twirl a blond strand of hair around my finger. "But there's a more pressing question I've been meaning to ask."

"Shoot."

When my stomach clenches into a fist, I say the words that've been bothering me far longer than I care to admit. "How do you know if your husband is cheating?"

Theresa checks the time on her watch. "I mentioned that

I could only squeeze you in for a few minutes today, so let's address that during our next session. It's a bigger issue that'll take more time."

As I'm walking out of her office, I stop in front of a flowering rosebush and remove my phone from my pocket. Holding my breath, I angle myself so that the morning's rays of gold light slash over my cheekbones at precisely the right angle. The photo makes my skin look washed out, and there's no life in my eyes. My upper lip looks a bit small; I should stop in at Mason's office for a touch-up before Georgia's wedding. After some teeth whitening and a blurring tool around my forehead and at the corners of my eyes to erase the fine lines, I'll finally look like the Erin I want to be, rather than the Erin I feel like today. I tag it #Can'tFixPerfect and #Nofilter and have thousands of likes before my second panic attack of the day.

CHAPTER FOURTEEN

BROOKE

I'm sitting in what has become my office, on the second floor, in the room overlooking the backyard. The sun has set, and the lights in the garden have kicked on, creating a wonder land of flowers, greenery, and auras of warm light. Jack said traffic was terrible, and he wouldn't be home for a few hours, so I've settled in to spend some time in my characters' heads. But before I can commit to writing, I have to check on Georgia.

Any word from Robert? I text.

She texts back seconds later: *Nothing.*

She must be hovering over her phone, waiting to hear from her fiancé, the poor thing. I'd be a wreck if I were in her shoes. As I think about her position more, I realize this is the fifth time she's experienced poignant loss in her life. The first two times when she lost her parents, and the last three times when terrible circumstances struck her significant others.

Does she feel the pain as poignantly each time? Or does the shock and grief wear off eventually?

Let me know if . . . I check my wording, delete, and try again. *Let me know when you hear from him. If you need anything, I'm here for you.*

Sliding on my noise-canceling headphones, I listen to the sound of thundering rain as I dive into another world. I'm in the zone, happily losing track of time. My fingers fly over the keyboard, and my heartbeat slows to a natural rhythm in my chest. Words are cascading onto the page. I've been waiting for this moment, when it feels as if a faucet's been turned on, and the flow is full and fast. It takes me only two hours to revise the pages I'd already written, to add Georgia's charismatic flair to my main character, Grace Dent. I changed her name, though kept the first letter so I'd instinctively know it was Georgia when I sat down at the computer to write. There's a secondary character too, who reminds me so much of Erin that I'm going to run with it. She and her husband are having major problems, and are going to be suspects in Grace's husband's death.

I'm writing the scene where they've all gathered on a rented houseboat to celebrate Grace's fortieth birthday. It's dark. There's a noise. A man, cloaked in shadow, is on deck, reaching out . . .

A flash of light streams through the window in front of me, taking me away from the world on the screen and jarring me back to my own. It had been bright, almost like the sweeping of a car's lights, but that's not possible. A towering retaining wall separates our yard from the street beyond. The bedroom's completely dark, the only light glowing from my computer.

Outside, near the fence between Georgia's yard and ours, a shadow shifts in the bushes. It's too big to be a cat or dog.

Removing my headphones, I get up slowly, narrowing my eyes as I peer through the window. I wait for movement again. Nothing. This is the second time today that I've seen something shadowed but couldn't tell if it was really there or not. Maybe I really should try to get better sleep.

The moment I sit back down, the bushes move again. Someone is in the large bush on our property, near the fence I share with Georgia. Whoever it is, they're tall; the top of their head peeks above the bush, and it's full-grown. From their position, they could easily see into Georgia's living room window.

I text Jack: *There's someone in the yard.*

Heart racing, I dash down the hall toward the bedroom to lock myself in when I realize the back door is unlocked. At least I can't remember locking it when I'd come in earlier. Even if I were to hide in the bedroom, someone could come walking right in.

I check my cell. No return text from Jack. My fingers hover over the Emergency button, and I'm about to press it when I realize I have no reason to be afraid. This neighborhood is protected to the extreme. Jack made sure of that when we bought the place. No one can get in. Whoever is in the yard must be someone trustworthy, someone who lives around here.

As thoughts of Georgia's death threat stream through my head, I tiptoe downstairs, turning off the lights as I go. If someone's out there, I want to be in the dark, and I want *them* to be in the light. I want to be able to see everything they're doing, while I remain hidden.

When I reach the first floor, I pause in the pitch-blackness, listening, watching the yard. Then, when I think it's clear, I creep past the couches, past the dining room table, and into the kitchen.

I'd been right: the back door had been unlocked.

Slowly, listening for any strange sound, I slide the lock into place. Then, when my pulse begins to slow, I crouch low and steal through the living area once more. But this time, the person's not in the bushes. He's striding across the lawn. He's walking toward the back patio, holding something behind his back. I can't see his face.

Seized by panic, I stumble into the kitchen, scramble through the drawers for a knife, and clutch it in my fist. When I look up, the man's gone. Not on the back deck or the lawn.

My breath comes out in pants as I scan the yard, and the areas around the pool pinpricked with light.

Where'd he go?

The back doorknob jimmies.

He's trying the door.

Flooded with awareness, I backpedal, watching the handle turn back and forth. Every sense heightens. I have to call the police. They have to know I'm home alone with an intruder. Clutching my phone in one hand and the knife in the other, I dial Jack and dart upstairs, taking the steps two at a time. Once inside the bedroom, I close the door quietly and lock it. Jack's call goes to voicemail.

I'm dialing the police when a single plank of hardwood creaks on the other side of the bedroom door.

"9-1-1, what is your emergency?" the dispatcher chirps in my ear.

I cup my hand around the bottom of my cell. "Someone's in my house. Send help. Please."

"Brooke?" It's Jack. In the room. "Where are you?"

"Oh, thank God." My knees buckle as I clamber to my feet. "It's all right, it's my husband," I say into the phone, breathless. "I'm sorry to have bothered you."

When I exit the closet, Jack's standing in the doorway, his hands hanging oddly from his sides. He's wearing black pants and a gray dress shirt. A shadow . . .

"What are you doing in the closet?" he asks. "With a butcher knife?"

He doesn't come closer or envelop me in a hug the way he usually does. Was he in the bushes? Is he acting strange because he knows I caught him?

"I was scared. I was working, and saw someone outside, in the bushes." I hold up my cell and hope he doesn't notice my shaking hand. "I called you twice."

He stares, his blue eyes focused on the knife. "I left my phone in my briefcase."

"Oh." That seems honest enough. "Did you see anyone in the bushes when you came in? Someone was at the back door."

"*I* was at the back door," he says, incredulous. "That's the door I've been using when I come home from work."

"And you didn't see anyone else out there? Dressed in black? Tall?"

"No, I didn't see a single soul. Honestly, Brooke, I don't know what's gotten into you lately. First, you ditch me to stay with Georgia and Erin on the yacht, and now I come home to find you hiding out in our bedroom, wielding a knife. You've been acting very strange. I had a feeling Georgia would rub off on you from the start, remember? I told you that you shouldn't be hanging around with a rumored murderer. Next thing I know, you're going to be plotting *my* demise."

I'm not sure how my hiding in the bedroom translates to killing him in cold blood, but I don't refute what he's saying because I *have* been acting strangely. I haven't been the quiet and demure Brooke that Jack knows and loves.

"I don't think psychotic behavior rubs off the way you're suggesting." Dropping my cell onto the bed and the knife to my side, I walk up to him and snake my free hand around his middle. He's stiff and unyielding. "Besides, I wanted to stay behind on the ship for research purposes. Georgia and Erin don't know it yet, but they're inspiring my characters. It was for work, sweetheart."

"Good. I would hate to think you were befriending them. They're the type of women who'll smile to your face then stab you in the back. You know I have a talent for reading people, Brooke. I see right through Georgia and Erin, and at the core, they're no good." He eyes me wearily, then plants a fatherly kiss on my forehead. "All I know is that I'm glad you're here, in my arms again, safe and sound. How did it go last night?"

"Oh, God." Pulling out of his arms and plopping on the edge of the bed, I spin the knife handle in my hand and recall the events of the night. "Robert's gone."

"What do you mean, 'gone'?"

"He disappeared. Georgia doesn't know if he fell overboard or if someone pushed him or if he took off as soon as we disembarked, but she hasn't heard from him all day."

Jack swipes his hand through his silver hair. "Jesus, that doesn't bode well. Did she call the police?"

I nod. "But they won't take a report until it's been at least twenty-four hours."

"Poor bastard." He heads to the closet and kicks off his shoes. "He probably thought he had at least a year until she killed him off. She's getting faster and faster."

I look after him. "You think Georgia is responsible?"

"It's likely." I hear him fussing with his shirt. "Her track record isn't the best."

"But she looks genuinely scared. I don't think she's acting."

When he emerges from the closet, in baby blue boxers and a white T-shirt, he stops in front of me and stoops to kiss my cheek. "Everyone is acting, baby."

And then he leaves to sleep in his bedroom—the one he occupies down the hall.

CHAPTER FIFTEEN

BROOKE

THURSDAY

Jack left for work early this morning without so much as a goodbye. Normally, I would've been peeved (he could've at least written me a sweet note), but I woke up with new, vibrant words whirring through my head. Forgoing coffee, which is not normal for me in the morning, I nearly run into the office, flip open my laptop, and start writing. I'm five pages in, right at the part where Grace's fiancé's body is discovered in the bay, when my phone bleeps with an incoming text. It's Georgia.

Police are on the way. Filing the missing person report. Come over?

There's no way I would miss this.

Of course, I text back. *Be right there.*

By the time I put on something nice, but not too formal—white jeans, blue polka-dot blouse, tall wedges—and stride into Georgia's home, Erin's already there, making herself at home in Georgia's kitchen, whipping up something that smells like a bacon and veggie egg scramble. She's wearing a candy-apple red apron that reads, WINE NOT? She waves as I walk in, then goes back to chopping something with the largest knife I've ever seen. It's definitely serial killer material, and I wonder what Erin's slicing that requires such a sharp knife. Georgia hugs me tight, thanks me profusely for coming by, and then situates herself in the middle of the couch like a queen, her feet planted perfectly in front of her, chin raised slightly, hands in her lap.

She doesn't look like a woman who's about to report her fiancé missing two days before their wedding. A normal woman would be rattling apart. But I'm quickly learning that Georgia's far from a normal woman.

The night my father died, I was an emotional mess. Cried my eyes out. Vomited when my stomach cramps became too much to bear. My father had been out that night, drinking with friends from work. At least that's what he told my mother when he rolled in after midnight. I'd stayed up with her watching *Some Like It Hot*, one of her favorite classics, and eating popcorn. He'd dropped his keys on the porch. Begun banging, banging, banging and hollering for us to open up. Mother told me to get to my room and put on my headphones. Listen to my music real loud. It was going to be a bad night. But between songs, in those few seconds of muffled silence, I heard the sound of skin meeting skin and the crack of my mother's skull hitting what turned out to be our granite island.

That was the night I learned how it feels to love and hate someone simultaneously. The night I learned how a butcher knife feels sinking into a man's organs.

But Georgia sits poised and graceful, like a raven on a branch with golden streams of early morning light slanting over her slick black hair. She appears undisturbed. Far from what I'd been when I lost someone I loved.

Within minutes, the two police officers who'd come over before stride into the house and take their seats opposite Georgia. This time, Linard takes out his phone and asks to record the conversation. Then, when Georgia begins retelling the events of the other night, he taps out notes on his iPad.

I notice Erin watching Georgia carefully from the kitchen. Erin doesn't appear to be upset by Robert's disappearance or the detectives' presence, although her actions speak otherwise. Every few seconds, the hard chop of the knife drops onto the cutting block, and the detectives turn her way to make sure she's all right. On another sharp chopping sound, I get a really good look at Erin. Her cheeks have a healthy, rosy glow, her lips are shiny red. It's as if she put on a face-full of makeup this morning to prepare for the detectives' arrival.

Putting her best face forward.

I remember Jack saying they'd smile to my face and stab me in the back and wonder if he'd been right. I should watch my steps more closely.

I make myself busy by taking everyone's coffee orders and tailoring the drinks to each person's liking. While I'm puttering between the kitchen and living room, I listen carefully to the question-answer session.

"If you didn't sleep with your husband the whole night through," Linard asks, "when did you realize he was missing from your bed? I'd like you to clarify that time line, if you could. We really need to get a bead on the last time someone saw him."

"Yes, of course. Robert went to bed earlier than I did, around ten, and then around midnight I joined him."

"And you're sure he was beside you when you went to bed?"

"I'm sure, Detective. We made love, went to sleep, and then after about an hour, he got up to use the restroom. I fell back asleep pretty fast, but he must've stayed up because next thing I know, I reach out for him, and he's not there. I get up, hear something in the dining room, and find Brooke. That was around two, I guess."

I'd been listening all along, but my ears perk up at the sound of my name. And I know, unequivocally, that the first time Georgia told me about that night, she left out the part about Robert using the restroom. Why would she do that? Seems like something harmless that she would've mentioned. Unless it wasn't harmless at all.

I get the feeling she saw something that night too . . .

"Would you mind telling us what you saw for the record?" Linard asks me.

"Not at all." As I get closer to the living room, Georgia pats the cushion beside her, and I feel a little like I'm snuggling up to a predator. "I was in bed, alone, and heard something banging against the side of the ship. I looked out, thought I saw something moving alongside us, but I really don't know. It was dark. I got up, went out on deck, and I think, in the distance, there might've been a boat pulling away."

Without looking up from his iPad, Linard makes a soft sound of agreement.

"When I came back in," I go on, "Georgia was there. We talked for a minute, and then I went back to bed. When we woke up, she said he was gone."

"What did you two talk about?"

She'd told me to sleep like the dead.

I glance at her profile, the gentle slope of her nose, her full lips, and wonder if she's capable of murder. "Nothing really. She asked me what I was doing up, and I told her. She wished me good night. That was it."

"What did you do after that conversation?" Pangburn asks Georgia.

"I went back to bed." She slides her hands beneath her thighs. "When I woke up in the morning, I talked to Raul about where Robert might've been—I thought perhaps he'd stayed in a guest room—and called the police."

Again, Linard makes a strange sound from the back of his throat. "What makes you think Mr. Donnelly would stay in a guest room? Had he done that before?"

"Sometimes, after we fight, he sleeps away from me."

Linard locks eyes with her. "Had you fought that night?"

"Yes," she says quickly.

"Before or after you'd made love?"

Feeling the pressure, I swallow hard. Georgia doesn't seem to flinch.

"After, if you must know," she says. "He was . . . having trouble, if you know what I mean. It doesn't happen often, but when it does, he gets upset, as you can imagine. He likes to blame his inability to perform on me. That night, it was probably from drinking too much earlier in the evening."

But she'd said Robert hadn't drunk to excess. Does she know how her story just cracked like an egg?

"I see," Linard says, nodding slowly. "If your fiancé did get cold feet and take off somewhere on his own, do you have any idea where he might've gone?"

Georgia seems to ponder this for a long while.

"No," she says finally. "No idea."

"Nearest relative, perhaps?" Linard presses.

I'm sure he could look up this information on his own, but he's asking Georgia purposefully, probably to determine exactly how forthcoming she's going to be. It's interesting watching Linard question Georgia. Like a spider readying its web with varying degrees of stickiness, hoping a fly buzzes through and gets caught on just the right part.

"His parents live in New York, but he doesn't talk to them anymore. He doesn't have any siblings that I know about."

Eli and Andrew didn't have close ties to family either, and I wonder if that's her go-to for husbands. Is it because she enjoys being the only stable person in her man's life? That way all of his attention is given to her? Or is it because no one will ask questions when he's gone? And she gets to keep all the money for herself.

"Friends?" Pangburn pipes in. "Cousins?"

"Or mistresses?" Linard shrugs. "We have to ask."

Through the space between us, I can feel heat radiating from Georgia's body. "Robert doesn't have any mistresses, Detective, and he doesn't have any extended family that I know about either. As for friends, I'm sure there are a few people at the yacht club he'd call acquaintances. He's there often enough. But you'll have to dig around on your own for that information."

As Linard rattles off questions pertaining to the yacht, I realize this might be my chance to search the office for more information. I have to find out what she's hiding in that chest.

There might not be a better time than this . . .

"If you'll excuse me," I say to Georgia, rising slowly. "I need to use the restroom."

"That's fine. It's toward the entry, down the hall on the right."

Exactly where I thought it'd be. Toward the office, behind her, where she won't be able to see me.

Perfection.

Checking to make sure Erin can't see me from her position in the kitchen, I steal inside and click the door shut behind me. Beyond the office walls, I can hear Erin clanking things around, and muffled conversation as the detectives and Georgia rally back and forth.

I won't have long.

First thing, I head to the chest on the shelf. It's in the same place it'd been in before. Setting the chest on the desk, I open the middle drawer to search for the key, the way Georgia had. Loose papers and pens and Post-its and paper clips litter the bottom of the drawer. I remove them in clumps and and set them on the desk. *There.* A shimmer of gold peeks from beneath a receipt. Snatching the key, I shove it into the lock and turn, lifting the chest's lid. More papers, receipts. I scan the names and numbers fast, trying to make sense of something. Anything. I skim my hand along the inner edge of the chest, and brush against a tiny scrap of paper that's fallen away from the others. Pinching it between my fingers, I hold it up to the light.

5550143.

It's written in pencil with a delicate hand. A phone number without the dashes. As I grin, feeling victorious, a strange, skin-crawling feeling settles over my bones.

I look up, and gasp. The tiny paper flutters to the floor.

Erin's standing in the doorway drying her wet hands on her apron, staring at me with a strange grin on her face. "What'd you find?"

Forcing myself to stay calm, I slowly replace the papers in

the drawer and close it. I do the same for the chest. I can't play this off. She's caught me reading Georgia's personal documents. I'll have to rationalize my actions . . . somehow. My mind races as she stares expectantly, waiting for a response.

"Georgia asked me to open the chest to get her a number, but I don't know what she's looking for in this mess." Forcing a smile, I shrug. "Next time I'll tell her that someone else should do her bidding. Put this back for me, would you?"

I hand her the chest, but when I think I have a chance to pick up the paper, she turns around, watching me. I kick the paper further beneath the desk.

As I pass Erin and stride back into the living room, I can feel the weight of her eyes on the back of my head. Needing to keep my hands busy, I remove the detectives' empty cups of coffee and take them to the kitchen sink. Erin seems to watch me all the while, and I wonder if she's going to tell Georgia what she caught me doing in the study.

"I think that's all for now, Ms. St. Claire," Linard says as both detectives rise. "Keep trying his phone. If you hear from him, please call me immediately."

Georgia remains seated, her knees pressed firmly together, ankles crossed. "You should question Raul. He was the one piloting the yacht. He might know something he's not telling me."

Linard nods. "Anyone else we should look into?"

Erin.

As I watch her exit the office and meet my eyes, a wave of heat flares through me. She and Mason were there last night, and Mason is friends with Robert. Do the police plan on questioning everyone who'd been on the yacht? Jack really doesn't have time for that, but maybe I could help out instead.

"I don't think so." Georgia worries her bottom lip between her teeth in an innocent, Marilyn Monroe–type of way. "What if we don't find him before our wedding?"

"Ms. St. Claire, I would suggest you continue on with everything as planned, hoping he'll return. It's still quite possible he simply had cold feet. We hear about these types of scenarios all the time."

"You do?"

He nods slowly and makes his way around the couch. When he meets the other detective, he mumbles, "If I valued my life, I wouldn't come back," under his breath.

CHAPTER SIXTEEN

ERIN

The moment the door closes behind the detectives, Georgia lets out a long, exasperated sigh and stretches her arms over the couch.

"They think I killed him, just like the others," she says, dropping her head back against the cushion. "They're going to make my life hell. They're never going to leave me alone."

Brooke locks the door and slowly makes her way toward the living room, her heels clacking over the tile. She's got a strange look in her eye that reminds me of the one Mason has when he comes home late from work. It's guilt. Plain and simple. She knows I caught her snooping through Georgia's things, and she doesn't know if I'm going to blab to Georgia. Come on. Of course I am. As for Mason, that's a conversation we need to have with our therapist present.

As Georgia groans and presses the heels of her hands into her eyes, I start mixing a martini.

"No, don't," she says, sitting up with a jolt. "What time is it?"

"A little after ten." I shake faster, sloshing the ice against the metal canister. "But it's five o'clock somewhere."

"Damn. My wedding dress. I—I'm sorry, I forgot. I have to pick it up before noon."

I pour the martini anyway, and toss it back. It's cold and smooth and perfect. Brooke eyes me curiously, so I offer her the remnants of the drink in the shaker.

"I thought you already picked it up," I say to Georgia, recalling the way she'd gushed over her dress last month.

She dumps her phone into her purse and slings it over her shoulder. "I went for my final fitting, but there was a problem. I'll explain on the way. Brooke?" Georgia asks, turning to her. "Want to take a ride?"

"To see your wedding dress?" Brooke asks with her usual perky enthusiasm. "I'd be honored."

As we're packed into Georgia's Alfa Romeo and speeding through the city, she explains how she'd ordered a one-of-a-kind dress from an up-and-coming designer, Monica Normande, in Los Angeles. Georgia had been sent swatches of fabric and embroidery, and had three fittings once it'd been sent to a private boutique in the city. However, at the final fitting, Georgia had noticed the hem wasn't even in the back. Rather than settle for something flawed, she had demanded it be fixed, even though I'm sure no one would have noticed anyway. She's not sure of the reason for the delay, but she'd been told to pick it up today, two days before her supposed wedding.

As if she didn't have other, more important things to worry about.

Zipping off Broadway onto Laguna, Georgia clutches the

wheel in a death grip, glancing behind her into the rearview. "You know what the craziest thing is? Those detectives are wasting time questioning *me*, asking where *I've* been, and digging into *our* relationship, when they should be out there looking for *him*. I bet they're not even searching. They've probably already made up their minds."

"It's hard not to," I say, steeling myself against a hard turn. "Your reputation certainly precedes you. Brooke, I'm sure you heard about Georgia before you met her. What'd you think?"

She makes a shocked, strangled sound from the backseat. "I—I'd heard about what they call you . . ."

"The Black Widow," Georgia offers with a scoff. "I should've gone for a black wedding dress instead of white. Would've fit people's expectations."

"The real estate agent mentioned a few details," Brooke goes on, "but I wanted to know you for myself, to make my own opinion."

"And?" I poke, feeling mischievous for putting her on the spot.

"I can't speak for your previous husbands, because I didn't know them, but after seeing you with Robert, I think you love him very much." She chooses her next words carefully. "I can't picture you lifting a finger to hurt him."

I frown, sagging into the passenger seat as Georgia pulls up to the boutique. Must Brooke have the right answer for everything?

Putting the car in park, Georgia glances at Brooke through the rearview mirror. "And that's why you're growing on me. Thanks, babe."

How am I going to tell Georgia that I'm doing a special on her, which could shake the foundation of our friendship, when

Brooke spouts perfect answers from her perfect mouth? Keeping this interview from Georgia is like having a massive canyon between us, and I constantly feel as if I'm leaning over the edge, teetering, about to fall into the abyss below. She has to know so I won't be constantly thinking about it anymore. Mason said it'll be like ripping off a bandage. Hard at first, but if the wound is going to heal—if our friendship is going to come out the other end of this unscathed—it needs to be out in the open.

I'm going to tell her today. Soon.

The boutique is larger than I would've thought from its frontage. Although the building is narrow, with first- and second-floor bay windows displaying headless mannequin brides, the space is long and overflowing with racks of couture gowns. The walls are covered with white shiplap, and the air is thick with the scents of lavender and vanilla.

"This is expensive, but so worth it," Brooke says from behind me. "It's utterly gorgeous. If I were to get married again, I'd do it in this."

Turning, I stare at the Regina Charlemagne she's brushing her fingers against. It's a shimmering shade of silver, dusted with diamonds, with a V-neck that would drop to Brooke's navel. It would look absolutely stunning on her petite frame, accentuating the perkiness of her breasts, the flatness of her stomach, and the evenness of her skin tone. But I refuse to tell her any of that.

"Eighty thousand dollars. For a Regina Charlemagne? I wouldn't pay more than thirty," I say snootily, and move along toward the dressing area, which is curtained with swags of rose-colored fabric. "The real dresses are this way."

We pass only the best of the top designer's gowns, and I remember how simple it was to choose the gown for my wedding. Mason had insisted that he come shopping with me, even though I'd wanted my wedding dress to be a surprise. In the end, it was better to agree than start a fight, so he tagged along and freely gave input on every dress I tried on. I felt very Julia Roberts from *Pretty Woman*. He demanded they wait on me hand and foot, serve me champagne, and ooh and aah when I came out of the dressing room. I'd had my eye on the first one I tried on: a form-fitting lace gown with a ten-foot embroidered train. It was elegant and regal. Timeless. I felt like it emphasized my best qualities. Mason, on the other hand, had wanted to see me in a strapless gown, drop waist, diamond-encrusted belt, and a flare at the knee. He'd been right in the end, of course. The dress was beautiful in the pictures.

As Georgia speaks with a woman at a small counter in the corner of the store, the skin-crawling feeling that someone is eyeing the back of my head washes over me. Must be Brooke, I think, and crane around, expecting to catch her eye. But she's perusing a rack of dresses against the wall. Brushing my hand over the back of my neck to smooth the hairs standing on end, I glance out the front window.

Across the street, someone is standing between two cars, staring at the store. Right through the windows. Right at me. I can feel the heat of his eyes, even through his dark sunglasses. He's wearing jeans and a black jacket that's zipped to his neck, and a black baseball cap with an orange Giants logo.

Why is he staring?

He could be homeless, with nothing better to do. He could be crazy. But something tells me he's not either of those things. Actually, judging from his height and the wide span of his shoulders, he could almost be . . . *Jack*.

"Erin?" Georgia calls behind me.

"Yeah?" I don't break eye contact.

That man really could be Brooke's husband. But I've never seen him dressed so casually, and if he saw us come into the store, why wouldn't he simply drop in to say hello? Why isn't he moving? That's probably the most perplexing thing of all. It might've been normal for him to remain stationary momentarily. Perhaps he's meeting someone, waiting for a dog to do its business, or reading a sign on the boutique's building.

In my gut, I know he's not doing any one of those things. He's watching us. And from the way he's standing there in plain view, unmoving, he wants me to know it.

No, it's not Jack . . . is it? Narrowing my eyes for clarity, I peer across the street through the passing of people and cars. If it is Jack, I need to tell Brooke that she's married to a creeper.

"I'm trying it on again, just to be sure," Georgia says, snapping. "Follow us to the back?"

I turn momentarily, to watch where she's headed, and when I turn back around, the guy's gone. Vanished as if he'd never been there at all.

"What are you staring at?" Brooke asks from beside me. She peers out the window, trying to follow my gaze. "Erin?"

I wait a beat, searching the people passing the front of the shop. "It's nothing. I thought I saw someone you knew—someone *we* knew—but I must've been mistaken."

Georgia's dress, on the other hand, is magnificent. It's clear that she loves the look of a corset top and a cinched waist and drama. The dress has all of these in spades. Whenever Georgia breathes, her chest swells over the top of the subtle heart-shaped neckline, adding spice where it was designed to be sweet. Her waist appears impossibly tiny as the bottom of the gown flares at the hip, falling to the floor in gentle waves of glimmer.

Spinning slowly, Georgia lifts her arms from her sides. "What do you think?"

"Angelic." Brooke gawks, covering her mouth with her hand. "Perfection."

Oh, I bet Georgia's head exploded just then.

I smooth down a nonexistent kink in the back. "There. Now it's perfect."

"If I only had a groom to go along with it." Georgia seems to tear up as the seamstress—or perhaps she's the designer—checks the hem a final time. "I don't care what the police think, he didn't get cold feet. I can't shake this terrible feeling that something's seriously wrong. Something happened out there on the water."

"I believe you," Brooke says. "If he's out there, we're going to find him."

Kiss uss.

"What are you going to do?" I ask, because suddenly Brooke is acting like she has all the right answers. "Take the yacht out to look for him?"

Brooke nods. "If that's what it takes."

I had forgotten for a moment that Brooke writes murder mysteries. To her, this is all a game, a story with loose ends that need to be tied up.

"I'm with you, Georgia. Whatever it takes," I parrot, and squeeze my best friend's hand.

After Georgia changes and arranges for her dress to be delivered to her home, we leave the shop and step into the early afternoon sunlight. The marine layer has burned off, leaving clean air and a reprieve from the cool sea breezes normally sweeping over the city. Searching for the strange man, I clutch my purse beneath my arm and look down Laguna in one direction, and then the other. Nothing seems out of place, nothing out of the ordinary.

Georgia unlocks the car and rounds the back. "What the hell."

Brooke's at her side, looking over her shoulder eagerly, like a sidekick. "Another one? What does it say?"

I don't have to look to know what they're talking about. Judging from the disdain and irritation in her tone and the excitement in Brooke's, Georgia must've had another note from one of her many admirers. Maybe even the creepy man who looked startlingly like Brooke's straitlaced husband . . .

Georgia lifts the paper from beneath the windshield wiper and unfolds it carefully. Something falls into the palm of her hand. With a squeal, she drops it to the ground, where it rolls under the tire. Whatever it is, it's covered in blood.

"Oh, no, no, no." Delicately, she picks it up again. It's a finger. Not just any swollen, bloody finger. Robert's. Identifiable by the silver and diamond-encrusted ring he always wore on his right hand. "His—this is his . . . his ring. I'm going to throw up." Unfolding the paper, she reads aloud, the words seeming to punch out of her gut. "WANT YOUR FIANCE BACK? HOLD UP YOUR END OF THE DEAL. THIRTY MILLION WIRED BY MIDNIGHT. GO TO THE PO-LICE AND HE'S DEAD."

CHAPTER SEVENTEEN

ERIN

As Georgia heads back toward the safety of Presidio Terrace, she mumbles to herself, cursing, slamming her hands against the steering wheel at every red light.

"Georgia," Brooke begins.

"I'm not going to the police, I can't," Georgia blurts, silencing her. "I know that's what you were going to say. If I do, they'll kill him. We're beyond that now. I have to handle this myself. Do you guys see that black Mercedes a few cars back? Is it following us?"

Craning around in her seat, Brooke keeps an eye on the Mercedes as my phone buzzes with an incoming text. It's Mason: *Detectives are here asking questions. Where are u?*

"Damn it," I whisper as Georgia turns sharply.

I'd planned on inviting Georgia over, and once Brooke went home, I'd break the news about the special. She'll understand how important this opportunity is to me, and she does owe me a monster favor.

"It went straight at the light," Brooke says. "You're not being followed."

Georgia breathes a sigh of relief.

I don't text Mason back and a few minutes later, Georgia turns the corner onto our street. I notice Penny, who has stopped trimming her lawn with scissors long enough to stand on the corner, gawking at the police cruiser in front of our house. Carol, the woman who lives in the house with the bright red door that barely meets neighborhood standards is with her, hands planted on her hips disapprovingly. Patsy shuffles to meet them, her pants pulled up embarrassingly high.

As the gate rolls shut, I glance back, catching a glimpse of a black car darting by. The Mercedes Georgia had been worried about? I'm not sure. There are so many of them in the city. Better not to mention it and fray her already worn nerves.

She pulls into her driveway momentarily, letting us out, and Brooke retreats to her home, head hung low. Georgia doesn't even say goodbye to her new friend. I bet Brooke is feeling wretched.

Before shutting the door, I lean inside and meet Georgia's gaze. "I hate to bring it up now"—I shoot a glare behind me at the police cruiser— ". . . but remember that favor you owe me?"

She shifts uncomfortably in her seat. "It's come back to bite us in the ass."

"I know, but it was a favor nonetheless."

"What do you want?"

"I was given an opportunity at the station—they want me back after all."

THE SINFUL LIVES OF TROPHY WIVES   153

A smile breaks her frown. "Good for you. But what does it have to do with me?"

"Will you give me an interview?"

Just like that, her frown returns, deeper this time. "Seriously? You know why I can't—"

"I know, I know," I interrupt. "This isn't the best time to talk, and believe me, I know how much I'm asking of you, but I—I need this. We can iron the script out later. Will you do it? Please?"

"Fine." She sighs heavily. "But after this, the debt I owe you is paid."

"Of course." The debt she's referring to was a favor. Something I did for her when she was in dire need. "Consider us square."

I point at the note sitting on the dashboard. "Are you going to pay Danny what he's asking?"

Danny Johnson . . . the hitman we hired to "off" her husbands.

"It's not possible." Zoning out on the garage door, Georgia grips the steering wheel tight. "I can't move that much cash by midnight. If Andrew hadn't changed his will right before he died, leaving everything to charity, I would've had enough to pay him upfront, the way I did after Eli's death. But now, with how much time has passed and the interest he's demanding . . . it's too much. I don't have it."

"And as for Robert," I say, shaking my head. "I don't know what's going on, but you shouldn't have to pay a dime. If he can't follow simple instructions, that's not your fault. Or mine."

"Exactly."

"I wish I could help you," I say "but . . ."

"Mason would kill you," she finishes for me. "I know. I'm

going to request a meeting. See if we can come to some kind of agreement."

My pulse quickens. "Georgia, no. That's not a solution. Just let me stew on it for a bit. I'll think of something."

"There's no other way, Erin. He's not going to stop, and you know it. I'll be smart. I'll make sure it's a public place— somewhere there's lots of people and ways I can escape if something goes wrong. But I have to do something. I won't forgive myself if something happens to Robert."

"You shouldn't go alone. We've never met him in person before. Once you see his face, you'll be able to identify him to the police. What makes you think he won't come after you next?"

She seems to chew over what I've said. "Because I'm the one with the money. I'll let you know my plans, Erin. Promise."

We part ways and I cross the street in a hurry, thinking about Georgia meeting this dangerous man. Anything could happen. She can't go alone. But I'm paralyzed with fear at the mere thought of going with her.

"They're in the living room," Mason says when I reach our entry. Gripping my elbow, he guides me inside, though there's no urgency in him. His tone and hands are steady. He leans down and whispers hurriedly in my ear. "We can't afford to get roped into all this."

"What's going on?" I whisper back. "What do they want?"

He closes the door behind me. "She killed him."

"*What?* Who?"

"You had to have seen it coming."

I peer into the living room at the two detectives' backs. They've settled into the couches in positions where they have a perfect view of our patio and pool. They're talking with each other.

"They think *Georgia* killed Robert?" I squeak. "How do they know? I mean, what makes them think that? Did they find his body?"

"No, no, that's not what they're saying yet—it's early—but you know that's what happened. She doesn't exactly have a stellar record."

I lower my voice further. "But they weren't even married yet."

"Clearly she's getting ahead of herself."

I remember how we'd joked about "bonus points" if Robert were killed with the sinking of his yacht. My phone burns in my pocket. As soon as I'm away from Mason, I'm deleting the pictures of breakfast from my Instagram account.

Mason grips me around the shoulders with sudden urgency. "Listen, we don't have much time. We have to get back in there, but I came home right after I left you on the yacht. I didn't go into work. You came home in the morning, and I was still asleep."

I look into his dark eyes, first one, then the other. "I actually tried to ping your location, but the service was turned off. When I texted you right before I went to sleep, you said you were still at the office."

He casts a glance at the detectives. "No, *Erin,* I didn't go to work. You wanted to make sure I'd made it home all right, so you checked my location on your phone, the way you always do, and it showed I was home the rest of the night. Got it?"

"Yes, but . . ." Confusion wars within me. "Where were you, really?"

"We don't have time to talk about it now, but you need to say this for me. You can do that, can't you? Erin, sweetheart?" He cups my cheek in his hand the way he used to do eight years ago, when we first started dating. I can't remember the last time he did that. "You ready to talk to the police? Or do you need to take some time to get yourself together? I can tell them you're freshening up or something."

I shake my head, though I can't seem to move the rest of my body. "I—I can. I'm ready."

"Good." His jaw is clenched tight and he's lost all light in his eyes. "That's my girl. Come on. Let's get in there and show 'em what a power couple looks like."

We walk into the living room hand in hand. When Mason's in front of the detectives, he's a new man, full of professionalism and cordial smiles, his shoulders relaxed, his tone even.

"This is my wife, Erin," I hear him say. "But you said you met before, at Georgia's house. Honey," Mason presses, "could you get these men something to drink? Water? Tea?"

Water would be great, I think. I'm parched.

But he hadn't asked if *I* wanted something to drink at all.

The detectives decline in a flurry of mumbles and take a seat on the couch in front of the windows. Mason's at my side a moment later, leading me to sit beside him on the couch behind us. I nearly stumble into the coffee table.

"My wife," Mason says on a laugh, wrapping his arm around me. His voice has an edge to it, but I doubt the officers will catch it. "Such a klutz. Her legs are continually bruised from running into all our furniture. But let's get down to what you two gentlemen are doing here. We're worried sick, aren't we, sweetheart? We'll do whatever we can to help."

"Yes," I say. It's all I can think of through the murk that's taken up residence in my mind. "Terrible."

I feel Mason's glare heat the side of my face, but I can't look at him. Not now. The detectives would surely pick up on the uncertainty and doubt and frustration I feel about him at this moment. As if through a tunnel, I hear the officers talk about the yacht and questioning Raul, the helmsman of the boat. They mention Georgia a handful of times, but I can't piece anything together until Mason squeezes my hand.

"Honey, Detective Linard asked you a question."

"Hmm?" I shake my head slightly. "I'm sorry, I didn't catch it."

"How well do you know Ms. St. Claire's fiancé?" he asks, an iPad sitting illuminated on his lap.

If I tell the truth, will it give them reason to believe I had something to do with his disappearance?

"We would hang out often," Mason answers for me. "Perhaps weekly we'd gather for dinner at one of our homes."

"A few more questions and we'll be out of your hair," Detective Linard says, looking up to meet my gaze squarely. "Georgia said only Mrs. King stayed overnight on the yacht. And you, Mr. King? Where did you go after you left the party?"

"Here," Mason says rather too quickly.

Linard swipes up on his screen. "Georgia said you had to work late."

"That's right, I should've clarified," Mason answers. "My wife stayed without me, while I called the office and got the information I needed to work from home. It was late, I was tired, so I changed my mind. I came straight here, called my wife, worked on a few files, and went to sleep. It was an uneventful evening."

Mason squeezes my hand so hard I think he's going to break it in two. But I can't fill in the details of a night that didn't happen, not when it's been thrust on me this way. Lies are bitter going down.

"Where do you work?" the detective asks Mason.

"King Plastic Surgery in Lower Haight. We're directly adjacent to Wave Surgery Center, which offers outpatient services. Our facility is state-of-the-art to ensure that each patient receives the highest quality of care and technology."

"Sounds like you've memorized the brochure," the squattier officer says. "You're the owner, then?"

"That's right." Mason's palm begins to sweat. "I work long hours. Which is what it takes to build a successful business. Things are going well, though. Better than expected. We've increased the services we offer and have grown two hundred percent in patient numbers this year alone."

"Impressive," the detective says. "I'm assuming you have a large staff."

I laugh at the innuendo. When no one else joins me, I clear my throat and force myself to quiet. *Large staff.* If they only knew. Mason's been researching penis extensions for years. As much as I tell him it's fine, he's fine, he doesn't need to undergo such a dramatic surgery, he won't let it go. Like a dog with a bone, that guy. I mentally chuckle at the images now flying through my head.

"We do," Mason says proudly. "Three surgeons besides me, with five assistants, and a handful of office staff."

"Who answered your call?"

His finger ticks against my hand. "Excuse me?"

"You said you called the office." Linard looks up from his iPad. "Who'd you talk to?"

"Forgive my asking, but why is this important?"

He drops my hand and folds his arms over his chest. He's

hiding something. But what? There's no way he had anything to do with Robert's disappearance two nights ago.

"We're gathering as much information as we can, Mr. King, to try to bring Mr. Donnelly home to his fiancée." Detective Linard swipes across his screen. "Back to the night in question. Do you remember who you talked to at your office?"

"I'm afraid I don't remember," Mason says.

"But your office typically closes at six, correct? And what time would you say you left the yacht?"

"Late. I didn't check the clock, so I don't want to give you a specific time and be wrong. Wouldn't want you to think you'd caught me in some kind of lie. But my office staff regularly works late. Still, I don't know what my calling the office has to do with Robert going missing anyway."

Linard makes a throaty, patronizing sound. "How would you classify his emotional state when you saw him last?"

"I wouldn't pretend to know what another man feels before he gets married." Mason is a ball of tension beside me, perched on the edge of the couch, his face a stony mask of irritation. "Nervous? Scared?"

I want to ask if he felt either of those emotions when he married me, but I keep my mouth shut.

"Do you recall him saying or doing anything unusual?" Linard asks. "Anything out of character that you can remember?"

"Nothing."

Something in the finality of Mason's tone warns that this conversation is over. Linard must pick up on the cue because he shakes hands, bids us well, and leaves without saying if he'll return. As friendly—innocent—neighbors must, Mason locks the door and sets the alarm with a curse.

"That was intense," I say, rubbing my hands over my arms to stave off the chill. "I'm glad they're gone."

"For now. They'll be back."

He heads upstairs, leaving me reeling. He doesn't think that's *it*, does he? I follow him into our room, heart in my throat. I find him in the closet, undressing. He's already down to his socks and checkered boxers, and plowing his way through the buttons of his white dress shirt.

"So . . . where were you?" I ask.

He curses under his breath as he jerks out of his shirt and flicks it into the basket. "You sound like the detective. He was quite the prick, wasn't he?"

"Don't change the subject, Mason."

"Fuck, Erin." He throws his hands into the air and lets them hit against his sides. "I'm done being interrogated for the day. Let it go."

I watch him shrug into a black T-shirt and shorts and slam his feet into his running shoes. "Where are you going?" I ask.

"To the gym." Standing erect once more, he whirls on me, closing the distance between us with a single aggressive step. "Unless you want to make this into a fight. Is that where this is headed?"

I try to exhale heavily, but a pathetic stream of air pushes out instead. "I don't want a fight. I just want to know why you wanted me to lie for you. You weren't at home, were you?"

"No."

"And you weren't at work . . ."

"For fuck's sake!" He jerks his thick mop of jet-black hair. When he brings his gaze back to mine, his expression is marred by fury. "You think I had something to do with what happened to Robert."

"No, of course not, I—"

"I had *nothing* to do with what happened to that asshole! I don't know where he fucking went, but I doubt your best friend could say the same." He gestures aggressively with his hands, barely missing my face. "You want to know what happened to Robert, look across the *fucking* street! Jesus, Erin, you really have a penchant for pissing me off."

As he continues on his rampage, spitting and snarling and charging through the closet to the bathroom, I follow on his heels, struggling to find something to say that will make him understand. But his words are sick and mean and as he leans over the sink, spewing hatred, all I can think about is how I would tag this image of him. He whirls on me, jabbing his finger in my face. #EveryCoupleFights or #IShouldn'tHaveSaidAnything would work, but as I'm thinking about whether I should push further, he's on me, against me, using his body to edge me back toward the wall. His eyes don't resemble Mason's anymore and I'm cringing and crying and wishing he would hit me so this would all end.

"I don't think you had anything to do with Robert going missing," I say feebly, as his body presses against mine. "I swear, I don't."

"You don't *now*, do you?" he barks, spit flying on my cheek. "Now that I've made it crystal-goddamn clear. Finally something sank into your thick-ass head. Why do you have to push me to this point every time, Erin? Why do you do this? You couldn't let it go. Had to keep going, keep poking with those incessant fucking questions. Now I don't even feel like going to the gym. You got me all riled up."

I wait for him to back away, to leave so I can breathe again, but he doesn't move. He stands over me for what feels like ten slow minutes.

"Ask the question, Erin," he seethes, his chest rising and

falling heavily against mine. "I know there's one more in that brain of yours. I've been with you long enough to see it's written all over your ugly-fucking face. Ask it now or forever hold your peace. And I mean it, bitch. If you don't ask it now, I never want to fucking hear it."

I've pushed too far. There's no going back from this. He's not going to let this go.

"If you weren't . . ." I begin.

He slaps me on the side of the head. "Speak up! I can't hear what you said!"

Shock and humiliation and pain surge through my body. In all the arguments we've had, Mason's never hit me. I've been afraid he would, of course, many times. But he's never actually done it. And he hit me on the side of the head. Not the eye or the cheek or the jaw. No, he hit me where my hair would cover any mark. It's as if he's thought this through before. How to get away with it. Wouldn't that make an interesting Instagram tag? Bet he would get more than a hundred views in five minutes . . .

"If you weren't here, and you weren't at work," I push out, fighting back stupid, shameful tears as my head throbs with heat, "who'd you spend the night with?"

He laughs hoarsely into the side of my face. "None of your goddamn business. That's who. Bring this up again, to *anyone*, and I'll knock you the fuck out."

CHAPTER EIGHTEEN

BROOKE

FRIDAY

I'm upstairs working, typing away, falling in love with Grace and the secondary characters who help her get into trouble. I skim over the last few pages I've written and fix a few typos. Not bad. My editor might even say this is my best work. Feeling proud, I remove the headphones from my ears to silence the sound of rain, close my eyes, and take a deep satisfied breath.

Bang! Bang! Bang!

Someone's downstairs.

I'd been so much in the writing zone, I hadn't realized the sun set in the last few hours. I'm sitting in the dark, only the blue glare of the computer screen lighting the room. Afraid to click on the office light, I tiptoe into the hall, checking both ways to search for Jack.

Shouldn't he be back by now?

It must be after nine. I don't know how it happened, but I

completely skipped dinner. It's as if the writing zapped me into some kind of time warp.

Bang! Bang! Bang!

Someone's at the front door.

It's dark downstairs too, with only the moonlight streaming through the back windows. Hadn't there been candles lit earlier?

"Jack?" I call out.

Bang!

Just one hammer of a fist against the door. An answer to my question.

With the house as quiet as a tomb, I tiptoe toward the front door, and grip the doorknob tightly. My heartbeat pounds in my ears. The knob turns in my hand. The door opens wide.

Robert is standing in the entryway, covered head to toe in blood. Clots mat his gray hair into thick, disgusting locks. His face streams with a steady flow of crimson. He reaches out for me with both arms extended, pleading for help, for mercy.

"Brooke!" he screams, clutching at my arms.

I fight him off, backpedaling. He charges inside, wailing in pain, blood pooling to the floor at his bare feet.

"Brooke!"

He has me now, squeezing my arms, his blood soaking my skin.

"Help . . ." I try to scream, but my voice is weak, and my throat aches. "Help me!"

My eyes flip open. Jack is beside me, holding my arms, blocking me from hitting him. I'm sitting at my computer. No one is screaming. No one is covered in blood. Robert's not here. My heart hammers against my ribs, and I'm out of breath. It was a dream. A terrible nightmare. No amount of rubbing my eyes will eliminate the image now burned there. But I'm safe. Jack's here. Outside, the sun has just risen, and is barely peeking through the cloud cover overhead.

"You fell asleep at your computer again," he says, brushing his hands up and down my arms to soothe me. "Nightmare?"

I can't go into detail about what I just saw in my mind's eye without sounding crazy . . . or morbid. "I—I was being attacked. It was awful."

"Well there's no reason to be afraid. You're safe. I'll protect you." He embraces me in a long hug that forces me to lean back against him. Rather than comforting, his arms are rigid, his chest hard beneath my head. It's like being hugged by a tree. "Did you write through the night?"

Nodding slowly, I pull away and scrub my hands over my eyes. I'm still in my clothes from yesterday. I'm in desperate need of a shower.

"I—I must have. Why are you still here? Shouldn't you be at work already?"

"It's Friday. I thought I'd take the morning slow." He picks up the mug he must've set on the desk before he woke me and takes a long drink. "Georgia's here."

"What?" I straighten. "Now?"

"Mmm." He buries his acknowledgment in a gulp. "Wanted to know if you'd go with her somewhere. I'll tell her you'll be down in two minutes."

Just like that, he's out of my hair. I dart into the closet, change into dark-washed jeans and a black shirt, and then clean my face, brush my teeth, and tie up my hair into a loose ponytail with tendrils falling down the sides. As I'm charging downstairs, Georgia's and Jack's laughter echoes through the house. He laughs from deep down in his throat, the way he does when something really tickles him. I haven't heard him laugh like that in a long time. A month, maybe. I wonder if the stress of the move and our work is taking a toll not only on me, but on Jack and our marriage.

When I reach the living room, Georgia and Jack are lost in hilarious conversation. They don't even notice I've entered the room. For reasons I can't explain, I look over the hearth to the painting that hides many faces in its colors and textures.

"I haven't laughed like this in years," Georgia says sweetly, brushing his shoulder before cupping her own face. "Brooke didn't mention how funny you were."

"There was a reason for that," I mumble under my breath.

"My cheeks hurt." Her laugh fades into innocent little giggles. "I needed this today, Jack. Thank you for making me remember what it's like to live in the moment."

"Don't mention it." He glances over his shoulder at me. "I'm taking off, Brooke. See you tonight for dinner?"

"Of course." I watch Georgia watch my husband walk out the door, and something deep down in my gut pinches. "Jack said you wanted to take me somewhere?"

"Something like that," she says urgently, taking my hand and sitting me down on the couch beside her. "I want you to come with me to Pier 39 for the day."

I feel my face scrunch because I can't picture Georgia there amongst all the tourists with their cameras and big families and expensive cheap food. "All right, but isn't that place a tourist trap? You sure you're up for it?"

She nods slowly. "That's exactly what it is, and exactly what I need. I've been so stressed, and to be honest, I'm going out of my mind. I need a distraction. Something that'll take me away from this place for a bit. It'll be loud and packed with people. I have to meet someone there for something, but that won't take long, and then afterward we'll get clam chowder in a bread bowl for lunch and watch the seals sunbathe on the edge of the pier. Sound good?"

"Sounds great," I say. "Should we invite Erin?"

She moves toward the door. "I already did, but she has a therapy session with Mason that apparently can't be rescheduled. Shall we?"

She's making this trip sound simple and innocent, but with everything going on—Robert's disappearance, the death threats, the ransom note, and the phone number on that scrap of paper—I can tell she's hiding something major.

And I'm going to find out what it is.

CHAPTER NINETEEN

ERIN

"I don't know why you dragged me here," Mason whispers, the deep baritone of his voice echoing off the open ceiling in Theresa's office. "Therapy is a waste of time."

If Mason were a toddler, he'd be stamping his feet, destroying the backseat of the car, and clawing for purchase at everything within arm's reach. Instead, he's a grown-ass man with a scowl and a piss-poor attitude. His arms have been folded all the way here, he's barely said two words to me, and even now, as I sit next to him on the modern couch, flipping a *Cosmopolitan* magazine, I can feel annoyance radiating from his body.

"No it's not," I say, checking to make sure Theresa hasn't sneaked in behind us. "We can all use it."

Especially people with anger issues. But I keep that nugget to myself.

"You're really drinking the Kool-Aid," he says. "Can't believe it."

"I loved Kool-Aid as a child. Didn't you?"

"Only the cherry." He glances at me, and something smolders down in his eyes. The hint of a smile curves his full mouth. "Seriously, Erin, I could think of a million things I'd rather be doing right now than sitting here waiting for our therapist."

His hand finds my knee, and for a moment I'm tempted to succumb to his plan, but when the door clicks behind us, I'm reminded why we're here. Mason is lying about where he was the evening Robert went missing. And I have a feeling he's cheating on me. Clearly Theresa suspects infidelity too. We're broken, and we need to fix "us."

As Theresa's floral scent wafts into the room, Mason removes his hand from my knee, replacing it in his lap.

"Sorry for making you wait," she says, sliding into the chair across from us. "I'm so glad you both came in this morning."

She's wearing a pale blue pencil skirt dotted with tiny bouquets of red roses and a matching red cardigan over a blue tank. Her stilettos are nude, making her legs seem impossibly long. Her dark hair is twirled up and piled on top of her head, and today she's stuck a pencil through the loose mop. I glance down absentmindedly and pick a piece of lint off my leggings. For the first time since taking a hiatus from the station, I miss dressing like a businesswoman.

"Where would you like to start?" she asks, her tender gaze flipping between us.

"How about the way Mason lied to me, and the police for that matter, about his whereabouts," I say, feigning indifference as I sit up straighter. "That seems like as good a place as any."

"Whoa." He laughs nervously. "Nothing like not easing into things. Can't we start with something smaller? Like how I'm such a workaholic or need to cut back on my drinking?"

"We only have an hour." She shrugs unsympathetically. "What makes you uncomfortable with discussing your whereabouts?"

His legs begin to twitch. "I'm not uncomfortable. I just thought we would *ease* into this conversation."

"The detectives came to see us about Georgia's husband's disappearance," I blurt. Mason's hand moves to my knee. He squeezes, a cue he'd like me to look at him, but I ignore the request. "They asked point-blank where Mason was after he left the yacht that night, and he lied to their faces. And he lied to me too. Asked me to corroborate his story. I don't know for sure, but I think that's a crime."

Theresa turns to Mason, a quizzical hitch of her eyebrows making her appear ten years younger. "How did you answer their question, Mason?"

Sighing, he removes his hand from my knee and shoves both hands beneath his thighs. "I said the truth. I was at home in bed. I called the office on my way home, had them email over some paperwork, worked until ten, and watched *SportsCenter* until I fell asleep."

"And that's truly what happened?" she asks.

"No," I blurt, before he can lie. "He wasn't home. He wanted me to *tell them* that he was home. That's different. He told me he was at work. I'd simply like to know where he was, that's all."

"It sounds as if it's the deception that has your wife upset," Theresa explains. "Can you understand that?"

"Of course I can. I'm not a moron." Turning toward me completely, Mason drags one leg over the other and glares.

"But you think I had something to do with Robert's disappearance. The doubt is written all over your face. You don't trust me, and that's what I have a problem with."

How could he possibly think he can spin this around in his favor? Has he lost his mind? I'm not the one lying. I can't look at him without feeling like my heart is going to beat out of my chest, so I stare straight ahead, at Theresa, our mediator, my saving grace. "If saying I don't believe you were at home or at work means I don't trust you, then fine. I don't trust you. Forgive me for wanting to know where my husband was the night my *friend's* fiancé went missing."

"I'd really rather not tell you."

Tears sting my eyes. "Fine. That's fine."

He's cheating. I know he is.

He throws his head back and groans obnoxiously. "There goes the surprise. I was in the city buying something for you. All right? Can we drop it now?"

"For me?"

"I was . . ." He shakes his head rapidly. "Jesus, I can't do a fucking thing without you questioning my motives, not even something that is going to benefit our marriage. You really do enjoy sucking the pleasure out of *everything* . . . except me, of course. Because if you did that, we wouldn't need fucking therapy."

"Easy, Mason," Theresa coos. "We want to keep our words encouraging, and our minds open. If you were truly doing something positive for your marriage, perhaps you can give a few details, and still keep the surprise?"

I hold his gaze and see a flicker of something there. I don't know if it's truth or lie or laughter, but it's a spark I've seen before.

For our fifth wedding anniversary, we made reservations

at JW's, my favorite Italian restaurant in the city. The place was painted deep red, wall to wall, with tiny lights hanging down from the ceiling as if it were raining specks of illuminated glitter. Coolest effect ever. After dinner, Mason took my hand and led me to the powder room, where he pinned me up against the door and made love to me. When we left the cramped room together, hand in hand, cheeks flushed pink, it was clear from the waitress's disapproving glare that she knew what'd happened. Mason's eyes lit up the way they are lit up now when he said, "Dessert was better than the dinner."

I wonder what he's hiding now . . .

He leans over, planting his elbows on his knees, and rubs his hands together briskly. "I was at Tiffany's."

"What?"

"I wanted to do something nice for you. I thought I'd buy that necklace you've had your eyes on."

"Mason, the Tiffany's on Post Street closes at six, and the one on Market closes at five. You left the yacht later than that."

He pounds his fists against his knees. "See that? No trust."

Theresa blinks slowly, calmly. "Would you mind clarifying so she's not confused? Did you go to Tiffany's in the East Bay, perhaps?"

"No," he bites out. "A guy said his girlfriend was a supervisor at the store on Post. She offered to make an exception and open up the store for a private showing so I could surprise you."

Now I'm the suspicious asshole. "You could've told me."

"And spoil this wonderful surprise?" He sneers.

"You really got me that necklace?" Grazing my hand over his knee, I give it a reassuring squeeze. "When were you planning on giving it to me?"

"I don't know." He meets my gaze once again. This time, the light is gone. "I suppose I was waiting for a special night."

Then I might've been waiting forever.

"Sounds like you're really making headway," Theresa says. "Our time is nearly up. I think that's a good place to leave off for today."

Mason lifts his hand. "Can we address something else before we go? Something that's going to save our marriage more than these sessions? Can we get Erin on some anxiety pills? Heavy duty ones. She needs to pop those things like M&Ms."

CHAPTER TWENTY

BROOKE

This morning, as the sun rose, I'd thought it was going to be a beautiful day. Instead, it's only gotten colder. Thick plumes of moisture have moved in fast, blanketing the city in clouds of gray. The wind has picked up, and tourists have started bracing for the cold. A twenty-something woman walks by, holding her screaming toddler's hand as his hat flies off his head, and street artists scramble to clip their paper canvases to cardboard. Once we're down the pier and between the businesses, the wind appears to die and we're offered a reprieve from the weather.

Georgia hasn't said much since we arrived. The area is bustling with people, as we knew it would be. Perhaps she's not comfortable making conversation with this many people around who could overhear and somehow misconstrue her words.

"How are you holding up?" I ask as we walk past a sign offering whale tours. I wonder if Georgia is thinking about what else might be floating out in the bay. "Have you heard anything from the detectives?"

Fiddling with the strap of her Louis Vuitton bag, Georgia stares at every single person who passes us, her expression grim. "Detective Linard called yesterday evening, but he was only checking in. Nothing new yet."

"Did you tell him about the note?"

She looks at me as if gauging whether to let me in on whatever secrets are swimming in her head. "I can't. For Robert's sake, I have to try to figure this out on my own."

"The letter seemed really cryptic," I say, treading carefully. "Do you know what the person meant by 'hold up your end of the deal'?"

"Whoever sent it is clearly crazy. I have no idea what he was talking about. I just want my fiancé back. This was supposed to be the happiest time of our lives." She checks over her shoulder, and seems to focus on something behind us. "I miss tiny, insignificant things about him, you know? Like the way he would kiss my forehead, or place my hand on his knee while we watched movies. I'm not trying to say we were perfect all the time, because there were definitely days when I'd wished he'd stay out on his yacht more often . . . but I never wished for this."

The sadness in her eyes seems genuine, but that's not possible. Two husbands dead. A future third mysteriously disappeared. No one could believe she's simply unlucky in love, not at this point.

"I can understand what you're saying. Jack makes me feel safe, which is important to me. I know he'd never hurt me.

But I like the fact that he works so much because when I'm home alone, I can finally be myself. I can let my guard down. I don't have to worry about being perfect."

"The pressure's always there, isn't it," she says. A statement, not a question. She checks behind her again, and sucks in a deep breath. She increases her pace. "Listen, I'm already hungry. Why don't we head into Eagle Cafe for an early lunch? It's always been one of my favorite restaurants in the city."

"Sounds great."

We head up to level two, where we're spoiled with amazing views of the bay, the pier next door, and the seals who've gathered to sunbathe in the pale light of the sun. The place is relatively empty, so we're seated at a table beside the windows.

"Perfect," Georgia says, though she doesn't sit when I do. Instead, she clutches the rail of the chair and rolls her fingers over the back nervously. "I just realized I left my wallet in the car. Would you order me the steamed clams and the fresh salmon? Oh, and an iced tea. Give me five or ten minutes?"

"Don't be ridiculous," I say, pretending to be offended. "Your lunch is on me today."

She scans the faces of the other people in the restaurant, her darkened gaze finally coming to rest on someone or something outside. "Thank you, but I wouldn't feel right about that. I'll be right back."

When the waitress makes her way over, I order what Georgia requested, including a calamari appetizer and a Cobb salad for myself. I'm looking out the window at the seals lounging lazily, barking at one another like old married couples, when I spot Georgia striding over the pedestrian walkway into the parking garage. It's not hard to spot her in a crowd. She walks with confidence, her head high, steps sure, and she's decked out in red and pink, like a shining beacon on this dreary day.

I watch her disappear into the shadows of the garage and thank the waitress when she delivers our drinks. Sipping the iced tea, I happen to catch a glimpse of Georgia as she steps out of the elevators onto the fourth floor, where she'd parked. Rather than continuing toward her car, she checks over her shoulder, twice, and then walks gingerly beside the concrete railing toward a large post.

She stops with a jolt. At first, I can't see what's stopped her, can't tell what she's looking at. But then I see him. Dressed in black pants, and a matching hoodie. He has his hands in his pockets.

She's meeting someone.

The ransom.

"Shit." My gut clenches. "It's going down *now*?"

I don't know whether to stay where I am and record the incident in case something goes south or run to meet her so she has backup. But what would I do in that situation anyway? Probably make things worse. Heart pounding, I fish my phone from my purse and start recording.

They talk for one minute and ten seconds, according to my phone, before the energy changes. Georgia's pointing at him now, nearly jabbing him in the chest. She's heated, though even when I zoom in, I can't read her lips. The man takes a step back, hands still in his pockets. She digs through her purse and comes out with a tiny piece of paper. The man doesn't take it. He looks at it and spits.

She takes a step back. He pulls out a gun, pointing it directly at her chest.

I jump from my seat and flag down the waitress, blurting something about forgetting my purse in my car, although it's slung over my arm. Charging across the pedestrian walkway, I pray for the man to show restraint, for Georgia to come out of this alive.

Taking the stairs two at a time, I'm at the top of the fourth flight, exhausted, panting, when I hear Georgia's voice. She's panicked, but not screaming. She's holding it together. He hasn't fired. I won't do her any good if I can't breathe. I need a second to compose myself. To make a plan that'll get us both out of this mess.

Her voice echoes through the garage. "I told you, I wired it last night, like you asked. Same account as before."

"No, bitch, you transferred ten million, but that only covers the original amount for Andrew," the man growls. "You still owe ten for interest on that mark because you made me wait so damn long, and twenty for the newest one."

Andrew? What does this have to do with her late husband? I thought this was all about Robert . . .

Slowly, I inch forward, so that I can see around the concrete pillar in front of the elevator. From here, I can see the man's body, tall and strong, but his face is masked in shadow. Adrenaline spikes through me.

"I was late paying for Andrew. I know, and I'm sorry about that. There was nothing more I could do, and I can get you the interest if you give me more time. But Robert was *never* supposed to be a mark," Georgia says, her voice strong, rather than desperate. "You must've misunderstood. That's your mistake. I'm not paying twenty million for that. Just let him come back to me and we'll forget all about this. Please. We can straighten the rest out later."

"No, we're going to take care of this right now."

In a flurry of movement I can barely track, the man snatches Georgia around the waist and hauls her against him, pointing the gun into her side, just below her breast. She begins to scream, but he whacks her over the head, silencing her, and then snakes an arm around her neck. He's pinned her back to his front. They're facing away from me. I could run up behind him, tackle him, knock the gun away. But if something goes wrong—oh God, there's so much that could go wrong—we could both be dead.

I creep around the pillar, closer, tiptoeing, searching for signs of others who might be able to help, but there's no one around. Somewhere in a parking level below, tires screech. The sound of a horn blasts through the air. In a level above, a car alarm goes off.

I'm closer . . . twenty feet away . . . ten . . .

My breathing is so loud, it's going to give me away. Short, shallow breaths punch out of my lungs and my heart races. Georgia's whimpering now, struggling to get away from him, but he's strong. Much too strong for her to overpower alone.

"I'll make you a deal," he says into her ear. "You're going to pay me the thirty you still owe. That's nonnegotiable. But if you want your fiancé back, you'll need to pay double the original asking price."

"But it was twenty originally . . ." she whispers, disbelievingly. "I have to pay you *forty million* to see Robert again? How do I even know he's still alive?"

"Because I fucking say he is," he growls. "You have until midnight to wire the money. You go to the police, he's dead. You tell anyone *anything* about me, he's dead, and I'll come for you next. You got me?"

"Got it," she says, breathless, as she fights against him. "Please . . ."

He relayed his message, now why isn't he letting her go?

I'm a few steps away, so close. I'm going to hit him upside

the head. Knock the gun away. And then we're going to run as hard and fast as we can away from this maniac.

My phone rings in my purse.

I freeze. He turns, and we lock eyes. Heat flashes through me and my legs turn to lead. Georgia stamps on his foot, and when he bowls over, she knocks the gun away. It hits the ground with a crack and spins over the concrete toward the ledge to the street below. They go for it at the same time.

"No!" I scream. "Georgia, run!"

But as she darts for the gun, her eyes are wild and desperate, like those of an animal that's been caged for too long. I run hard, and when he crouches to pick up the weapon, I leap onto his back, coiling my arm around his neck. He makes a throaty, strangled sound, and slings me off his shoulders. I hit the concrete hard as the gun goes off. The sound is deafening, echoing on and on through the garage. Birds scatter overhead, flying toward the pier.

Everything goes quiet.

I meet Georgia's eyes. She's on the ground, gun pointed in the air as if the man was still standing there. But he's on the ground beside me, splayed in a pool of his own blood. His body is steaming. Or maybe that's from the gun.

My hands tremble. "What have we done?"

As if she's just realized she's holding the murder weapon, Georgia drops it and scrambles to her feet. "Brooke, get up."

But I can't stop staring at the man on the ground beside me. Dark hair the same color as mine. Almond-shaped eyes. Wide chin. Scar slashed across his cheek.

"The po—the police," I mumble, trying to make sense of things. "They're going to come, and they're going to know what we did. We can't leave him here."

She tugs on my arm. "Brooke, we have to go. We can't stay."

My legs won't work. They've turned to jelly. It doesn't make any logical sense because I should be running far from here, especially if the police are coming, but I don't want to leave this spot. I just need a minute to think . . . to clear my head. As my vision blurs, I see Georgia move around the scene in a fog. She wipes off the gun and drops it near the lifeless body, then rifles through the man's pockets, taking what she finds there and shoving it in her purse.

Shouldn't she dispose of the gun? The bay's right there. Or maybe cameras are watching. Would tossing a gun into the water make her look too guilty?

In my haze, I can't make sense of the right thing to do.

She's at my side again, patting my face. "Can you hear me, love? We have to move or we're going to be in a world of trouble. We're in this together. It's you and me now, so I can't leave you here by yourself. You have to come with me. Can you do that? My car's right over there. Come on, girl. You can do this."

You and me.

We killed him . . . together.

I'm going to be sick. As we're pulling out of the garage, I roll down the window for fresh air and hang my head out. The sound of seals barking on the pier gently bleeds into the wail of a siren, reminding me too much of my childhood. I look up to the fourth level, where I imagine the man's blood circling the parking lot drain.

Guess there are certain things we can't escape in this life.

Everything really does come back full circle.

CHAPTER TWENTY-ONE

ERIN

"Let me in!" I rap on Georgia's front door. I know she's in there with Brooke, but she won't come to the door. "Georgia, it's me! What's going on?"

I heard the engine of her car rev as she turned onto the street, and I saw the way she raced into the driveway. Mason said I should leave her alone, give her space to make new friends. But he doesn't know what's going on.

And something definitely went wrong.

"Georgia!" I bang on the door again. "Come on!"

She jerks open the door, but instead of greeting me, the way she usually does, she storms back into the living room. Brooke's on the couch, head between her knees, blowing in and out heavily as if she's fighting off a panic attack.

I lock the door behind me. "What the hell happened?"

"We just need to calm down so I can run through this. I need to hear how it sounds when spoken aloud." Georgia paces behind the couch where Brooke is having a semidramatic meltdown. "Erin, tell me how this sounds. Danny Johnson—some greedy, crazed man—kidnapped Robert and wanted a ransom for his safe return. He asked me to meet him at the Pier 39 parking garage, told me to come alone, and not to alert the police."

Brooke lets out a pathetic whimper that sounds vaguely like agreement.

"But I couldn't bear to go alone because I was too afraid, so I asked Brooke to come with me and watch from afar. We got a table at the restaurant, so she would have a straight shot of the interaction. But it went south fast. I refused to pay him. He pulled out a gun."

Gasping, covering my mouth with my hand, I settle into the chair across from Brooke. She looks up at me, her eyes glossy with tears. She nods as if she hears my unspoken question.

Georgia stops pacing, gently rests her hands on Brooke's shoulders, and finally meets my gaze. "She saw what was happening and ran to the garage to save me. She surprised him from behind. We fought. The gun went off. We were very lucky to get out of there alive."

Brooke nods weakly.

Holy shit, this is bad. I'm so glad I wasn't there.

"And then," Georgia goes on, "we didn't know what to do, having just killed a man, so we freaked out, and left. The detectives were so eager to talk about fight or flight when it pertained to Robert getting cold feet. Now we can claim it for real. We acted on instinct. We ran. It's understandable. But now—now we have come to our senses and will call the police."

"Are you okay?" I mouth to Georgia. "This is crazy."

"I'm fine—we're fine. A little jumpy, a little spooked, but we're okay. I'm glad all of this is finally over."

Her words reverberate in my head. *This is finally over.*

She means more than this single event. She means no more death threats. No more someone following her around, trying to scare her. No more having to worry whether this man is going to continue blackmailing her for additional money, beyond their spoken contract.

Georgia can now close the book on Eli's and Andrew's deaths. Put a period and move on. I would consider the entire process successful.

It's not that we were excited to be rid of Eli and Andrew, but once they became abusive, Georgia knew she had to do something. She couldn't go on living that way, and since they'd signed prenups, divorces would've left Georgia with nothing. They left her no choice, really. They couldn't have expected her to live in fear that way forever.

I'm simply thankful I was there to assist in her time of need. All it took was joining a few abusive spouse chats and forums on a handful of social media outlets. People who get out of dangerous situations are always eager to talk to others about what they "should" do to be free themselves. When I'd mentioned divorce wasn't an option, and that my husband was incredibly wealthy, one woman in particular was very supportive and helpful, asking to meet me at Starbucks. After talking briefly about her own situation, she gave me a slip of paper with a row of digits written on it. I'd texted the number right away, thinking it was for a divorce attorney or battered women's shelter.

Instead, I'd been given something far more powerful. It'd bonded Georgia and me. We'd been friends before, of course, starting from the day we bought our homes in Presidio Terrace, one month apart. But after we held her husbands' lives in the palms of our hands, our fates became forever intertwined. She can't turn on me, and I can't turn on her.

We're in this together.

"Have you told her . . ." I ask Georgia, even though my gaze jumps to Brooke. ". . . everything?"

Georgia nods. "She's in the thick of it with us now. Through and through."

I exhale heavily—secrets are heavy things to carry—though my chest tightens with nervous energy. How did Brooke take the news when Georgia told her that we hired Danny Johnson to kill Eli and Andrew? Did she tell her that Danny was supposed to kill Mason this time, but royally screwed up by taking Robert instead? Damn that guy. Danny had been such a thorough hitman before, so careful to make both Eli's and Andrew's murders look like an accident and a suicide. Why would he suddenly disregard the plans to take Mason? Did he think Georgia would pay more money for his return? Or was he truly a moron?

I'm not sure of the reason for his mistake, but now I'm left with Mason, who is alive and well, and Georgia's panicked that the only man she ever truly loved is gone from her life forever.

Talk about karma.

I'll ask Georgia *exactly* how much she revealed to Brooke later, in private, because in this moment we have to focus on locking down our story.

"The police are going to ask for the ransom note," I say quickly.

"That's the easy part," Georgia says. "I can use the latest one with Robert's finger in it. In that note, Danny asked for thirty million and he told me not to go to the police."

"Good," I say. "Your story will check out."

Brooke blows her nose into the tissue she'd been tearing apart in her lap. "The police are going to bring us in for questioning. They're going to try and arrest us for murder."

"You can't be that naïve, Brooke. They're not going to arrest you if you were defending yourselves." I drag a piece of hair over my shoulder and fiddle with the end as I think about the police poking their noses around here again. "According to the story you're going to feed the police, that guy attacked an innocent woman. And he kidnapped her husband. Georgia's the true victim in all this—it might be the way to clear her name once and for all."

"Exactly." Georgia sits beside Brooke and rests her hand on Brooke's knee. "We have to call the cops, because now that our adrenaline from the attack has worn off, our consciences must kick in. We have to show we're good people who do the right thing."

"Are we?" Brooke asks wearily. "Are we good people?"

Georgia better not answer that.

"We're trying, and that's all anyone can expect of us." Georgia sighs deeply. "Now that I'm able to think clearly, the parking garage must have video footage of us leaving around the time of the incident, so we have to call not only for that reason—they're going to come knocking anyway—but because this means Robert is out there somewhere, being held captive, and his captor is dead. Who's going to bring him food and water? Robert's not going to last long now."

"As soon as the police ID the body," I say, "they'll use their resources to track down his last known residence, contacts, everything. If Robert's out there, the police will find him."

"If?" Georgia parrots. "I can't think about a future without Robert. He's out there. He has to be."

"But you took Danny's wallet," Brooke says. "Identifying a body takes time. According to some of my book research, identification can take weeks."

Georgia drops her head in her hands. "If Danny was telling the truth, and Robert's still alive out there, he won't last that long. Damn it. I shouldn't have taken the wallet, but at the time, I thought it'd be better if the police couldn't ID him because he'd be just another dead guy in a parking garage. I thought there'd be no way to link him to us."

"Where is it?" I ask, and twist around when Georgia breaks away from Brooke to run to the kitchen island.

Digging furiously through her purse, Georgia removes a dusty brown wallet and holds it up for inspection. She pinches the leather between her fingers as if it's a putrid piece of trash she's removed from the gutter. "What should I say? Why would I have taken it?"

"Panic," I blurt. "Say you freaked out and lost your mind. People do all kinds of weird things when they're under extreme stress."

Disgust curling her upper lip, Georgia opens the wallet. "He's changed a lot from his picture. Time has not been kind. Fort Walton Beach, Florida, address. Wonder what he's doing in California?"

"Extorting you for millions of dollars, that's what," I say.

"He wanted forty million to bring Robert back! Can you believe it? Greedy bastard. How could I have come up with that kind of money by midnight?"

"You didn't owe him a penny more, Georgia."

Eli's murder was $10 million, paid through a fake charity account called World Wish Foundation. Andrew's murder was the same price, if you don't count the $10 million in interest Danny was demanding, which Georgia refused to pay. Mason's death was supposed to cost $20 million, and I'd planned to make a "donation" for that amount through Georgia's charity. If Georgia and I had paid Danny everything, he would've banked $50 million.

Quite the entrepreneur, that guy.

Too bad he's dead. Who's going to take care of Mason for me now? After Robert's discovered dead or alive, and some time has passed, I'll have to deal with Mason in my own way.

Brooke's phone goes off. She checks the name, and then looks up innocently, a deer caught in headlights. We're going to have to groom her a lot more if she's going to be talking to the police. "It's Jack. What should I say?"

"Nothing," Georgia and I say in unison. Moving to sit beside her, I take the lead. "Nothing more than the story Georgia just told you. Don't add or omit any other details. Your stories have to be solid."

"I'm calling the police now," Georgia says, "so if they check the timing of the calls, they know we called the police at the same time she told her husband. Erin?"

I turn to her. "Yeah?"

"Still want that interview?"

"Yes, but you don't have to—"

"Think there's a possibility we can run it late tonight? Show everyone that I just survived a terrible ordeal, right before what was supposed to be my wedding day. It'll garner a lot of sympathy. Then, when the police find Robert, you can cover our heartfelt reunion. Tie everything up with a bright red bow."

"I don't know, Georgia. I'm not sure the timing is right. Are you sure you're up for it? I mean, after what just happened don't you want to take a Xanax and bury your head under the covers until Christmas?"

"I'm sure." She smiles, but it doesn't reach her eyes. "People will watch because they love to hate me. They'll hear Robert disappeared and think the Black Widow has struck again. I'll use the gossip and morbid interest that swirls around me to get people to tune in to the show . . . and then we'll make the focus on what happened to us today, and the fact that Robert is still out there, missing. Maybe people will feel bad for me. Maybe they'll see a photo of Danny's face and say, 'I saw that guy leave this area or that' or 'I saw something strange happening at this address.' I know I'm grasping at straws, but if there's a chance someone has seen Danny or Robert, and this show brings my fiancé home sooner, it'll be worth it."

As Georgia walks through the kitchen, phone to her ear, and Brooke begins telling Jack about their ordeal, I get the feeling everything is going to turn out right after all.

CHAPTER TWENTY-TWO

ERIN

The police take Georgia's and Brooke's statements, and as they leave, for the third time this week, I'm reeling. I don't think Presidio Terrace has ever gotten this much police action. I'm sure the neighbors are pissed. We must be in violation of some homeowners association code. I'll have to look it up when I get home.

Georgia handed Danny's wallet over to the police. Officer Linard eyed her curiously when she explained the panicked state she was in when she snatched it. They're going to search Danny's home and surrounding areas for signs of Robert. They said the show might help bring attention to his disappearance.

Jack came straight from work to console Brooke, who looked a bit stronger with her husband there. He seemed to fold her against him, and wrap her in a cocoon-like embrace. For a split second, I envied her marriage, longed for that.

Mason went to work after our therapy session, and I haven't heard from him since.

It would be nice for Mason to want to check up on me every now and then. But perhaps he knows I can handle myself. I'm not as fragile or emotionally unstable as Brooke appears to be. It's clear she's had some sort of trauma in her past that's rearing its head now, with the death of this guy. Her answers to the officers' questions sounded a bit rote, a little too rehearsed, but the police will assume it's because she's been frightened.

Poor thing, they'll say. *She's gone through quite an ordeal.*

As expected, the police said they were checking video from the parking garage. I don't think they suspect we hired Danny Johnson. We're going to come out looking like victims in all this.

Striding into Georgia's bedroom, I plop on the edge of her bed, give my hair a good fluff, and touch up my makeup. I miss Monique styling my hair every day; she's pure magic. The station sent one van with Monique, Rob, and a woman I've never seen before. Apparently they determined that Georgia's bedroom has the best overhead lighting and preferred I conduct the interview there.

I don't care where it takes place, as long as it's a hit . . . and that it brings Robert home, of course.

Now that Monique is working on Georgia's hair and makeup and the crew is busy setting up, her bedroom is a flurry of movement. While Georgia perches like some exotic bird in front of a large vanity in the center of the room, her blue dress bedazzled with flecks of red and yellow, Monique touches up her lips. She moves to this side and that, crouching to get just the right amount of lift. Rob cues up the camera, fiddling with the angle and snapping a few practice pictures to get the lighting just right. He pushes a love seat in front of the door leading out to the private patio.

"Hurry and grab those vases. Set them on the ground. By the love seat. Good," a woman says from behind me. She forces her way into the room, nicking my shoulder without a single apology. "We need flowers. Long-stemmed white ones. *Pure* white, not that dingy yellow-white." When Rob drags a potted plant so it peeks from behind the chair, she snaps, "Move!"

"Why white?" Monique asks, applying gloss to Georgia's lips.

The woman spins on her as Rob leaves the room. "Because we want Georgia to be the only pop of color in this space. And white screams innocence."

She must be Hillary Gleaves, the perky one Bill mentioned. The one who took my place, the bitch. She's everything I feared she'd be: lean, young, and fresh-faced, with a spark of ambition in her eyes. She's wearing a black, wide-legged pantsuit peppered with tiny white dots with a V-neck that plunges down near to her navel. She must've taped her nipples to the lapels—it's the only way they're not showing. I hope the tape tears her most sensitive skin when she tries to peel it off tonight.

The way she's snapping and pointing and snarling at the crew makes me think she would rather be a producer than an anchor. Maybe climbing the corporate ladder is her endgame. Wonder if Bill gave her the same revolting "opportunity" he offered me.

Brooke is standing in the bathroom doorway like a statue, champagne glass in her delicate hand, a strange, zoned-out look on her face. She hasn't said much since the police left. The cotton dress she's wearing is the palest shade of pink I've ever seen. Like wisps of cotton candy. Between the way she's standing—her legs crossed with her weight on one leg, her ankle twisting coyly against the floor, and knees squeezed together—and her feminine, girlish dress, she appears ten years younger.

Just when I thought it wasn't possible to hate her more . . .

"Hey, Br—" I begin.

"You ready to do this?" Georgia interjects, glancing at me out of the corner of her eye.

"Ready as ever."

"Brooke set up the mimosa bar on the bathroom counter." She slowly opens and closes her eyes so Monique can work her lashes against the brush. "They're not as good as Grounds & Greens, but close. You should have one before we get rolling."

"Remember to make her look natural. We want housewife, not home wrecker. Those lips are too garish." Hillary Gleaves snaps three times over her head. Her boob nearly escapes its polyester hold as she waves her hand. "Five minutes, people! Where the hell did he go to get my flowers? Napa? Are we cued up with the mics? Ready? Good."

I lean in close to Georgia, more to get Monique's attention than to share some deep dark secret. "How's the 'new me' measuring up?"

"She's intense," Monique whispers, "but she's good. Ratings are higher than they've been in years."

"Well that's . . . wonderful, isn't it?" I laugh tightly and smooth my hands down my throat when it feels like I'm swallowing fire. "What's she doing here anyway?"

It's as if Bill didn't trust me and sent his new favorite to ensure I'd do the job up to standard. I try not to feel insulted.

Monique shrugs. "Bill sent the list of everyone headed over today. Her name was at the top."

Cringing inside, I force a tight smile. "Want to run over your answers, Georgia? It might help with your nerves. Or you can borrow some of my meds?"

"I don't know what I'm going to say yet," she says, giving the dramatic V-neck of her dress a solid hike. "I looked over the questions you sent, but Hillary thinks it'll appear more genuine and organic if I answer at the spur of the moment. A little more shadow on my eyes, please."

Monique is caking on her makeup much too dark, if she wants my opinion. Not that she does, but that doesn't matter.

"*Hillary* thinks?" I parrot.

But I'm her best friend. Georgia's literal partner in crime. I guess to hell with what I think about being prepared. Perhaps she's not taking this special as seriously as she should be.

"She said it's important to not seem rehearsed," Georgia explains. "People won't relate to me if they think I've been fed the questions and answers."

"How nice of her to want to help you." Cheeks flushing with a rush of blood, I stand to confront this *stupid* woman. "I don't think we've met," I say, forcing myself in front of her and extending my hand. "I'm Erin King."

"Yes, I know." Her smile is flat. Faker than fake. "Ted has told me all about you."

Ted, the tool. I'm sure he had such kind things to say.

"Listen," I say, lightly touching her shoulder. "I understand you talked with Georgia earlier about the importance of appearing earnest in front of the camera. And while I understand what you're trying to accomplish, it's also important that she feels prepared. I don't think it's a terrible idea for her to run through a few of the questions I'm going to ask her."

"If she wants to run through *your* questions, that's fine." Casually glancing around the room, Hillary makes a light huff-

ing sound, and then shrugs. Behind her, Rob enters with arm-
fuls of white flowers and begins arranging them near the
couch. "But Bill has his own questions he wants asked, and
those should be on-the-spot. About time you show up with
those things. Ready, Mon?"

"*Mon?* Didn't know you two had gotten so close." I glare
at Monique, then back to Hillary. "Bill didn't send me any
questions."

"Oh? That's right. I was supposed to send them to you this
morning." She slips her phone from her pocket, scrolls, and
jabs the screen. "My bad. They're in your in-box now. Let's
get this thing rolling. I don't want to be here until midnight."

What the hell?

Why would he send the questions through Hillary? My gut
tells me the answer. Because he knew if he sent them to me,
I'd warm Georgia up to the questions. And it's clear he has his
own agenda for how this interview runs.

As Monique finishes applying a second layer of mascara, I
excuse myself to the bathroom to talk to Brooke. She's clutching the champagne flute as if she plans to crush it between
two fingers.

"How are you holding up?" I ask, embracing her in a quick
hug. For a moment, it seems as if she's quivering. But it's not
cold in the house, and when I brush my hand down her shoulder, her skin is warm to the touch. "You okay?"

"I'm all right. Worried about Robert. I hope they find
him."

"Me too."

"Do you think they will?"

"I don't know, but this interview should draw attention to
what's happened. We can only hope someone's seen him, or
knows where Danny might've taken him."

"I wonder if Georgia has thought about finding him on her own," Brooke says, after a long drink. "You know, going out there, to Danny's house, and looking for herself."

I hadn't even thought about the possibility that she would do something like that without the police's help. I suppose I should ask her after everyone leaves. If she wants, I could go with her, be the friend I should've been earlier, when she was attacked by that madman.

"Let's get started," Hillary yells. "Places, people!"

Hillary snaps one, two, three times in a helicopter move over her head. I sit on the edge of an upholstered chair beside the love seat in front of the windows leading out to Georgia's private patio. She leans into the love seat's cushions, resting her arms on the back as she crosses her legs. Monique leaves the room, and Rob is ready to start filming. A stationary camera is set up at another angle nearby. There'll be a camera on each of us, so as not to miss a single reaction.

Hillary moves behind Rob, surveying the scene, and I know she won't be in my anchor position long. From the way she's studying every angle of this special, she has her sights set on directing. Despite my envy—God, I hate that it's the word that came to mind—I have to admit, Hillary created the perfect environment for the shoot. Georgia flares her blue skirt over her knees. Moonlight streaming through the windows envelops her beautifully. Georgia is the focal point, the vivid blast of color against a soft white backdrop.

I pull Hillary's questions up on my phone, skim past Bill's introductory email, my eyes catching on the title of the special.

Georgia St. Claire: The Sinful Life of a Trophy Wife.

Doesn't sound like this is going to be sympathetic to Georgia at all. But I suppose that was to be expected. Whatever it takes to hook viewers in. I scroll to the list of questions, and read furiously through them.

Holy hell.

This isn't what I had in mind at all. This isn't what I signed up for.

"Erin . . ." Georgia reaches over and squeezes my hand. "We got this."

I look up from my phone. The camera lights blink red.

Good God, we're live.

CHAPTER TWENTY-THREE

BROOKE

"Good evening, I'm Erin King, and thank you for watching . . ." She pauses, glances at the phone in her lap, and clears her throat. ". . . Georgia St. Claire . . ."

It's silent for so long, I don't know whether she's going to continue at all. Hillary stamps her foot behind the camera and glares. Georgia leans toward Erin and whispers something. Whatever she says seems to jar Erin back to reality.

"Thank you for watching tonight's special, *Georgia St. Claire: The Sinful Life of a Trophy Wife*. We are in the prestigious gated community of Presidio Terrace, conducting an exclusive interview with the rumored Black Widow, who some believe has killed two husbands over the last ten years. Tonight we will set the record straight and hear from the Black Widow herself, for the first time in a live interview. Good evening, Georgia."

Now she's rolling, and I'm not sure what made her stumble in the first place.

"Good evening." Georgia's voice is strong, laced with confidence, as always. "I'm happy to answer any questions I can—anything to bring home my fiancé, Robert Donnelly."

"I wanted to touch on that for a moment, to brief the public on what's been happening over the last few days."

As Erin goes over the details of Robert's disappearance and our horrific incident earlier, her voice seems to muffle and zone out, as if she's moved into a tunnel far, far away from me. My ears fuzz with static. My vision swims. I brace myself against the bathroom door and finish my mimosa. The sweetness from the sugar on the rim lingers on my lips as the alcohol left in the bottom of the glass burns my throat. I'm not sure how long I'm standing there, slowly swaying back and forth, focused on the blinking red light of the camera, but when I finally regain awareness, Erin's brought everyone up to speed.

"How tragic," Erin says, shaking her head solemnly. "You're lucky to be sitting here right now."

"I am." Georgia swallows hard. "But I can't count my blessings because I don't have my fiancé, the love of my life, here with me now. Whatever sins I've committed in the past are mine, and mine alone. It's not fair that he should have to atone for them. He's innocent—a good man, and he doesn't deserve this. If anyone has *any* information that can help bring Robert Donnelly home, please, I beg you, call the police. I just want him back where he belongs."

"Your wedding was scheduled for tomorrow." Erin glances down at her phone and frowns. "Do you have any hope he'll turn up in time to marry you?"

Georgia flinches. "Of course. No one knows what tomorrow brings."

Erin looks down at her phone again, and this time there's a pregnant pause before her question. "People know you as simply the Black Widow. What's your real name?"

A soft blush rises to her cheeks. "My full legal name is Georgia Jane Coventry–Dalton–St. Claire. Legally, I still carry my maiden name, along with the last names of each of my husbands."

"Well that's fitting, considering you still carry their money as well." As the words leave Erin's mouth, scolding and harsh, her expression softens, almost apologetically. "Some of the viewers may not know the details of your past, so I'd like to enlighten them a bit. Were you ever formally charged with the murders of your husbands?"

Frowning, Georgia presses her lips together firmly. "I was never charged. Because like Eli, and Andrew, and now Robert, I'm a victim in all of this."

"Their killers have never been brought to justice . . ." Erin goes on. "I just want to be clear."

"Oh yes, let's make sure everyone has the complete picture." Georgia uncrosses and recrosses her legs as if she's suddenly uncomfortable. "Eli and Andrew were not murdered. There are no *killers* to be found. Eli slipped and fell down our stairs. Andrew shot himself. Robert . . ." She hesitates, her chest ballooning with a deep breath of air. ". . . was kidnapped by the madman who attacked me earlier. He's still out there, and I won't rest until I find him."

Between the tension, the shifting of her eyes, and the way Georgia's voice is now laced with doubt, I realize this is ratings gold. The story of Erin's career.

Erin glances at the phone in her lap. "Georgia, would you say you have a lot of enemies?"

Georgia slides to the edge of the love seat. "I'm starting to think so, yes. Comes with the territory, I suppose."

"What do you mean by that?"

"People have a hard time being friends with someone they envy." Georgia's eyes bore into Erin's, and I feel the tension sparking between them. "Don't you agree?"

Erin purses her lips in annoyance. "You were married to your first husband, Eli, for a year. Remind us how he was murdered."

"He *died*, Erin. It wasn't murder."

"But the autopsy revealed large amounts of medication in his bloodstream at the time of his death. He'd been drugged."

"He'd just had knee surgery, and was in a lot of pain. The doctor had prescribed him those painkillers."

Erin skims her finger over the phone's screen. "Your second husband? How long were you married that time?"

"Andrew. Eight months."

"You were home asleep when he shot himself?"

She nods decisively. "I was."

Erin reads something on her phone and grimaces. "You received ten million dollars upon his death. Is that right?"

"Actually, I didn't receive a dime from Andrew. He donated all of his money to charity. He was a very noble man."

From what I've read online, Andrew was a philanthropist who often donated millions of his hard-earned dollars to charity. But he was also abusive, and according to what I've been able to dig up, he was charged with domestic violence on more than one occasion—not with Georgia, but I'm certain he was abusive to her as well. I'm assuming she didn't want to report him because of the negative attention she'd receive. Easier to kill him, apparently.

"That's very kind of him," Erin says. "And you've been very generous with your money as well. You donate to all kinds of charities, don't you?"

Georgia's jaw clenches.

Behind me, Hillary snickers. She must have somehow realized from the expression on Georgia's face that it's over. The audience must be able to see through her by now. She's a gold digger who married older men for money, and then killed them off one by one.

"And . . ." Staring at her phone, Erin seems to falter. "Now Robert. He'd be the wealthiest of all your husbands, wouldn't he?"

"Stop," Georgia bites out. "I can't do this—I need a minute."

"I think we all need some time to process this information," Erin says sweetly, glancing into the camera. "We'll return after this short break."

At the cue that they've cut to commercial, Georgia is on Erin before she can blink, her finger pointed into Erin's chest. "What the hell was that about? We're trying to save *Robert*, not incriminate *me*."

Erin holds up her hands in surrender, her phone clutched between her fingers. "I'm sorry, Georgia, I don't have a choice."

"Dissecting my past like this was *not* part of the deal. We were supposed to be focusing on Robert, bringing attention to what happened, and pleading to the public to come forward if they know something."

"This is what they think is going to bring in the most viewers."

"And it's gold," Hillary pipes in. "Pure television gold. You're doing amazing, by the way. Building up suspicion without admitting guilt. It's the perfect balance."

Georgia points at Hillary. "See? This is the stupidity I'm worried about. Erin, you know me, probably better than anyone, and you know what's at stake. You know I can't afford to have everyone think I had something to do with what happened to Eli and Andrew. Now Robert!" Standing with a jolt, Georgia rips the mic pack from her waist and drops it to the floor with a thud. "I didn't think I'd have to explain myself this way, not to you. The interview's over."

"Georgia, let me explain—" Erin starts as Georgia heads for the door.

"I don't think so." Hillary Gleaves puts out her arm, stopping Georgia from leaving. "When you committed to doing this, you agreed to the terms, and that includes finishing the interview. It's live. We can't just cut it partway."

"I do what I want, when I want," Georgia says, snapping over her head to mimic the way Hillary had earlier. "You're on my property and I'm officially asking you to leave. Oh, look, now you're trespassing."

Hillary's lips curl in the most sinister way, and I suddenly know why they didn't want Georgia to be prepared with questions beforehand. Why they painted her eyelids exceptionally dark. They probably suggested she wear such a low-cut top.

They never intended on hearing Georgia's truth, the way she'd hoped.

They're going to make her out to be a gold-digging killer. And, well, she's not a saint.

"Oh, darling," Hillary says, laughing cynically. "We're not going anywhere, and neither are you. Sit your rich ass down or you'll be hearing from our lawyers."

I'm moving toward the door when Erin rises off the chair and steps between Georgia and Hillary. Out of the corner of my eye, I catch a subtle twist of the camera, and a whisper from Rob, the cameraman. *They're being recorded.* I freeze, feeling the hostility snake between them. The last thing I want is to be caught in the crossfire.

"Hillary," Erin says, "it's over. We need to let her go. It's the right thing to do. We don't want to push her if she's uncomfortable. That's not the way we do things."

Hillary chuckles. "Thanks for the advice, but if they wanted the show to continue running the way it was with you, they would've asked you to come back. They didn't. They wanted *me* to fill your shoes, but"—she leans in close to whisper— "they're cheap and ugly, like you. So we're doing things my way."

As she turns, Erin lurches toward her with a roar and yanks back on a smooth rein of her hair. I leap into action to stop the fight but wind up tangled in the middle. Hillary cries out, teetering backward, and loses her balance on the edge of her stiletto heel. She lands on her backside with a thud, knees buckled, legs spread, clutching at Erin's hands, which are still attached to her hair. Someone laughs. Someone screams. I can't tell which sound is coming from whom.

"Erin, stop!"

I don't know who yells her name, or who eventually releases her death grip on Hillary's hair, but when the smoke finally clears, Hillary is across the room, mouth open in a scream, her finger stabbing in our direction. Chunks of her hair are wound around Erin's fingers.

"Keep that bitch away from me!" Hillary spits. "I'm filing charges, you psycho! You'll never work at the station again. Monique, call the police!"

"You're not calling the police. Not in my home," Georgia says. She's planted firmly between Hillary and Erin. "You want to call the police, do it on the curb."

"You're just as crazy as she is!" Hillary snaps at Rob and Monique. "We're out of here. We got what we wanted in the end anyway."

Even though she didn't say the words, she doesn't have to.

They were able to capture Georgia's weakness and refusal, along with a catfight between the Real Wives. It only goes to show how much Georgia has to hide. If she were innocent, why would she resist answering questions? Why wouldn't she be completely transparent?

Hillary knows she got the final blow.

And it just aired live for the whole country to see.

CHAPTER TWENTY-FOUR

ERIN

SATURDAY MORNING

I storm into the station, hands clenched into fists, feeling as if I'm going to rattle apart. I don't know if Theresa prescribed a low dosage of anxiety medication on purpose—maybe everyone starts out this way so as not to shock the system—but I'm not feeling any better. In fact, I've never felt more volatile, more shaken. If people would stop screwing with me, I'd have a better chance at knowing what normalcy feels like.

This early, the only people who'll be here are the morning show staff and, if I'm lucky, Bill. He's the one I really want to see.

Winding my way through cubicles, I don't make eye contact with a single coworker. Over the speakers, the morning show anchors' voices blare the top news stories of the day. I don't care about current world events. I have my eyes on the prize: Bill's office. I don't bother knocking when I reach the door. I push inside and slam it behind me.

He lifts his arms from his sides and smiles as if he's happy to see me. "I was just going to shoot you a text. I'd hoped to see you this morning."

"You put me in one hell of a position." I'm breathing hard, my chest rising and falling in short pants. "You should've sent me the questions beforehand so I could've prepped her. That was wrong, and you know it. We've *never* handled a live interview like that before. We've always given the subject the option of seeing the questions."

"You've never interviewed a murder suspect before. It was crucial that it appear completely candid."

"You wanted to catch her in a lie."

He grins slyly. "Of course we did. Have you forgotten we're in the entertainment business?"

"We're the news!"

"But if it doesn't keep the public's interest, they'll click, click, click, to the next best thing. We want to stay on the air, we have to compete with everything else out there." He stands, raising the blinds behind him, revealing the morning show's set. Lucy and Miguel are on air, illuminated by blinding lights, talking and laughing curtly. They hate each other, though they play nice when the cameras are rolling. "You think people watch this particular segment because they want to see the news? No, they watch because they know there's tension between those two. They don't know if they're fighting or fucking, but they tune in to see the friction anyway."

My heart pounds. "But Georgia is, or was, my friend, Bill. I don't know what more you expect me to film now, but I'm done."

He whips around. "It's not your call to make. I already talked to Georgia. We're going through with it."

"What?"

"Just got off the phone with her. We're finishing the special the way we planned before."

"Her fiancé is gone." My thoughts reel. "The police still don't have any leads." I know because I spent most of the night on Google, searching forums and news outlets, praying someone would come forward with new information. By dawn, my worst fears were confirmed: no one knows where Danny might've been keeping Robert, and I might've lost my best friend for nothing. "There's not going to be a wedding without a groom, Bill. What do you plan on filming?"

"The devastation on the Black Widow's face when she's standing at the altar, and he doesn't show up."

"Maybe you're not hearing me clearly." I can't help but laugh. "Without Robert, Georgia's not going to be standing anywhere near an altar."

Bill snatches a folder off the corner of his desk and waves it around. "Our lawyers say otherwise. She signed an interview release agreement."

"I didn't—"

"Hillary Gleaves took care of it."

Must've been before I arrived. *That's* the reason Bill sent her. Not to set everything up, or make sure the lighting was right, but to lock Georgia into an agreement he knew I wouldn't consent to.

"No interview release agreement would force Georgia to go through with her wedding," I think aloud. "What did she agree to?"

Bill grins slyly. "Two interviews to be included in a single two-night special. One interview the evening before the wedding and one on the actual day."

"Two interviews in a two-night special." I shake my head, disbelieving. "And you ran the first one live . . ."

"Which means she owes me an interview that'll run to-night." He raises his hands into the air triumphantly, like Moses parting the Red Sea. "It was brilliant legalese. She tried to claim we were in violation of the agreement due to invasion of privacy, but according to our lawyer, she doesn't have a case. I've already gone over the options with her. She can either complete the interview at her home, dejected, waiting for her fiancé to miraculously arrive . . . or go on with the show, wedding gown and all. That's more her style and you know it. If the police somehow pull a rabbit out of their hat and find her missing fiancé, we capture the sappy moment on camera. If he doesn't show up, that's even better. When it's clear Robert Donnelly's not going to show, you'll interview Georgia a second time, per our contract, and catch the raw emotion. Talk to her friends and family, get the real story, the one that viewers have been dying to hear." He presses his palms on his desk. "Don't look at me like that, like you want to slug me in the face. You came crawling back here begging for your job, remember? You want it, here it is."

I fold my arms over my chest, mind reeling. He's leaving me no choice.

"Take a look at this." He lifts a stack of papers off his desk and shoves them at me. "Ratings were through the roof last night."

"What?"

I skim fast as he goes on. "You had more viewers than your largest day as anchor. People ate it up. Not only the actual interview, but the fighting afterward. They were riveted. The network thinks the numbers will skyrocket for the wedding segment. Everyone wants to be there, to watch Georgia be jilted at the altar."

But Georgia can't possibly think Robert will show up in

time to marry her today. If anything, she'll be going through the motions for contract purposes only. If the viewers want raw emotion—shock and horror when the time to say her vows has come and gone, and Robert's still nowhere to be found—they're going to be disappointed.

But the numbers don't lie. With everything going on, I hadn't been checking my Instagram viewers, but I would expect those numbers to correlate with these. Tingling sensations whip through me at the thought. I'd begun to believe I was irrelevant, that viewers didn't care about me anymore. If what Bill is saying about the response to Georgia's program is true, tonight's special will definitely take my career to the next level.

"What's your plan?" I ask, because I know he has one. "You can't send Hillary to see her again."

He licks his lips sloppily, as if clearing away lingering flavors of breakfast. "We're going to set you up with a camera and mic you. You'll talk to her, dig deep, expose her secrets. This is big, Erin. The show of your career. After this is over, you'll be thanking Georgia Jane what-the-hell-ever for making you famous."

I'll be thanking *her?* I nearly jolt back from shock. It should be the other way around. The only reason she's infamous in the first place is her Black Widow moniker. And she has that only because of *me*. I was the one who contacted the hitman on her behalf. If it weren't for me, she'd still be married to Eli, miserable, walking on eggshells, bruises on her ribs because he'd been too much of a coward to hit her in the face, where the marks would be seen.

She should be thanking *me*.

Only, now that I think of it, she hasn't thanked me. Not once. She probably thinks this screwup with Robert was my fault, but it wasn't. I had no idea Danny would take him instead of Mason. How could I have known? A vile, bitter taste rises in the back of my throat.

I'll be thanking her . . . over my dead body.

"And," Bill says, closing the blinds once more, "you should be thanking me too. I didn't have to give you this show on a silver platter. I didn't have to run it at all."

"Thank you," I say. "Of course I appreciate the opportunity."

He plops into his chair and leans back, arms draped over the sides. He's staring expectantly, swiveling his chair so that his legs aren't beneath the desk, but beside it. Realization creeps in.

He wants repayment for his favor.

"Listen, Bill," I start, but he puts up his hand, cutting me off.

"I want to say that I appreciate and respect the work you've done as a news anchor for this station. I would never want you, or anyone else who works for my company, to feel uncomfortable at any time."

Is it possible I've misinterpreted his cues completely? Wouldn't it be great if this were all a stupid misunderstanding?

"I appreciate you saying that, Bill." I place my hand over my thumping heart. "I can't tell you how relieved I am to hear it."

Nodding, he leans back in his chair, letting it bounce back and forth a bit as his gaze rakes up and down my body. "That's why, if you're not comfortable getting on your knees to thank me properly, right here and now, you shouldn't work here anymore."

"Excuse me?"

"You want to come back, those are the terms. If you're uncomfortable with what's being asked of you, I'll have Hillary take your spot at Georgia's wedding."

Before, when I'd been in his office and the proposition was first insinuated, I'd hesitated. I'd wondered if I should or shouldn't or what that would mean for my career. But now, in this moment, the lights are too bright, glaring into my skull. The air is too dry, clogging my throat when I try to breathe. My clothes are too tight and scratchy. Something has changed, and I think it's me.

I've changed.

"Bill," I say, feeling steadier than I have in days, "thank you for the enticing opportunity you're offering, but I'd rather die on my feet than drop to my knees."

I turn on my heel and storm out of his office without looking back. I hear the squeak of his chair wheels and the creak of his door as he pushes it open.

"Keep hanging around with the Black Widow," he bellows after me, "and you just might get your wish."

CHAPTER TWENTY-FIVE

BROOKE

"I thought we were supposed to have dinner last night." Jack adjusts his tie in the bathroom mirror. "You didn't come home until after midnight, and didn't head to bed until almost three."

Didn't realize he was making mental notes about my sleep habits. "I know, I'm sorry. I got caught up at Georgia's. After the camera crews left, she needed someone to stay with her for a bit. Then when I got home, I felt really inspired to work on my book, and it was worth every minute—I finished. Sent it in before I went to bed. *The Nightmare Next Door* is out of my hands."

"Congratulations," he says dryly. No excitement. No embrace. "I bet you're thrilled."

I *am*, actually. Despite his poor attitude. He doesn't have a right to be upset about last night. It's not like we were going to have a romantic evening together.

But that's not the point, I remind myself. It's about up-holding the image that I'm a loving, doting wife, cooking din-ner for my husband at dusk. Going out with my criminally minded friend definitely taints the image he's shooting for. The parking garage incident gave him perfect fuel for his rea-soning that Georgia's a terrible influence. He hasn't asked me too many details about it because he wants to make it clear that the event should have no part of our lives.

But it did. It happened. And it's affected me deeply, bring-ing up events from my childhood that he doesn't even know about. It's as if Georgia sliced open a wound and now it's raw and bleeding again, hurting as much as it did before.

Gripping my shoulders, Jack leans in and smatters a line of kisses down my neck, taking my mind off what happened. My skin covers in gooseflesh as I tilt my head so he can continue his trek. I'm wearing one of his favorite dresses today—a sim-ple black, spaghetti-strap number with clear stiletto heels. I always thought it looked more like a slip than a dress, but it's not about what I think. It's about what others think. And when I wear this to what is supposed to be Georgia's wedding, they'll think Jack is married to a woman who is a little wild and carefree, someone who isn't afraid to dress risqué. They might think I'm kinky, and Jack would love that.

The truth is, we haven't had sex all week. He's been work-ing long hours each day, and I've been sucked into my manu-script and the drama of this place. Presidio Terrace is like a vortex, where negative energy and drama cling to the air like fog, swirling round and round our little cul-de-sacs.

I love Jack, I do. We work when we're together, because without saying a word, we understand the roles we're sup-posed to play in this marriage. Expectations are clear, under-stood, and executed. However, given all that, there are days I want to strangle the man. Maybe that's just what happens when we live with another human being, entwining our money and hearts and the stress of daily life.

I wonder if other couples have the problems we do.

"Can I ask you something?" But even as I say the words, I know I should keep my mouth shut. Maybe it's the dress, and the boldness I have to adorn myself with when I wear it. "Do you think marrying for money produces a different outcome than marrying for love?"

He removes his lips from my skin, leaving me cold. "You know what they say: love and money get people killed."

"That wasn't exactly the answer I was looking for," I say, applying a second coat of lipstick. "And I don't think that's the actual saying."

"What *are* you looking for, Brooke? A philosophical discussion about the reasons people get hitched?" He dabs on my favorite cologne, a spicy musk I've always loved on him. "Is this because of Georgia's wedding later? You know she's only going through the motions because she's obligated. Robert's not coming."

"That's what everyone keeps saying," I say, feeling bad for her, "but I think some part of her is still hoping for a miracle."

"That's not going to happen."

"I know. But do you think people who marry for money, instead of love, have the same kinds of problems we do?"

He leaves the bathroom, and from the sound of his footsteps, he's left the bedroom and headed downstairs. I'm expected to follow if I want to continue the conversation. I fluff my hair, grab my purse, and trail close behind. Only he doesn't continue the conversation at all. He doesn't say a word as we pull out of the driveway and pass a catering truck parked in front of Georgia's house. He doesn't mention the crews moving things in and out, busying themselves by preparing for an intimate reception that probably isn't going to happen. He doesn't speak a word until we've turned onto California Street, stopped in front of the Merchants Exchange Building, where Georgia is supposed to get married in a few short hours. Sometime during the night, it began to rain, and it hasn't stopped since. Puddles mar the sidewalk, and tourists run for cover beneath awnings of financial district buildings. Jack turns off the engine but doesn't get out of the car. He looks straight ahead, hands on the wheel, staring at the rain-dimpled windshield. It's just before noon, but with the clouds lumbering so low in the sky, blocking out any trace of the sun, it could be after nightfall.

"You think we have problems?" he asks finally.

I almost laugh, but when I see the steely glare in his eyes, I force myself to remain calm. There are times I wish he would chew more quietly. Hell, sometimes if I'm sitting too close to him, he *breathes* too loudly. He can snore and work long hours and not appreciate the work that I do to make our life beautiful. I'm sure I drive him crazy too, but we still love each other. We love each other despite our problems, and I was only wondering if he thought other couples, ones who marry without love, fight over the same things.

Taking his hand, I stroke the wedding ring I put on his finger almost a year ago. "Of course we do, sweetheart. No one is perfect."

He makes a strange, apathetic sound. "Up until this moment, I thought *you* were. Thanks for the enlightenment."

I'm gaping, watching him exit the car, shielding his face from the rain as he strides around the hood to open my door. Does he not think we have problems at all? Could he really have been oblivious to the strain his work has put on our marriage? More than that, does he really think I'm completely, blissfully happy being a wife who sits at home and stares at her computer all day?

He escorts me across the slippery sidewalk, using his coat over my head as a cover. Always the gentleman. He watches my steps carefully, matching my pace.

Squeezing my arm, he says, "Talk about this later?"

We can't start up this conversation now, when we're about to enter the Julia Morgan Ballroom and be swarmed with wedding guests. I nod and walk inside the building because the air is still caught in my throat and the words won't come. The building resonates elegance. I can see why Georgia picked this location, because she and the building are alike in that way. Past the foyer, bar, and lounge, we're led into the grand ballroom with floor-to-ceiling arched windows. The city glitters beyond the rain-smattered glass and I'm holding my breath as I take in the honeycomb ceiling, the rich paneled walls, and the stone fireplace at the end of the room. The space is alive with laughter and smiles and glasses clinking and light jazz wafting from the overhead speakers.

I know the role Jack wants me to play, the parade he wants me to put on. That's the thing about coming from a home with an alcoholic father: I know how to gauge people, how to read the energy in the room; I know what's expected of me, and I play my role well. Jack, for example, expects perfection. That's all. No more, no less. But only the *façade* of perfection, which I can handle. Because if people are envious of my nails and my hair and thinking about how our marriage is perfect, they're not asking about my childhood, about the way my father died, and how I learned to survive on my own for so many years. They're not asking about my brother, how he took the fall for my father's death, or the way he spent his life in and out of prison. If they're staring at my smile and my figure, they're not probing to see the worthless soul lurking beneath.

Drinks in hand, Jack and I work the room, introducing ourselves to Georgia's other guests. As I pass a couple I've never met before, I hear the woman say she saw Erin King from "the special last night" chasing away a news crew outside. I'm about to head out and talk to Erin when Jack seems to notice someone near the bar. Just as he places his hand on the small of my back to guide me there, I catch sight of Mason, knocking on a door attached to the ballroom. When it opens a crack, he slips inside, and then Georgia peeks her head out, a long veil draped down her back. She looks both directions and stands up on tiptoe to search through the crowd.

"I'll meet you over there," I tell Jack. "I'm going to see Georgia first."

I should ask how she's holding up. She can't possibly go through with the initial parts of the wedding for the sake of some stupid show. She's certainly not going to walk down the aisle without a groom there to meet her. While I don't mind enjoying the reception at her home afterward without having suffered through the actual ceremony, it'll feel a little morbid if Georgia's strutting around in a wedding dress waiting for her missing fiancé to show up.

I knock softly on the door and wait to be invited inside.

Nothing happens.

The volume in the bar heightens as I turn the handle and crack the door open. Sticking my head in gives me a clear shot of the room. Ornate, gold-rimmed mirror against the back wall. Curtains used to separate the space—probably put up with the express purpose of giving the bride a place to have some privacy. Georgia sits on a stool in front of the mirror, silk wedding dress slinking down her body, her hips swiveled around so she's facing Mason. He's standing in front of her, still as stone, hands hanging lifelessly from his sides. If he moved a step closer, his legs would be straddling her lap, his inner thighs touching the outsides of hers. As it is, they could be touching. I can't really be sure.

Whatever they're talking about is important, and very private.

I listen hard.

"I've been trying to get you away from Erin for days," Georgia says, desperation lacing her tone. "We don't have long . . ."

She motions for him to lean in, and mumbles something in his ear. I can't pick up what she's saying. Mason nods, turning toward her as if to kiss her cheek. She looks up at him, batting thick false eyelashes. Something passes between them. Shock pummels me hard, a fist to the gut.

Mason and Georgia . . .

"I didn't know how to tell you without Erin finding out . . . it's so hard to get you alone." Gazing up at him, Georgia clutches at his arms desperately. "You deserve better, Mason. You deserve to be happy."

He shakes his head. "There may have been a point when I thought I could leave her, but realistically, it's not going to happen. She'll lawyer up so hard, I'll be robbed blind. I'll be left with nothing. My practice . . . everything I've worked my whole life for. She'll take it all."

I cover my mouth with my hand so my breathing doesn't give me away. How could Georgia even think about moving on to someone else—Erin's husband, no less—when she hasn't even married Robert yet?

"And that's better than the alternative?" She places her

hands on his thighs, a gentle motion. "Mason, I care about you, deeply, and I don't want to see you get hurt. You have to leave her."

Something brushes my arm, tickling me. I swipe away the sensation.

Then I see the sleeve of Erin's coat, draping over me as she leans in to listen. She stares at the crack in the door, mouth open slightly, eyes glinting with disbelief before flipping to rage.

She heard.

"Erin," I whisper. "Maybe you should—"

Swallowing hard, she seems to compose herself by pulling back her shoulders and adjusting the minijacket over her arms. And then, blowing out a deep breath, she pushes open the door. I follow her inside, ready to break up a fight.

"Mason, honey," she says sweetly. "Could I speak to you for a moment?"

He jumps, his gaze flipping between Georgia and his wife. "Of course. Thanks for the talk, Georgia. I'll come by sometime next week and trim that unseemly tree in your front yard. Wouldn't want Erin to fine you for being in violation of the association's code."

As he walks out of the room, taking Erin's arm along the way, I'm reminded of secondary characters I wrote in my latest book. Matthew is cheating on his wife with their neighbor. Has been for years. His wife knows. Has known from the first transgression. But she puts up with his cheating because deep down, she doesn't believe that she deserves any better.

They split in the end, after a hellish divorce. They wind up losing their house, their dignities. Matthew gets violent, his wife gets even. I don't know how Mason and Erin's story will end, but I get the feeling it's going to be just as nasty.

Georgia turns back to the mirror, fluffing her veil. "How much do you think she heard?"

"Enough," I say softly. "Enough."

Her phone rings from the table beside her. She picks it up on the first ring, holds it to her ear, and then lets out a soul-cringing wail as she slides helplessly to the floor.

The police have found Robert.

CHAPTER TWENTY-SIX

BROOKE

SATURDAY AFTERNOON

When the police told Georgia that Robert's body had washed up along the rocks in front of Fort Point, I had to Google the location. Apparently, Fort Point is a masonry seacoast fort tucked beneath the Golden Gate Bridge. Built before the Civil War to defend the bay against warships. It's now a land-mark with tours running through it daily, probably every hour. I didn't even know it existed until we turned just short of the Golden Gate Bridge and wound along Marine Drive, on the edge of the bay. Storm waters crash over the boulder seawall, spraying the road, drenching our car.

Ahead, in front of the fort's parking lot, police cruisers line up, creating a black-and-white barricade to stop pedestrians and bicyclists from continuing their paths to the fort. As the wipers sweep over the windshield, Georgia sits silent in the pas-senger seat, holding her knees. The rain reflects off the windshield, making it appear as if the drops are running down her face and gouging into her porcelain skin.

"Thank you for taking me," she says, her gaze landing on the yellow blanket draped over a boulder. "I wouldn't have been able to drive myself. I'm too shaky."

"Of course. Anything I can do to help."

"Everyone will be at my house after this," she says, smoothing away a wrinkle in her wedding gown. She couldn't be convinced to change. "I told the wedding guests we'd have the reception no matter what. I can't be alone right now. Is that normal?"

"I think when you're dealing with loss and grief anything is normal. If being home alone is too difficult, it's all right to ask people to be there with you."

"The crews were setting up all morning. There's more than enough food for everyone." She pauses, hand to door handle. "Do you think the police know what we did? What really happened?"

What we did. I shudder at the thought.

Somehow, I've gotten myself linked to the ransom and the fallout of her refusal to pay it. I still don't understand. If she'd only given Danny Johnson what he wanted, Robert would be in a tuxedo, standing in front of the Julia Morgan Ballroom hearth, his hand in hers. It's not as if she's hurting for money, or couldn't somehow pull it together between all of her investments. But I suppose I shouldn't judge her or her actions under these intense circumstances. Until I'm walking in Georgia's red-soled Louis Vuitton shoes, I can't say what I would do. We each handle stress in our own way. I know that better than most.

"You keep saying 'what really happened,' like there are

two versions to the story. The truth is, there's only one: Danny Johnson kidnapped your fiancé. He tried to ransom him for millions of dollars. When you tried to confront him, he attacked you. That's what happened, Georgia. That's the truth."

"Yeah, you're right," she says, pointing a shaking finger to the black tarp-like object lying beside the yellow blanket. "What do you think that is?"

I peer through the rain-splattered windshield. "I can't tell. Do you need more time, or—"

"No, I'm fine. Happy wedding day to me." She shakes her head with a sick laugh. "Let's get this over with."

As we approach the police cruisers, I notice the detectives right away. They order a few officers to bring us umbrellas, which we cower under together, and join us at the edge of the seawall. While the rain's dropping straight down, lancing into my umbrella, the mist and sea spray are hitting me sideways. We'll be drenched in minutes.

"Is that your wedding dress?" Linard asks, surprised.

She lifts the small train from the back. "Today was our day. This wasn't exactly the reunion I'd been hoping for."

"I'm sorry to tell you this, Ms. St. Claire, but one of Fort Point's workers found your fiancé about an hour ago." The detective outstretches his arm to keep us a safe distance back from the waves as they crash and blast through the air. "Currents are strong through here. The storm must've pushed his body over the rocks."

"Can I see?" Georgia looks up at the detectives, face wet with a mixture of tears and rain. "I have to see him for myself."

One of the officers shakes his head as Detective Linard squats near the boulder and lifts the yellow blanket. Robert doesn't look like the man she was about to marry. His chest, face, and neck are bloated and discolored, and he's missing his eyes. Georgia moves in close, knees buckling when she's seen too much. I cradle my arms around her shoulders as Linard replaces the blanket.

"How—how do you know it's him?" she asks feebly.

"We found this in the pocket of his coat." Linard hands over a silver business card case with Robert Donnelly's name engraved on the lower right corner. When he catches Georgia staring at Robert's face, he says, "Birds must've gotten to his eyes. He's also missing the ring finger on his right hand, though from the marks, we believe that was cut or sawed."

I wonder what Georgia did with Robert's finger and ring. Did she keep them? Bury them in her front yard, beneath her rose bushes? Perhaps he lost his eyes at the same time he lost his finger. Maybe it wasn't birds at all.

When Georgia gags, Linard says, "I'm sorry, Ms. St. Claire. I told you not to come. You could have met us at the station."

"No, it's fine, I'm fine." She sways into me. "I needed to be here to see for myself. I told you I wanted to know everything. Thank you for your candor. May I ask—what is that?"

She points to a pile of black tubing piled up next to Robert's body.

"It's an inflatable raft. We think it had a motor on it at one point."

Now Georgia knows I'd been honest earlier. I'd seen the boat that had taken Robert away.

Linard turns to me. "During our initial questioning, you reported seeing what you thought to be a boat pulling away from the yacht. Could this have been it?"

I stare at the deflated pile of black inky tubing. "I suppose so, yes."

"Do either of you recall anyone following you at any time?"

Georgia and I shake our heads as she says, "No, I'm sorry, Detective."

Deflated, his shoulders hunch forward slightly. He's having a hard time with this case. I wonder if he's feeling pressure from his superiors. "Is there anything else you'd like to add at this time, Ms. St. Claire?"

"I—I don't think so. This is all such a shock . . ."

"We'll be in touch." When she nods shakily, he says, "I'd like you to call if you think of anything. You still have my number?"

"Of course."

But I doubt Georgia would ever ring him.

When he's out of earshot, she leans his umbrella against the cruiser and we make a mad dash for the reprieve of the car. Once inside its safety and warmth, she flings wet hair about her face and turns to me.

"We have a problem," she says, strength returning to her voice. "The timing is too perfect. We kill this Danny Johnson guy, and then my Robert turns up here. It's not a coincidence. No, I have an awful feeling in my gut that there's someone else involved, and that someone, when he heard his partner wasn't coming back, dumped Robert in the bay."

"It's also possible that the timing's coincidental. Maybe Danny Johnson dumped Robert in the bay that night and when his body wasn't washing up on shore anywhere, he thought he'd get as much money out of you as possible by *pretending* he was still alive."

"I don't know," she says hesitantly. "Something just doesn't feel right about this."

"You've lost your fiancé. I can't imagine anything feels right at all." I brush my hand down her arm to soothe the worry I can see brewing in her eyes. "It's over now, Georgia."

She worries her lower lip between her teeth. "I want to believe that, but I don't know. If that guy was working with someone, they still might come after me."

I don't want to say the words and acknowledge the truth, but . . . "Do you want to go back out there and tell the detectives your theory? They might be able to offer you protection."

She scoffs. "Did you see the way Linard looked at me? He's not going to protect me. If anything, he'd try to use me as bait to catch the person who's still out there. I can't go to Erin . . . not anymore. She's liable to blab all of this to her network friends. I don't know who I can trust. They say people come into your life when you need them most, Brooke. I'm so glad you moved to the neighborhood."

"Me too," I say, and take her back to Presidio Terrace Prison.

CHAPTER TWENTY-SEVEN

ERIN

SATURDAY EVENING

Mason, I care about you, deeply . . . you have to leave her.

Georgia's words scream through my head so loud and repetitive, like a gong being blasted against my skull over and over again. I want to scratch the skin off my face. Rip off my fingernails. Scream until my voice box explodes.

After Georgia ditched out with Brooke a few hours ago—going God knows where—I demanded Mason take me home. Rather than stay with me, like a good, loyal husband would, he didn't even get out of the car. Said he was going into the office to work on a few things.

Work.

My ass.

Slamming the car door on the way out, I'm about to charge inside and bury my head in a vat of vodka when something else Mason said echoes through my head.

I'll come by sometime next week and trim that unseemly tree in your front yard . . .

What the hell had he been talking about? I know it was a cover, but still. What made him think of one of her stupid trees? As his car exits the neighborhood, I stalk across the street, squeezing between two unmarked white vans. Florist and caterer, I'm guessing. I pass a woman in a white apron and two men carrying in the cake, and nod to them as if I'm supposed to be there.

"Hi. Hello. Good to see you. Beautiful day. Terrible about the groom."

I wait until I'm alone in the yard, then, standing beside the front windows, I find the tallest, widest tree. It's scraggly, but I always thought that was simply the type of tree she'd planted.

She wants it cut? My husband wants to do it for her? How about I help them both out and trim it myself?

Storming back across the street, I punch the code on the panel for our garage, and when the door opens with a squeal, I charge inside to search for the pruning shears. I'm not about to trim the tree with scissors—I haven't lost my mind that badly.

I care about you deeply.

The hell she does.

Georgia's starting to feel invincible, isn't she? Untouchable, like she can do whatever she wants. As if no one can touch her. Not even the detectives. I should've let Bill bring in all the cameras he wanted. Interview every person attending the reception, slant the story any way he could to boost ratings. Still doesn't mean I'd do him any favors, but it'd drop Georgia down a peg or two.

Someone has to put her in her place.

I'm always happy to be that person, to even out the playing

field. First step? Hacking away at the ugly tree in her front yard.

Shears in my hand, fire burning in my gut, I'm stomping down my driveway when I get the feeling someone is watching me. It's so extreme, it stops me cold. I scan Brooke's house, then I look to Georgia's, and a few of the others on the street. Workers buzz around in and out of the house, but they don't seem to care about my presence. No curtains ruffle. No one seems to be interested in what I'm doing.

Down the street, a police cruiser comes into view, rounding the corner before rolling to a stop in front of my house. Feeling transparent, as if they somehow know I'm about to murder her tree, I hold the shears behind me, and traipse backward, waving, until I drop them on the floor in the garage.

"Ms. King," an officer says, exiting the car.

There are two, dressed in black suits, hair slicked back with enough gel to make them look like Ken dolls. They're stepping over the curb, forcing smiles, prematurely extending their hands.

I shake them both when the men approach and hope they don't sense that my insides are trembling. Should've gone inside and taken my pills when I first got home. "What can I help you with, Officers?"

"I don't know if you remember," the taller one says, "but I'm Detective Linard, lead on the investigation into the Robert Donnelly missing person case. I came by a few days ago."

"Yes, of course I remember."

"This is Officer Pangburn, who's assisting on the case." The officer smiles as Linard motions toward my front door. "Mind if we talk to you for a moment inside?"

My spine goes rigid. "Sure."

When we're situated on the couches in the family room,

the detectives sit silently, their analytical gazes taking in *everything*. Just like the last time they were here. Can they see how hard I worked to make my marriage thrive? Can they sense where he slammed my head against the wall? Do they realize this home is solid on the outside and crumbling on the inside?

"Is your husband here?" Linard asks, finally meeting my gaze.

"No," I say, "but he should be home shortly. For now, I suppose, you'll have to settle for talking to me."

I should offer them water or coffee or tea, but I suddenly don't feel like being the doting housewife. Flushed with nervous energy, I use a small decorative pillow to fan myself. It reads #BLESSED in squatty black letters.

"I don't want you to get the wrong idea, Mrs. King. You are exactly who we wanted to talk to," Linard says. "But first, are you all right?"

"Of course. What's this about?"

How much do they know? Have they ID'd Danny Johnson? Have they dug into text messages? He swore he deleted them, and I did as well, but you can't trust a crook. Hell, I can't even trust my husband.

The detective removes an iPad from his messenger bag and begins flicking the screen. "I'm not sure if you've talked with Georgia St. Claire in the last few hours, but her husband was pulled out of the bay."

"Oh, that's terrible. I had no idea."

Did I act it well enough? Did it seem like I genuinely cared?

"The last time we saw you, we inquired where your husband was on the night Robert Donnelly disappeared," Linard goes on. "Your husband said he was here working before calling it a night."

"That's right." I continue fanning, harder now.

At least those were the words he spoke out of his lying mouth.

I can feel Officer Pangburn's gaze boring into the side of my face with scorching intensity. I can't bear to look him dead in the eye. They must know Mason lied—and that I lied to cover for him. They're going to think he had something to do with Robert's death, but they have no idea how deep the rabbit hole goes. If they really started digging, I would go to jail. If they get creative, they could concoct a story where Mason's at fault and I'm an accomplice. Either way, I lose everything. Lightning rods of heat shoot up my spine.

Linard presses. "You've turned rather red, Mrs. King."

"Thermostat needs to be turned down." I grit my back teeth. "Can we get to the point, Detective? There's some landscaping work that demands my attention."

Pangburn checks his watch. "It's nearly six o'clock."

I smile and nod, scared of what I'll say if I try to explain.

"Mrs. King, on Tuesday night, while you were on Robert Donnelly's yacht, your husband visited a hip-hop club off Perry Street in the South Beach area."

"Hip-hop?" I shake my head to make sense of what he just said. "Mason?"

"According to their video surveillance, your husband arrived at the club around eleven in the evening. He came alone, however he left the club with a woman—a tall brunette—when the club closed hours later."

He waits for me to respond. I'm fuming inside, digging my nails into the pillow, where he can't see. It's not only Georgia. There's someone else . . . a brunette who likes hip-hop, apparently.

"Do you have any idea who that woman might've been?" Linard probes.

"No, but I'm going to kill her," I say under my breath.

"Excuse me?"

I shake my head and force a smile. "I don't know who my husband might've been with that night. He told me he was home."

Now he's made me sound ridiculous.

"And the first time we met, you informed us that you tracked his location to the house. You lied to us, one way or another. Did you not track his location at all, or did it show he was away from home?"

I drop the pillow into my lap. "I did track his phone and it did show his location was here. He must've left his phone behind—that's the only explanation, but—was she—were they . . ."

I can't finish.

"They left holding hands," he says gently, reading my mind as vomit rises in the back of my throat. "I'm sorry to have brought your husband's infidelity to light, but we had suspected he might've had something to do with kidnapping Mr. Donnelly."

"Don't be ridiculous." I sneer. "He had nothing to do with what happened to Robert. My husband might be unfaithful, but he's no killer. What would make you suspect him in the first place?"

"You, if I'm being honest."

Damn it.

He spins his iPad around for me to see. "Can you explain this? It's an Instagram post you made earlier in the week . . ."

His words trail off as I stare at my ridiculous joke made at

Grounds & Greens with Brooke and Georgia. *Bonus points if the captain goes down with the ship*, Georgia had said. I should've put my damn phone away.

"It was a joke. A poorly timed one, but still. We had no way of knowing he'd be kidnapped."

"Somebody might have known." Officer Pangburn lets the accusation hang.

But all I can think about is Mason wrapping his arm around some brunette. Holding her hand. Nuzzling against her neck. I can see her throwing her head back, chestnut brown hair fanning over her shoulders as she giggles sweetly. Even though I don't know what she looks like exactly, I can see her smile, the light in her eyes, and I hate both of them so much I could explode.

At some point, between Pangburn and Linard asking about Georgia and Brooke and my marriage with Mason, I zone out. When I drift back to reality a few minutes later, I realize Mason is free and clear from any guilt or fear. I'm the one struggling, upset, anxious, and he gets to run around the city, banging anyone he wants.

He doesn't get to run to his office every time things get tough.

That ends now.

The detectives are finished with me. They've gotten what they wanted. They dropped a bomb into my marriage and now they're going to watch it explode. After the officers drive away, I snatch my purse off the kitchen counter and head into the garage. As the garage door rolls up, I open Find My Phone, and search for Mason's cell.

I'm going to find the lying son of a bitch and demand answers.

It's time he faces the consequences for his actions head-on.

CHAPTER TWENTY-EIGHT

ERIN

Mason's cell is unavailable. Figures. When I need to find him, something's wrong with the service. Last known location was work, two hours ago. My fingers rap against the steering wheel. I've tracked his cell countless times, and it's never unavailable. Wait . . . now that I think of it, I tried to locate him the night Robert disappeared.

The night he had his arm around some brunette floozy in the city.

His phone had been unavailable that night too. When I asked him about it, he hadn't even been able to give a reason why he'd turned it off on the app.

He and his side chick must've laughed behind my back.

Stomach souring, I slam the car into reverse and peel out of the garage, narrowly missing one of the unmarked vans parked in front of Georgia's. I shove the car into gear and squeal the tires as I speed down Presidio. I pass Carol stand-

ing in front of her stupid red front door—she painted it that
way to irritate me, I know it. I rev the engine, turning the
corner. She lifts her hand in a wave. I flip her off, and she
gapes.

I ignore Malik's ridiculous salute on my way out the
gate—he probably hasn't even served our country—and fight
traffic through the area known as Presidio Heights. By the
time I get to Mason's office building thirty minutes later, I'm
fuming. Too many taxis striding the line between my lane and
theirs. Too many trolleys with tourists hanging on to the rails
like they're starring in some kind of television show. Too many
pedestrians and fire engines and—*God*, I can't breathe.

Times like these, I think this city is going to kill me.

Reaching into the depths of my purse, I pull out my anxiety pills and pop two back, dry. They clog in my throat, and I
choke, coughing and hacking as I circle the block. When a
parking spot comes open across the street, I veer into it,
nearly clipping the car behind. Once parked, I search Favor-
ites on my cell. Mason's contact photo shows him smiling
smugly, holding up a glass of scotch on the rocks.

Rat bastard.

Someone hollers at a dirty man crouched in an alcove
across the street. He's sprawled on a spread of newspapers,
his nasty backpack slouched next to him. He's a few feet from
the entrance to Mason's building. The homeless are ruining
this city. Absolutely disgusting.

The call goes straight to voicemail. I ping Mason's location
again. Now there are two dots at this location: his and mine.

Breathing hard, I sprawl across the console and passenger
seat, and stare up at the windows. Floor one, two . . . three.
From my angle, I can make out Mason's desk, filing cabinet,

Ficus in the corner. He's in his chair, leaning toward his desk. He swivels a bit, and then rolls back, hitting the window.

I gasp.

Someone is on his lap.

A muffled whimper escapes my lips as I squint, peering harder through the dark. It's definitely Mason. His dark hair is buzzed short. Can't mistake that hard jawline. A woman claws her fingers over the back of his head as she moves to deepen their connection. Her legs—long and lean, pale and smooth—are straddling his lap.

As if I'm watching a car accident play out in slow motion, I can't look away.

I'm going to be sick.

His hands cup the round of her hips. Her dark hair covers her face, obscuring her features, but she's gorgeous—she'd have to be to capture Mason's attention. And if her figure is any indication, she's young. And tight.

"Don't you know you're in the fucking window?" I bang my hands against the driver's window. "Mason!"

As if he could hear me, the bum rises off the sidewalk and weaves through traffic until he's standing at my passenger window.

"I'm hungry." He slurs. "Got 'nyfing to eat?"

"Go away, you're blocking my view!" I bang against the window with the palm of my hand. "I don't have anything!"

He bends so he's staring me square in the face. His two front teeth are missing, and there's not a single hint of light in his eyes. He might as well be dead. A walking zombie.

Poking his dirty finger against the window, he points to the passenger seat, to my purse. "Change?"

A wave of rage and adrenaline and fear attacks me all at

once. I beat my hands against the window. "Leave me the hell alone! I'm having a mental breakdown!"

He mumbles a curse, bangs on the top of my car, and stumbles back through traffic to his hole. Mason and whoever was with him are gone.

A shriek of terror rips from my lungs. *He's cheating, right now.* I grip the steering wheel tight and mash my head against the rich Italian leather. *He was with her that night. I lied for him.* My heart thunders out of my chest with the heaviness of what his lie means for my marriage, for the investigation. I scrub the tears from my eyes and my hands come back with traces of mascara.

Glancing into the rearview, I swipe away the black marks on my face. My eyes are as void and lifeless as the homeless man's. Mason has stripped me of any light I'd had when he met me. I'm dead inside. Might as well be sleeping on the street. Only I won't be, because I'll take him for every damn dollar he has.

Something bright catches light behind me. In the rearview, a Porsche convertible shines like a ruby-red apple from the glow of the overhead streetlamp. I lift off the seat to snag a glimpse of the license plate.

The numbers are nothing special. But the plate around it reads: YACHT BOSS.

But what would Robert's car be doing—no, not Robert's, I realize, as vomit rises in my throat. It's *Georgia's* car now. The window. The ass grabbing.

I retch onto the passenger seat.

CHAPTER TWENTY-NINE

ERIN

The reception started at eight, and is already in full swing. I've maintained my cool. Kept everything stuffed inside. Watched people walk in and out of Georgia's house for over an hour. I thought maybe I wouldn't go. I'd only cause a scene. But once I saw Mason waltz into the house, smile at me the way he has every day of our marriage as if nothing was wrong, I knew there needed to be a crescendo to this night. A confrontation inside the walls of our home wasn't going to cut it.

I want to see Georgia in her wedding dress, lonely and crying in front of her nearest and dearest friends. I want an audience, an outlet for my anger.

I'm standing in front of the windows watching it all go down when Mason stomps downstairs. I can smell his cologne from here, spicy and masculine, and I bet he's using it to mask *her* scent. Out of the corner of my eye, I can tell he's wearing his best blue suit—my favorite on him. But I won't tell him that tonight.

"I think we need to have a talk," he says from the entry. He's spinning his wedding ring around his finger. The gold must be burning into his flesh.

"I don't think this is the best time," I say, smoothing my hands down the front of my dress. "We're about to head to Georgia's. Can we talk later?"

"Sure." He lowers his eyes to the hardwood.

Infidelity must be a heavy load to bear. I don't feel bad for him, not at all.

Beats from the music at the party blast through the house so loud, the air quakes. Or maybe I'm trembling from the inside out. Perhaps it's not the music at all. Hard to tell these days. I'm dressed in my favorite blue dress. Bought it a year ago. Been waiting for a special evening out to wear it. Doesn't get more special than my husband's mistress's wedding reception in honor of her dead fiancé.

"I need a drink before heading over," he says. "Want one?"

"How about two?"

He chuckles. "You sure you can handle a double?"

"Aren't you the one who thinks two is better than one?"

He shrugs stupidly. "I guess. Have you taken your anxiety meds? Probably shouldn't mix alcohol with 'em if you have."

"Suddenly you care about my well-being?" I mumble as he heads toward the kitchen.

"What was that?" He turns back. "I didn't catch it."

"Nothing."

I can hear him in the kitchen, popping the decanter, and pouring two generous glasses of his favorite scotch. He returns and hands over my glass, then takes a long drink. I did take my meds, and I don't care if they crash and burn with the scotch in my stomach. We stand in silence, a canyon of lies and doubt and malice stretching between us.

"Have you heard from those detectives?" Mason asks. "The ones who came by before?"

"No, not a peep," I lie, finishing the drink. "I'm guessing we won't be hearing from them until they make a determination about the cause of his death."

Mason shakes his head solemnly. "Poor bastard. Drowning sounds like a painful way to go."

"Versus what, Mason? Gunshot wounds? Strangulation? How would you like to go if given the choice?"

He makes a strange, scrunched face. "I don't know, I guess it wouldn't matter as long as it was quick. What about you?"

"Me?" I grab my clutch and head into the foyer. "I'm going to live forever."

Chuckling, Mason glances out the narrow window flanking the front door. "Brooke and her husband are on their way to the reception."

I open the door. Jack is in a dark suit—black or navy, I can't tell—and Brooke is wearing a dark, floor-length silk dress. "Looks like she's wearing a sheet."

"I think she looks great. You should try dressing up like that sometime."

Whirling around, I stare into Mason's eyes for the first time since I discovered his affair. He's more handsome than I've ever seen him, the bastard. Freshly shaven. Hair cut close to his scalp. Suit fitted perfectly over his muscular frame.

"You'd look good in it," he blubbers on, and then: "Better than Brooke."

Liar. Cheater. "Thanks."

Somehow, all the anger that'd been boiling inside me earlier flips to apathy, and a strange sense of calm washes over me. Other than the constant rattle in my bones and the feeling that I'm going to spontaneously combust, I'm fine. Not angry about the affair one bit.

He must notice my unease with the way this dumpster fire of a conversation is going. "What you're wearing is fine too." He lifts my hand from my side and twirls me around. "New dress?"

Does he watch Georgia as closely? He certainly has taken notice of Brooke and her fancy, slippery dress. Maybe he plans to seduce *all* of my friends.

The thought washes over me like a wave, heavy as lead.

As we walk across the street holding hands like a couple in love, I'm rather proud of myself. Not a tear has fallen since I watched Mason screw Georgia against his office window. I haven't set fire to or bleached his clothes. I haven't taken a sledgehammer to all the windows in the house or threatened to kill him. I can walk next to him, holding his hand, without digging my nails into his palm.

There are other, better ways to seek vengeance.

I can't divorce him—that's not an option. He would only find someone younger and fitter, some gold-digging slut who'd marry him for his millions and pretend to ignore the bald spot growing on the back of his head. No, what I have in mind is a little more sinister.

Too bad Danny's not around anymore.

CHAPTER THIRTY

BROOKE

It's so dark on the short walk from our home to Georgia's that I can barely put one foot in front of the other without feeling like I'm going to trip and fall. Jack extends his hand like a gentleman, guiding my steps, protecting me from wrenching my ankle. As we step up on the walkway, tiny orbs of golden white light illuminate our path.

"It's breathtaking," I say.

Looking at me tenderly, Jack lifts my hand and kisses the back. "That's exactly what I was thinking." He stops me and forces me to face him. "Brooke, I know you've been preoccupied this week, and it's probably had a lot to do with the amount of time I've been working, and the pressure of turning in your book mixed with all of the drama circling Georgia . . . but I want you to know that I love you. No matter what. I thought moving here was what you wanted."

"It was." I squeeze his hands. "It is."

"If it's not, if this is too much for you, we can move anywhere you want. You name it. As long as we're together, I don't care where we are."

"I was thinking," I say carefully, "about heading home. Going back to Louisiana for a while. I have a feeling my mother is going to need me soon. Would that be all right with you? Could you get away from your company that long?"

"If it means a lot to you, I'll make it happen."

He wraps me in his arms and lifts me off my feet, and for a moment I feel like I'm in a fairy tale. I'm not scarred by my past and Jack's not a tech genius with all eyes watching him all the time, and we're not perfect. We're just two people trying to make it work. And we might fail at getting it right some of the time, but at least we're trying.

"Brace yourself for the crowds in there," he says, turning to glance through the windows. "The vibe's going to be interesting."

He's not wrong. Everyone's going to be in shock and probably grieving, but dressed for a wedding, with the décor and the bride in white.

As we head inside, the gag-inducing smells of perfume and cologne and body odor hit me first. Then the screeching bleats of a saxophone over the happy plinking of piano keys and incessant laughter and condescending glares and people violating my personal space. My heart races, pushing adrenaline hard through my veins, and for a moment I don't know if I should be here.

A stranger turns to me, grinning. "Good evening," she croons, batting her fake lashes. "Lovely night for a party, isn't it? This place is beautiful—packed! I can't even get through to the kitchen!"

"It is lovely," I say, and push past her, deeper into the house.

We move on from one group to the next. They're wearing tuxedos and formal gowns, pearl necklaces and phony smiles. Someone bumps into my shoulder, spilling champagne down my dress. They bumble an apology and swipe clumsily at my shoulder in a poor attempt to wipe away the mistake, but then they're gone. As I move toward the kitchen, a draft blows into the house. The front door has opened again. Pam walks in, cradling her Yorkie under her arm, then blends into the crowd as they "ooh" and "aah" over her pup.

Erin squeezes through the open doorway behind her. Stopping momentarily, she scans the crowd with a scowl etched into her face. She's dressed in a gorgeous floor-length gown that cinches at the waist and flares at the knee. Deep blue. V-neck. Sleeveless. Hair curled into thick tendrils, draping down her back. She looks more uptight than usual, if that's possible. Her jaw is set as she narrows her eyes at each woman who passes. She's examining the room quickly, her hands balled into fists. I can see her nostrils flaring from my position near the couch.

She must be looking for Georgia.

I spot Georgia across the room, slipping out the back doors leading to the patio. I can't believe she's still wearing her wedding dress. If her aim was to become the talk of the party, she's succeeded. She's not crying, as I assumed she would be. Instead, she appears angelic, clear-eyed and smiling, thanking one person for coming, pointing out the food and drink lineup in the kitchen to another. A brunette wearing a retro twenties dress covered in beads follows her out, champagne flute pinched delicately between her dainty fingers.

I should go check on Georgia.

"Sweetheart," I say, gently touching Jack's arm, "would you mind grabbing me a drink? I'm going to find the restroom."

Because if I said I was going to talk to Georgia, I'm sure I'd hear a lecture about how I'd rather spend time with her than with him. It's easier to lie than to deal with Jack's fallout.

After a kiss on the cheek, he's fighting his way to the bar, and I'm weaving through the crowd toward the patio. Outside, white lights cover every shrub and wrap around every tree trunk. They stretch over the pool, from cabana to gazebo on either side, illuminating the water with ripples of silver. Fires burn in pits on either end of the patio. Guests huddle around the concrete rings, cackling like geese, tipping back their pink and orange drinks. It smells like rain and bonfire smoke. Thunder rumbles over the thumping beats of the music, and the guests huddled near the fires barely notice, continuing their meaningless conversations about handbags.

I find Georgia seated at one of the fire pits with a brunette. Her back's to me, but her voice floats on the evening breeze.

"I want to thank you again for making that purchase so easy," the brunette says, firelight dancing over her face. "Porsches have been my favorite cars for as long as I can remember. I'd hate to say it was good timing, because I understand why you were selling, but I can promise you I'll take good care of it."

Georgia leans back in her seat to get more comfortable. "That's very sweet of you. Do you have any trips planned? Robert used to like dropping the top and cruising up Highway One."

I pause in the shadows, listening, a few steps shy of joining their conversation.

The brunette beams. "I showed my boyfriend earlier today, actually. He loved it. Says we should take it out this weekend."

Georgia nods thoughtfully. "You'll have a wonderful time."

"Oh, I almost forgot, you left the license plate on the front. Did you want to come by my office, or—"

"Just drop it in the mail."

When there's a natural break in the conversation, I round the couch and extend my hand to the brunette. "I'm Brooke Davies," I say. "I live next door."

"She's a writer. Murder mysteries," Georgia elaborates as the brunette shakes my hand. "This is Theresa Wilson. She's a therapist in the city. I'd called her last week, on Erin's recommendation, to see about being treated for depression. And then my world went to hell, and here I am. More depressed than I was before."

"Nice to meet you," I say and take the seat next to Georgia. "Do you specialize in depression?"

"I'm a marriage and family therapist, mostly, though I see people who are suffering with many different kinds of issues."

What a stock answer.

"Well I'm glad you'll have someone to help you with your grief," I tell Georgia.

"Oh, she's not going to be the one helping me through this." Georgia and Theresa shake their heads in unison. "We're not a good fit. After the blowup that Erin and I had the other day, I thought it was best we see different shrinks."

"There you are, you bitch." Erin charges across the patio, jabbing her finger at Georgia. "You glassy-eyed, gold-digging whore. I thought we were friends!"

CHAPTER THIRTY-ONE

ERIN

I hear Mason's steps pounding behind me, and I feel him grasping for my arm, but nothing is going to stop me now. I held back the floodwaters in regard to Mason, but Georgia . . . all bets are off.

"Erin, calm down," Mason says, panic lacing his tone. "The alcohol isn't mixing well with your meds. You don't want to say something you don't mean."

"Oh, I mean every word I say." My gaze skips to Brooke, looking doe-eyed, as usual, and—my vision blurs. "Theresa? What are you doing here?"

Mason clutches me against his body, as if to protect me, but I'm not the one who needs protecting. I squirm in his grasp. My body has the sensation that it's floating, tingling, lifting right off the ground.

Theresa looks over my shoulder, then back to me. "Georgia invited me. She came in last week—you referred her, remember? It didn't work out, professionally speaking, but we started talking, and she invited me tonight. I thought, since I wasn't seeing her professionally, I would come as a new friend to offer my condolences."

I recall referring Georgia, but it feels strange seeing them here together. The two women in front of me know all of my deepest, darkest secrets. Every single one of them. I've never felt more vulnerable. The skin on my face feels tight, like it's going to crack and flake away.

"Georgia wouldn't know a real friend if it whacked her in the face." On instinct, I reach over and pat her on the side of the head. Only my aim is off, and I connect solidly, throwing her off-balance. "Damn it, I didn't mean—"

"What the hell's the matter with you, Erin?"

Mason jerks on my arm, but I don't acknowledge his presence at all.

"I want an apology." I stagger as one of my stiletto heels twists on a seam in the concrete. Mason steadies me by the elbow, but I smack his hand away. "Right now. In front of Brooke and Theresa, I want you to apologize for what you've done to me."

She narrows her eyes, squinting. "What have I done to you, Erin? Enlighten me. What could I possibly have done to deserve the public shaming you dished out on national television?"

Chewing on the side of my lip, tasting blood, I press forward, tugging against Mason's grasp. "I saw you." I heave for air. "How about that? I saw your car . . . in front of his office. *I know*."

"Oh my God," Theresa gasps.

"What are you talking about?" Georgia yells. "You know *what*?"

Mason yanks my arm. "Erin, this is enough. Let's go."

"Oh, don't deny it. I saw you together!" Tears roll down my face as my body convulses. "I know you're having an affair! I saw your car in front of his office earlier this afternoon. I saw you in the window!"

"Erin, we're not—"

"I heard it from your own fat mouth this morning! You and Mason were in your dressing room before what was supposed to be your wedding, and you told him you loved him!"

"Whoa, whoa," Mason says over my shoulder. "She didn't say that."

I whirl on him. "Don't cover for your lover, it's too late now. I heard her loud and clear. She said she 'cares about you deeply' and she asked you to leave me."

"Love was *never* mentioned."

Brooke steps in between us, arms outstretched. "Clearly there's a miscommunication. Why don't we all slow down, cool off."

"That's why . . ." Georgia starts, and then stops. "You thought that me and Mason . . . that explains why you . . ."

"Why I put a hit out on him. Yes!" As the words punch out of me, I sway back and forth, suddenly dizzy. "I knew he was cheating. Suspected it for months. I just never thought, not for a second, that it was with you."

"Erin, we aren't sleeping together," she pleads. "You have to believe me."

Mason spins me around angrily. "What do you mean, 'put a hit' on me?"

Across the fire pit, Brooke gasps and moves to where Theresa is standing in shock. The earth spins beneath my feet, and spots dance in front of my eyes. I'm parched, and I have half a mind to steal the champagne flute right out of Theresa's hand.

"Oh, it's exactly what I said, Mason," I slur. "We hired someone to kill you, only he screwed up and took Robert instead. Ten million dollars. What a deal."

"She doesn't mean it," Georgia says to the group. "She's not in her right mind. Look at her. She can barely stand up right. The meds must be mixing with the alcohol."

"She's been drinking while taking the medication I gave her?" I hear Theresa screech as if her voice is booming through a tunnel. "She's going to need a doctor."

"I'll go for help," Brooke says, and disappears.

"What the hell, Erin." Mason's shaking me, his face in front of mine. His eyes and mouth are huge. Too big for his face. "I fuck someone else and you try to kill me? You're insane! I'm going to the police."

"You admit it!" I spin in a circle, arms over my head, victorious. Dizzy, I stumble against the brick fire pit and plop into the closest seat. Suddenly my head's too heavy to hold up, and Theresa's arms are around my shoulders. Her shoulder is soft, so I lean my cheek against it and rub it back and forth. "I told you!" I shout into the night. "Liar!"

"Shhh . . ." Theresa says, touching my forehead. "It's going to be all right. Help is on the way."

"Mason, you can't go to the police," Georgia pleads. "You don't understand. She's been drinking and taking those meds and she's saying things she doesn't mean. If the police question her, she might say . . . other things—things that could incriminate any one of us. And they wouldn't be the truth, necessarily. Who knows what she could say in her state."

"This is bullshit." Mason's voice lowers as he storms away.

"I'm not letting you leave this house until you calm down and talk to me," Georgia says, yanking on Mason's arm. He jerks away with a curse.

Something jingles. Sounds like keys coming out of a pocket. That tinkling, jostling sound. Now scuffling. Someone's fighting. My vision swims, then becomes clear. Georgia and Mason are tangled together. She's trying to stop him from leaving, blocking his path. He's screaming in her face, scowling and spitting.

"Mason's yelling at Georgia the way he does at me," I mumble to Theresa. "Very mad."

"Yes, he's angry," Theresa, says, smoothing her hands down my hair. "But it's going to be all right in the end. You'll see. Are you feeling light-headed?"

"Yup." All night. Now Georgia's screaming. She doesn't want him to leave. My vision goes topsy-turvy as Mason breaks away from Georgia and walks off. I clamp my eyes closed to stave off the nausea. "Where's Mason going?"

In the distance, a door slams, and then another. A thunderous roar echoes through the neighborhood, followed by more screams and a screeching sound. Tires, I think. I can't be sure.

"Erin," Theresa says; I almost forgot she was beside me. "You're breathing really heavy, and your heart's racing, and I don't know if you're going to remember this later, but I have to say it: I'm so sorry. This is all my fault."

"No, not your fault." I can barely formulate words. Sounds are tumbling from my numb lips. "You didn't sleep with my husband."

"But I did." She goes quiet as my mind processes what she just said. "It wasn't Georgia. I was the one sleeping with

Mason. We've been together for a year. He's been trying to find a way to tell you all this time. I bought Georgia's car— I was with him earlier today, when you saw us. I don't know what Georgia was trying to tell him this morning, but they have nothing going on. I'm the one you should be mad at."

My breathing goes shallow, and a cloudy red haze swallows my vision. "You?"

Theresa. The one I confided in, leaned on. The one who was supposed to be helping us with our marriage. She was probably sabotaging it all along.

"Bitch," I breathe. It's all I can muster.

She removes her arm from my shoulders and slinks out from beneath me, leaving me in a crumpled heap. "I'm sorry, Erin. I'm going out there to try to find Mason. Brooke's getting you help. Just stay here. It's going to be okay."

Like Georgia, Theresa disappears into the night. As I focus on my breathing, the ringing in my ears slows to an annoying hum. If I force myself to concentrate, things become clear. I can feel strength surge through my muscles. Whether it's adrenaline or fear, I grip the edge of the seat and stagger to standing. I stumble into the house and through the living room, clutching people's shoulders to assist me as I pass. They make strange sounds, as if I'm some sort of burden, but I don't care.

As I move, hugging the giant white pillars on the front porch, the world in front of me spins. People's faces blend together, warping from laughter to anger and back again. Across the street, a car peels out from our driveway, but it's dark and I can't see well. Lights and shapes tumble as if they're shifting in a kaleidoscope. My head hurts so damn bad. Something in the middle of the street takes form. Mason's car. Peering through the dark, I make out two figures inside. It roars down the lane, swerving, narrowly missing parked cars.

"Mason!" Theresa's voice. She's at the curb. Running along the sidewalk, arms waving over her head. "Mason, wait!"

The car screeches to a stop. Lurches into reverse. There's a struggle in the car. Georgia screams again. They're stopped in the middle of the road. I follow Theresa, running, stumbling along the sidewalk.

"Mason!" she screams. "Mason! I'm going with you!"

The car's engine revs, and then goes quiet. I'm close to Theresa, sucking in air and pushing it out, nearly hyperventilating. My skin feels like it's on fire. I'm scampering from one parked car to another, nearly falling off the sidewalk, pushing onward, closing the gap.

Theresa's up ahead. Between two cars. Waving. Illuminated by a glow—no, by headlights. Mason's car. She calls his name again. The sound is like nails on a chalkboard in my brain.

The car growls, tires screeching. It swerves. The glare of headlights is blinding, searing into my brain.

"Mason!" Theresa screams. "Wait!"

With one solid push, with every ounce of energy left in my body, I shove her in front of the speeding car. And then, floundering, I collapse onto the concrete.

CHAPTER THIRTY-TWO

GEORGIA

ONE WEEK AFTER THE ACCIDENT

St. Mary's Medical Center

Karen, my nurse, cracks the door open and peeks inside. "You have two visitors. Brooke Davies and Erin King are here to see you."

"It's about time they visit." Sitting upright, I pull the sheet up to cover my lap. "Let them in."

Not a single friend has been in to see me since the accident. Not one. As they enter the room together, I'm about to scold them for their insensitivity, but Brooke holds up a basket filled with fruit, crackers, cheese, olives, and dark chocolate, and Erin waves a gorgeous rose bouquet at me, and tears sting my eyes.

"Familiar faces . . ." My voice cracks. "I've missed you."

Erin leans in for a hug while Brooke waits at the foot of my bed.

"I'm so sorry . . . for what I thought about you and Mason," Erin says, taking my hand. "I shouldn't have said those horrible things about you. And I should never have blindsided you for that interview. I don't know what I was thinking."

"It's all right. All's forgiven." I smile warily, knowing what words need to be said. "I'm sorry for your loss, Erin. I shouldn't have let Mason leave the reception. I shouldn't have gotten in the car with him at all. Everything escalated so fast. I didn't want him to bring the police to the house and have them start asking you questions. In your state, I didn't want you to say something about Eli and Andrew . . ."

"I have to ask . . ." Brooke says quietly. "Why'd you do it? Why hire Danny when you could've just divorced them and started over? You married well each time. It's not like you needed *more* money."

Erin cocks her hip. "One can never have enough."

"It was more than the money," I say and open up like a floodgate.

I tell her about the abuse I suffered while being married to Eli and Andrew. How, once we were married, I became something they could control and possess. The countless nights I spent awake, wondering if the violence was going to reach the point where they'd "accidentally" kill me. The way I learned that bruises with a blue or purple hue were best covered with yellow concealer, then set with a spritz spray so the makeup didn't fade. The reason I changed my wardrobe to the many shades of the rainbow, so people would gossip about my eccentric sense of style, rather than the state of my marriages.

When I asked Erin to make the call to a hitman on my behalf. How I made sure the alarms were off so Danny could come into the house undetected. How I buried my head under two pillows when Eli heard a noise in the house and went to seek out its source. The way I trembled and prayed that Danny wouldn't kill me next. How many times I prayed, begging for forgiveness. When I asked Erin to make the call again. How much easier it was the second time around, with Andrew. How I truly loved Robert. He was the only one I'd ever really loved, the kindest man I'd met in my whole life. How I grieved for him with my body and soul.

"I'm not proud of what I've done," I say, unable to stop the tears from rolling down my cheeks. "But I'm glad I don't have to hide anymore. At least not from my best friends."

Brooke takes Erin's other hand and looks to me with a smile. "Who am I to judge? We all have skeletons in our closets. But deep down we're good people. Right, Georgia?"

I smile sweetly, remembering our earlier conversation. "Right."

"Are they still going to discharge you this morning?" Erin asks.

"That's the plan." I eye the clock above the television that's been showing reruns of *Friends*. It's the episode where Joey wears all of Chandler's clothes at once and does lunges in the kitchen. It gets me every time. "The nurse that just left said the detective is on his way over. Apparently he has some news for me. Have you heard anything?"

"About Robert's death or Mason's accident?" Erin asks.

"Either."

There's been so much loss . . . too much. After this, I'm burying my head in the sand for a long while.

"I—I haven't heard anything," Brooke answers. "Investigations are still ongoing, last I heard. Mason's and Theresa's funerals are next week."

I drop my head back onto the pillow. "I'm sorry, Erin. How are you holding up?"

She shrugs her shoulders up to her ears. "Fine. Mellow.

Think the meds are finally working properly. They've effec-
tively numbed my conscience."

Brooke chuckles.

"I'm kidding," Erin says. "It's been hard, but I'm doing all
right. Seeing a new therapist for grief counseling."

The door opens and Detective Linard strides in, cutting
our conversation short. "How are you feeling, Ms. St. Claire?"
he asks cheerily as the second detective walks in behind him.
"Leaving today?"

"This morning, hopefully. Erin and Brooke are going to
drive me home." I try to read the detectives' expressions and
come up empty. "The doctors have given me the all-clear.
They're processing the discharge paperwork."

Erin and Brooke step back against the window as the detectives move closer to the bed and perch on the edges of the
chairs situated there.

"I wanted to stop by this morning because we have a few
updates to brief you on." Linard rolls his fingers against the
edge of my bed. "Your fiancé's death has officially been ruled
a homicide. We received an ID on the man who attacked you
in the garage. His name was Danny Johnson. A thorough
search of his Florida home resulted in all kinds of information
on your fiancé. He'd been planning to kidnap him for approximately a month."

"Oh, that's terrible." My heart aches. "Just awful."

"Had he survived the attack, he would've been charged
with the murder of your fiancé." He measures my expression
before going on. "Now about the accident . . ."

"My head aches from the thought of it." I touch two fingers to my forehead for effect. "I hit the windshield right
here. I still have bruising."

"Mason King was driving the car that hit Theresa Wilson.

She was killed on impact. Your friend Erin was first on scene to give the witness statement." He looks to her, and she hangs her head. "After that, you claim there was a struggle over the wheel, and that you'd demanded he stop the car."

"That's right."

"And then you say he lost control of the car and hit a tree."

I pinch my eyes tight. "I can still hear the sound of glass and metal crunching as we hit. What a traumatic experience."

"Mr. King had alcohol in his system at the time of the accident." He watches me, before turning his analytical gaze to Erin. "Had *he* survived the accident, we would've charged him with vehicular manslaughter for Ms. Wilson's death. You might've been able to sue him for your medical bills. You may still be able to get those compensated since his wife is the registered owner of the vehicle."

"Oh, no," I say, feigning exhaustion. "That won't be necessary. I have insurance, and I'm going to be fine. I'm not severely injured."

"Then I think we're done here." He closes the cover of his iPad with a snap. "I hope you heal well, Ms. St. Claire. I'm sorry for your loss. And yours, Ms. King."

As soon as he leaves the room, Erin and Brooke approach the bed.

"Do you still think Danny was working with someone?" Erin asks me.

"I'm not sure, but something isn't right about the timing of that whole thing."

Erin nods, agreeing. "You should be careful after you're discharged. Maybe the detectives can sweep the house to make sure it's safe before you go home."

"I just want this to be over." I drop my head back against the pillow, drama-drained. "So badly."

"Then let's call the number that woman at Starbucks gave me," Erin says simply.

"What number?" Brooke asks.

"I don't know if I told you, but I was the one who found Danny Johnson. When Georgia reached the end of her rope and couldn't handle the abuse anymore, I joined a few online forums for abusive women on her behalf. Didn't take long for me to strike up a friendship with one of the women whose husband had died mysteriously months earlier. We met up at Starbucks, exchanged war stories, and she gave me a slip of paper with a phone number scribbled on it. It was the answer to our prayers—well most of them anyway. We could call the number again. See if someone answers. We'd know once and for all if Danny had a partner."

I lift my head and meet Erin's gaze. "That paper is locked away in the chest in my office."

"Not anymore." Erin lifts the scrap of paper from her purse. "I found it on the floor beneath your desk, the day the police came over to take the missing person report."

Brooke shakes her head warily. "I don't think the hospital is the best place to do this."

"We're safe here," Erin presses. "It's your call, Georgia, but if you want this over with, once and for all, this is the way to do it."

"I don't know," Brooke says. "Maybe, if Danny *was* working with someone, that person won't contact you at all. There's a chance, with all the police crawling around, he'll tuck his tail and disappear."

Something twinges in my gut. If Danny *was* working with someone, that person will want his money eventually. Danny demanded thirty million. His partner, if he had one, would know I hired him to kill my husbands. He could blackmail me for the millions I owed Danny . . . or more. Will I be able to put the possibility that he had a partner behind me and move on with my life? Or will I always wonder if there'd been some-one working with Danny behind the scenes? I don't want to be scanning shadows and worrying about whether or not I remembered to set my house alarm.

I should call the number on that piece of paper, to see if someone picks up the line on the other end, to finally end it.

"Give me the number," I say.

As Brooke paces nervously back and forth at the foot of the bed, Erin hands over the scrap of paper. Hands shaking, I dial the number into my phone, and wait.

Something buzzes in the corner of the room.

The phone rings on the other side of the line.

More buzzing. It's coming from a chair in the corner.

Brooke moves to the chair where her purse rests, unzips slowly, and lifts a generic-looking phone to her ear. "Hello, Georgia."

BROOKE

ONE YEAR LATER

Wonderful news, I type to my editor. *I'll keep an eye out for the contract.*

"Honey!" I call out, hitting send on the email. "Jack!"

"I'm here." Jack strides into the room and places his hands on my shoulders reassuringly. "Book news?"

"The publisher wants the next three in the series. Isn't that great!"

Stooping, he kisses my cheek. "Amazing. I knew they'd love the idea. You still haven't let me read the proposal you sent. Are you going to make me wait until the book's release?"

"Probably."

Because, like the novel I'd been working on last year, if I make Jack wait until the excitement wears off, he won't end up reading it at all. Then he won't see how closely I relate to some of the main characters. He won't notice that I know a little too much about certain elements of a crime. How to sneak in and out of a house undetected, for example. How to shoot a man and make it look like suicide. Or how to transfer money from a charity to an overseas account. I may not have pushed Eli down the stairs or pulled the trigger on the gun that killed Andrew—those were Danny's executions—but I was the one who gave him the ideas. The one who directed the scenarios from afar. I had plans and backup plans and backup plans for the backup plans.

"Well I'm proud of you. You're so talented."

"Oh, you have no idea," I say, and then laugh.

He squeezes my shoulders and kisses my forehead. "Can't wait to celebrate the success of your newest book when we land in New Orleans."

Before settling into our new home in Los Angeles, I've asked to spend a week in New Orleans, visiting with my mother. She took Danny's death hard, and I don't blame her. The anniversary of my brother's death is right around the corner, and I really should be with her.

Jack doesn't know that Danny was the man Georgia shot in the parking garage. As far as Jack is concerned, Danny is still in and out of prison in Florida. Some people believe married partners should share everything, and have no secrets between them. I wholeheartedly disagree. The only reason my marriage to Jack is successful is that certain things remain hidden in the shadows.

He also doesn't know Danny's last stint in prison was due to him witnessing a bar fight between a woman and her husband. Husband got violent. Danny got involved. He was sentenced to ten years. Voluntary manslaughter. Didn't have any remorse for his crime at all because when he looked at that woman in the bar, he saw our mother. In his own way, he was *saving* her. One night, not long after he was released, he

THE SINFUL LIVES OF TROPHY WIVES

called and said he'd found online forums for abused women seeking help, and talked with a woman in San Francisco who feared her husband would kill her. He said he was stepping in to help. Given Danny's past, I knew what that "help" entailed. But Danny was sloppy. Always had been. Filled with good intentions, but not a lot of thinking. I didn't want him to get locked up again, so I orchestrated the plan . . . as I did for Georgia, and then for Erin.

Those are the only women we ever "helped."

"I already made the reservation," Jack says, bringing me back to the present. "It's the perfect place. You'll love it. I thought we could invite your mother to dinner as well. I've already texted her."

"Perfect, darling." I blink back tears. "You're the best."

If he only knew how much taking control like that means to me. After my brother and I lived a life of uncertainty, never knowing if we were going to come home to our parents fighting or setting up a nice family dinner, we chose different paths in life. Danny decided he couldn't count on anyone but himself. On the other hand, I realized I needed someone to make me feel safe and protected at all times. I craved routine, and what some might call "stuffiness," because there isn't volatility in scheduled rigidity. Jack provides that and then some. We may have an unconventional marriage because we sleep in separate bedrooms, but we give each other what we lack. And there's love there, beneath it all. Always love.

Someone knocks on the front door downstairs.

"That's Erin and Georgia," I say, closing down my laptop. "I'll get it."

When I open the door, Erin holds up Malibu strawberry rum, Diet 7-Up, and a lime. Georgia's behind her waving around V8 berry and peach schnapps.

"We brought the party," Erin says and pushes inside, setting everything up on the counter. "I'm going to start mixing. Four glasses?"

"Three. Jack's in the bedroom packing up the last of his things."

Georgia plants her hands on her hips and scans our bare living room and kitchen as Erin searches through the cabinets for glasses. The movers have already taken the large items. All that's left are a few essential kitchen items, personal effects, and a handful of crates a third-party moving company is going to transport to Los Angeles. The red and white painting with the many faces still hangs in the living room.

"I can't believe you're leaving," Georgia says, gazing at me somberly. "Feels like you just moved in. Do you really have to go?"

A smile tugs at my lips. "It's not like we're moving across the country. We'll stay in California because of his work, but it looks like there's an opportunity for me in Los Angeles. It's not far. Only a ninety-minute plane ride. You can come down whenever you get lonely."

"That might be all the time."

"Unless she gets hitched again," Erin says with a giggle.

"I think I'm content being single for the time being. Can I ask you something, Brooke?" Georgia levels me with a serious stare. "You didn't move to the terrace until Eli and Andrew were gone, yet you were still able to—you know, take care of business. Why'd you need to buy this place when it came to Mason?"

"Danny and I talked about how to handle Eli and Andrew from the start. We were lockstep. Had every detail outlined. But when we discussed how we would handle Mason, Danny was adamant that we were missing our big chance. He kept insisting we could get more money if we went for Robert instead. He said we could make it a simple kidnapping and ransom." I locate a pitcher for Erin and slide it in front of her. She dumps in the alcohol, diet soda, and V8 juice. "But that was never our plan. We were helping women escape abusive relationships. We weren't basic criminals, who were only in it for the money."

"Darling," Erin says, stirring the pink drink, "you're far from basic."

"You know what I mean." I cut a lime and squeeze the halves into the pitcher. Droplets of juice dribble down my hand. "I tried to reason with him, but he was fixated. I thought my presence here would keep him in check. I was wrong." I push the glasses closer to Erin for her to fill. "He was greedy and went too far. There was nothing I could do."

Leaning over the counter, Georgia takes a drink and passes one to me. "I'd call it water under the bridge, but considering where they found Robert, I think it's too soon."

I kink my head to the side sympathetically. "I'm so incredibly sorry."

"What's done is done." She licks the side of her glass. "So you didn't move here because of Jack's work? Isn't that what you said when we first met?"

"That played a part in the decision, of course." I swirl my drink round and round. "It was easy to convince him to move because the Bay Area is the hub for anything technology-related, and the timing was right to be closer to his business's headquarters. But I'd also become stagnant in my writing and thought a change of scenery might spark inspiration. The move to Presidio Terrace killed a few birds with one stone."

I wince, waiting for the backlash from my last words. The comment was ill-timed under the circumstances. But Georgia and Erin don't seem to care and continue oohing and aahing over the pink-red color of their drinks. God, I'm going to miss them.

Erin takes the first drink and moans. "Delicious. Speaking of writing inspiration, will Georgia and I find ourselves in your newest book?"

I think of the story line, the murder, the women who are perfectly flawed, who think they have it all together, when really they're just trying to do the best they can with what they have. The leads could be anyone in Presidio Terrace. Pam, using a tiny Yorkie to keep her company because she's too lonely living in the huge house with her husband. Penny, edging her lawn with scissors because if it's not exactly right it'll bother her when she's trying to sleep at night. The lead could be me, using my career as a novelist as an excuse to search for retribution against men who abuse women. We're all the same, really.

"I think you might find some of the elements familiar," I say, turning my gaze to Georgia. "There's a sister and brother working together at one point. The sister had no idea her brother was going off the rails, sending death threats to people, and extorting them for large amounts of money. The sister never knew about any of that. He'd kept her in the dark. The friend was never supposed to be in danger or pay anything beyond the original contract. That was never part of the plan."

Georgia purses her lips as if she's deep in thought. "I bet the friend suspected that. She forgives the sister in the end and they become great friends, bonded by tragedy, don't they?"

"You'll have to read it to find out," I tease, sipping the sugary drink.

"It's on my reading list. I think Erin and I are going to start a book club with some of the other ladies in the terrace. Come back, and we'll read the book together. Throw you a proper book signing party." Georgia plops onto the barstool in front of me and empties half her glass in a single gulp. "Are you all packed?"

"Almost. The crating company is going to come in later and create custom boxes for our artwork, and a few of the chandeliers." I glance at the painting in the living room—the one Georgia had taken a liking to the first day I met her. Since that time, she's said it looks familiar but can't place where she recognizes it. Although I can't say for certain, I bet it's like seeing an outfit on a rack that you're sure you already own. A jacket that fits just right or a blouse with a pattern you absolutely love. To be honest, that's why I purchased the piece. Because it spoke to me on some subconscious level I couldn't understand. There's simply an element of the painting that appealed to me. And it's clear it appeals to her as well. "I'd like you to have that," I tell her.

She perks up, glancing into the living room. "What?"

"The painting. It's yours."

"I—I couldn't."

"It's done. I'll have the craters deliver it to your home tonight before we leave." My heart warms at the thought of it hanging in Georgia's beautiful home, where it'll be cherished. "I didn't bring a gift to Robert's funeral, but I should have . . . I simply couldn't think of anything appropriate, under the circumstances. It'd mean a lot to me if you'd accept it."

Sliding off the stool, she comes around the island and wraps me in her arms. "Thank you," she whispers and then returns to her stool as Erin downs her drink. "You don't have to leave, you know. You could stay and be housewives like us. Grounds & Greens every morning."

"Mimosa bar," Erin pipes in with a wink. "You have to admit, it's tempting."

"It is, and I appreciate the gesture," I say, "but I can't stay. I'll never forgive myself for Danny's mistake that night. Every time I see that engagement ring on Georgia's finger, I'll think of what I could've done differently to prevent what happened."

"Brooke, we all experienced loss this year," Georgia says. "Robert . . ."

Erin tops off her frost-rimmed glass, then does the same for Georgia's. "Mason . . ."

"My brother . . ." Then Erin tops off my drink. "But I was the only one who profited from the losses. It wouldn't be right for me to stay."

"Depends on how you interpret profit." Erin raises her glass in cheers. "To skeletons in closets that never see the light of day."

I raise my glass to meet theirs. "To good people."

Georgia meets my gaze. "Or at least people who are trying."

And that's all any of us can do.

ACKNOWLEDGMENTS

I have so many people to thank, but first, I must thank God for the amazing blessings he's placed on my path.

I'd like to thank the people who rock my writing world. My wonderful agent, Jill Marsal, for her support and guidance. Shauna Summers and Lexi Batsides at Random House, for their wisdom and insights that helped shape this book. Eternal gratitude to Jennie Marts, for late-night plotting sessions, cheering me on, and keeping the faith. Your friendship is invaluable. Thank you from the bottom of my heart.

Special thanks to my Spartan crew for their unwavering support, and to a select few, for allowing a few minor characters in this book to borrow their names: Martha Dent, Jeff Baldwin, Zulfiqar Malik, Lisa Wilson, Karen Dell Osso, Sheree Richter, Stephanie Maestretti, Stephanie and Andrew Barrious, Mike and Hillary Pangburn.

As always, much love to my family and friends, for asking how my writing is going, dropping champagne on my doorstep when I reach a milestone, hunting for my books "in the wild," or encouraging me when the words simply aren't there. You're the very best there is. To Justin, Kelli, and Gavin, immense gratitude and unending love.

PHOTO: © LILLY WALKER

ABOUT THE AUTHOR

Kristin Miller is the *New York Times* and *USA Today* bestselling author of more than thirty novels. After writing dark and gritty versions of "happily ever after" for more than a decade, she turned her hand to psychological suspense, a genre she has loved since childhood. She lives in Northern California with her husband and two children.

kristinmiller.net

ABOUT THE TYPE

This book was set in Caledonia, a typeface designed in 1939 by W. A. Dwiggins (1880–1956) for the Merganthaler Linotype Company. Its name is the ancient Roman term for Scotland, because the face was intended to have a Scottish-Roman flavor. Caledonia is considered to be a well-proportioned, businesslike face with little contrast between its thick and thin lines.